I0654817

John Burgoyne

Rudimentary Treatise on the Blasting and Quarrying of Stone

For Building and Other Purposes by Sir John Burgoyne. Fourth Edition

John Burgoyne

Rudimentary Treatise on the Blasting and Quarrying of Stone
For Building and Other Purposes by Sir John Burgoyne. Fourth Edition

ISBN/EAN: 9783337390730

Printed in Europe, USA, Canada, Australia, Japan

Cover: Foto ©Andreas Hilbeck / pixelio.de

More available books at **www.hansebooks.com**

RUDIMENTARY TREATISE

ON

THE BLASTING AND QUARRYING OF STONE

FOR BUILDING AND OTHER PURPOSES.

BY

LIEUT.-GEN. SIR JOHN BURGOYNE, K.C.B.,

ETC. ETC. ETC.

FOURTH EDITION.

WITH NUMEROUS WOOD ENGRAVINGS.

TOGETHER WITH OTHER USEFUL ADDITIONS RELATING
TO THE SAME OBJECTS.

LONDON
JOHN WEALE, 59, HIGH HOLBORN.
1860.

LONDON:
BRADBURY AND EVANS, PRINTERS, WHITEFRIARS.

ADVERTISEMENT.

For the present Volume, on a subject hitherto little treated of, I am indebted to Lieut.-General Sir JOHN BURGOYNE, Bart., who published the same as a contributory Paper in the elaborate and continuous Work, entitled "Professional Papers of the Corps of Royal Engineers," of which there are at this period 10 vols. large quarto. Sir JOHN BURGOYNE, with his usual urbanity, to aid its more general diffusion, has kindly sanctioned the reproduction of this Paper in the Rudimentary Series. For the very useful additional matter, and the sanction of this FOURTH edition, I have to offer, in behalf of the public and myself, thanks to the gallant author.

JOHN WEALE.

CONTENTS.

PART I.

QUARRYING AND BLASTING ROCKS.

PART II.

QUARRYING AND BLASTING ROCKS.

In a "Rudimentary Series," such as the one to which this volume belongs, perhaps no subject can be introduced with greater fitness than that of quarrying or stone-getting,—certainly one of the rudimentary arts connected equally with the duties of the engineer, the architect, and the practical builder. Any attempt to recount the history of the art would oblige us to extend our retrospect to a very early date, perhaps we should rather say to a dateless period; to call to mind the structural wonders of Tyre, of Sidon, and of Thebes; and to close the history with the confession that, however the mechanical modes of wielding the wrought masses may have received improvement in modern times, the primitive methods and tools of the quarryman and of the mason have, if we except the introduction of gunpowder, become no more altered in our hands than have the chiselled works of the ancient sculptors been surpassed by the productions of later ages. The one powerful assistant, however, to which we have referred, has been enlisted in the service of the quarry within a comparatively recent period, and its aid has certainly supplanted to a great extent the action of the wedge and the hammer.

Without this valuable auxiliary, the work of separating large masses of stone from their native blocks or beds must have been infinitely more laborious, and have needed also a skill of no mean degree. The art of applying gunpowder to this purpose has, however, remained very nearly the same since the first experimenter "jumped" and "charged" a bore in the stubborn rock, which till then had been attacked only with the chisel and the wedge.

B

The implements employed for quarrying by mere manual labour are simply the sledge hammer or mallet, the borer or chisel, and the wedges, besides trucks, and such gearing as may be required to facilitate the removal of the blocks when detached. Of these, the only one which needs any description is the chisel, which is an iron rod with a steel cutting end, welded at one extremity, and flattened to a wedge-like form at the other. The implements used in blasting are of a similarly simple character, and consist of the borer or jumping tool, the scraper for clearing the hole of the chips produced, the claying bar for driving in dry clay if the hole be too damp for the immediate introduction of the charge, the needle, which is driven into the charge, and remains while the hole is filled up with stones, &c., so that, when ultimately withdrawn, a channel is preserved communicating directly with the powder. While the needle, which is a long thin copper rod, remains in its place, the space around it is filled up, by means of the tamping bar, with stones, &c.

In the following paper, which is from the pen of Major-General Sir J. F. Burgoyne, we have a most useful collection of facts upon the subject of blasting, together with a complete account of the process and the materials employed, and several hints for the improvement of both, which we trust will receive all the attention due to their high authority and intrinsic practical value.

The operations which constitute the entire process of blasting are, boring the holes, loading, and firing.

BORING THE HOLES.

The best means of expediting the operation of blasting, would be by any contrivance that would render the boring of the holes more quickly executed.

The ordinary implements used for this purpose are, the jumper or cutting-tool, the hammer, and the scraper.

There is much discrepancy in the account given in different places, of the time required for boring holes; arising from differences in the precise quality of the rock, the mode of working, and the different bases of calculation.

The following, obtained from John Mac Mahon, Esq., of Dublin, is the result of some considerable experience in quarries of granite of good quality at Dalkey, in the neighbourhood of Dublin.

" 3-inch jumpers, used in boring holes from 9 to 15 feet deep; 2 men striking, and 1 man holding and turning the jumper, bored on an average 4 feet in a day, or 5 feet with a 2½-inch jumper, which was frequently used for boring the same depth.

" 2¼-inch jumper, for holes from 5 to 10 feet deep; 3 men as above would bore on an average 6 feet each day.

" 2-inch——holes from 4 to 7 feet deep; 3 men would bore 8 feet of such holes.

" 1¾-inch——holes from 2 feet 6 inches to 6 feet; the 3 men bored 12 feet.

" In working the two last classes, a strong boy will answer to turn the jumper instead of a man.

" 1-inch jumper, for breaking the fragments of rock to smaller pieces; 1 man bored 8 feet per day.

" The waste of steel and iron was nearly as follows :—a 3-inch jumper took for its bit 2 lb. of steel, with which it would bore 16 feet, on being dressed or sharpened 18 times; waste of iron 18 inches to each steeling, or 1⅛ inch for each foot bored.

   2-inch jumper took 1 ¼ lb. of steel.
   1¾-inch ,, ,, ¾ lb.
   1-inch ,, ,, 3 oz.

" They would all bore from 18 to 24 feet with each steeling, and require to be sharpened about once for every foot bored.

" The weight of the hammers used in boring with each class of jumper was as follows :—

  18 lb. hammers for 3-inch jumpers,
  16 lb. ,, ,, 2½ and 2¼-inch,
  14 lb. ,, ,, 2 and 1¾-inch,
  5 to 7 lb. ,, ,, 1-inch, used by one man.

" Churn jumpers, so called from the manner in which they are worked, from 7 to 8 feet long, with a steel bit at each end; general diameter, 1⅛ to 1½-inch. Two men would bore with them about 16 feet per day."

These last are much more efficient than those struck on the head with a hammer, and are sometimes used with a spring rod and line. They are applicable to holes that are vertical, or nearly so, and to rock that is not too hard : in the granite at Kingstown they were abandoned on account of the edges turning so fast, that the frequency of the necessary sharpenings gave the advantage to the use of the hammer:

where they can be used, the work will be performed at a far more rapid rate than even above mentioned. In boring artesian wells to great depths the application of the tool is entirely on this principle.

A still quicker mode of boring would be by *drilling* the holes, if it were feasible. It has often been proposed, but the cutting edges of the tools will not stand in any kind of stone.

Where charges have been exploded without blowing out the tamping,* it may be very desirable to bore the latter out for the purpose of introducing another charge; in such case the hole need not be of the size of that originally made, as 1-inch bore will be adequate at any time.

In clay tamping, a hole may be bored out with the jumper and hammer at the rate of about 26 minutes for 3 feet. Broken stone tamping will be bored out at the rate of 20 minutes for 3 feet.

A very few trials were made to bore a hole through clay tamping with an auger; the labour was less, as fewer men were necessary; the time consumed was somewhat more, but the tool was capable of improvement and the men were new to its use.

It is conceived that augers, properly constructed, may be used to advantage in re-boring through clay tamping for successive blasts from the same hole, to the gain of a saving in time and labour, and avoiding the application of water, which is necessary with any kind of jumper.

In case of a miss-fire it is a very dangerous practice to re-bore the hole, and has occasioned very many bad accidents; it is very properly usually forbidden altogether. If the hole be vertical, or nearly so, and the needle or fuse hole can be cleared, so as to *ensure* a thorough wetting of the charge, by pouring water down, it might be done with safety; but sometimes the very object of the quarryman is to save the powder,—a very unworthy one for which to incur the great risk of killing or maiming two or three workmen.

To prevent the loss of any large charge in this way, a hole is sometimes bored on one side, and within a few inches of the one that has failed, to the same depth as its charge, and being loaded and exploded, has had the effect of igniting the other also.

---

* The "*tamping*" is the filling up of the hole in which the charge of powder, &c., is deposited.—ED.

An apparatus for boring to considerable depths has recently been introduced into this country from mines in Germany* by Charles Vignoles, Esq., C.E., which it is believed is far more efficient than any hitherto employed in Great Britain.

This machinery has been in operation, it is believed, on the Manchester and Sheffield Railway, of which Mr. Vignoles was the engineer; its direct application being to bore into and ascertain the precise qualities of the strata through which the great tunnel (3 miles in length) will be carried, which is to form the communication through the mountain ridge that divides the eastern and western inclines of England.

The principal feature in the process is that the cutting tools are attached to a heavy weight, and worked by a rope, instead of by rods with screw joints.

The rope is wound round a cylindrical roller by a winch, and there are several ingenious contrivances in the details and parts of the machinery, that tend to facilitate the operation.

Upon the judicious selection of the position of the holes will in a great measure depend the useful effect of the blast; but two leading errors are committed by quarrymen or miners in general, viz., selecting an injudicious position for the charge, by which the action of the powder is exerted in the direction of the opening where it was introduced; and the adopting as a rule for the several charges, to fill a certain number of feet or inches of the hole bored, usually one-third of its depth, instead of employing given weights adapted to the *lines of least resistance.*

The *line of least resistance* is that line by which the explosion of the powder will find the least opposition to its vent in the air. This need not necessarily be the shortest line to the surface; as, for instance, a long line in earth may, from the same charge, afford less resistance than a shorter line in rock.

Supposing the matter in which the explosion is to take place to be of uniform consistence in every direction, charges of powder to produce similar proportionate results ought to be as the cubes of the lines of least resistance, and not according to any fanciful depth of hole bored.

Thus, if 4 ounces of powder would have a given effect

---

* It is said that boring on a similar principle has been long used in China.

upon a solid piece of rock of 2 feet thick to the surface, it ought to require 13½ ounces to produce the same effect upon a piece of similar rock 3 feet thick; that is,

Cube of 2-feet line of least resistance.		Charge of powder in ounces.		Cube of 3-feet line of least resistance.		Charge in ounces.
as 8	is to	4	so is	27	to	13½

or, what is the same thing, half the cube of the line of least resistance expressed in feet, will, on *this particular datum*, be the charge in ounces, as follows :—

Lines of least resistance in feet.		Charge of powder lb. oz.
1	. . . . . .	0 0½*
2	. . . . . .	0 4
3	. . . . . .	0 13½
4	. . . . . .	2 0
5	. . . . . .	3 14½
6	. . . . . .	6 12
7	. . . . . .	10 11½
8	. . . . .	16 0

These quantities being of common merchants' blasting powder, will be found adequate for any rock of ordinary tenacity; but a precise datum should be ascertained by a few actual experiments on the particular rock to be worked.†

Thus, with a 2-feet line of least resistance (A to B, fig. 1), whether 4 ounces or 6 ounces, or 8 ounces, are requisite to produce a good effect; with 3-feet line of least resistance, whether 13½ ounces, or 18 ounces, or 27 ounces, &c.

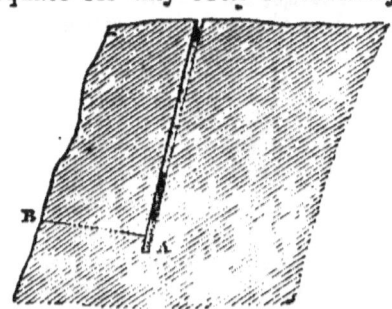

Fig. 1.—(Section.)

* To so small a quantity as ½ ounce a little excess might be added, but ¼ ounce, or ⅛ ounce more, will be sufficient.

† In the granite quarries of Kingstown (near Dublin) these charges were sufficient to open the rock where there were no fissures, apparent weakness, or other advantage; but where the line of least resistance was not that of the hole bored, the effect was either to bring it down, or only to crack it, according to the quality of the powder used.

On the results of these trials a scale may be adopted for guide in the service.

With regard to the first error above mentioned, that of leaving the action of the powder to be exerted in the direction of the hole bored, one consequence is that, with small charges, commonly a part of the explosion finds comparatively easy vent by that opening (in spite of the best tamping), and is wasted; and it is only the excess that acts in producing the effect required on the rock; whereas, if the explosion were forced through another direction, the whole of its power would be exerted beneficially. But the great objection is, that the rock is then so much more firmly bound all round the charge, as to oppose and lessen in a very great degree the extension of the effect of the explosion.

It must be understood that, even although the line of least resistance should be in the direction of the hole bored, the *depth of the hole* will by no means be the measure by which the proportions of powder for the charge can be taken according to the above rule, namely, as the cubes of the lines of least resistance.

1st, because the tamping, however good, or by whatever contrivance strengthened, cannot be equal in strength to the solid rock.

2ndly and chiefly, because of the various proportions of the entire depth of the hole occupied by different charges of powder: thus, ½ ounce of powder will occupy an insignificant proportion of the depth of even 1 foot of a 1-inch hole, and also the 4 ounces for a 2-feet line of least resistance would fill only 2 inches of a 1-inch hole, and consequently occupy one-twelfth of the 2 feet, and leave 1 foot 10 inches of tamping; while the 13½ ounces for a 3-feet line of least resistance would occupy of a 1-inch hole above 6 inches, that is, more than one-sixth, and leave only 2 feet 6 inches of tamping, and consequently of resistance, such as it is.

This might be remedied in one way, by applying holes of larger diameters for increasing charges, but, by so doing, an increased amount of the less resisting medium (the tamping) would be the consequence, which again renders the calculation, founded on a resistance of solid rock, incorrect.

There is another reason why the powder is ill applied when the explosion takes place in the same line as the bore, which is, that it is placed longitudinally with the line of least resistance, as at o, in fig. 2, and not perpendicular to it, as at P; when much extended, the elongated form in either is bad, but it is worst in the former case.

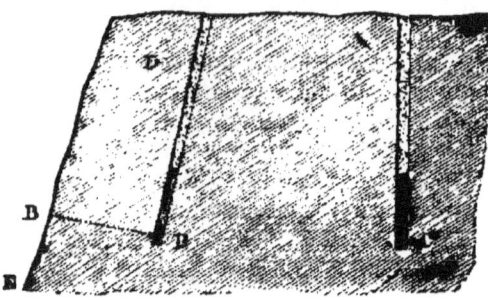

Fig. 2.—(Section.)

When the common mode of blasting is adopted, a loud report is heard like a gun (louder in general in proportion to the less *useful* effect produced), and fragments of stone are frequently thrown to a considerable distance; but when done judiciously, the report will be trifling, and the mass will be seen to be lifted, and thoroughly fractured, rent, or thrown over, without being forcibly projected.

It is the irregularity and extent of the violent explosion following the ordinary process, that renders it so peculiarly difficult to form an accurate judgment on the proper charges for each circumstance; the consequence is a practice purely empirical. The miner or quarryman will give as his rule either a proportionate depth of hole, or, aware how frequently that must prove erroneous, is driven to his usual answer, that he knows from the *appearance* of the situation, what to apply; that is, in fact, admitting that it is a matter of caprice, and provided a certain effect is produced, he is little aware how much time, powder, and labour, may have been wasted.

It is difficult to make ordinary quarrymen, or even overseers, understand correctly the meaning of the lines of least resistance: after appearing to comprehend it, they are frequently observed to confound it with the length of hole bored, or with some conceived necessary direction either vertical or horizontal.

With respect to the second error mentioned, it can easily be shown how very erroneous *must* be the rule of measuring the charge by any given proportion of the depth of the hole, since the quantity of powder will in that case depend, not only on the depth, but also on its *diameter*, with which it can have no relation: thus, if a 6-feet hole is to be bored, it may be an act of chance or caprice whether a jumper of 1½-inch gauge, or of 2 inches, or of 2½, were used; whereas the third of the depth, or any given number of inches of the 2-inch, would hold very nearly *double* the quantity of powder that would be contained in the 1½-inch; and of the 2½-inch, one half more than in the 2, and nearly *three times* as much as in the 1½.

Such a rule also takes no account of the quality of the rock, which in reality will cause the greatest difference in the effect; a given depth of hole being applied to hard or soft rock indiscriminately.

Although some allowances may be made in extreme cases, yet it will be found in most books and papers on blasting rock, that a *usual* charge is one-third of the depth of the hole; and the same will be found to be the actual prevalent practice.

As to the experience by which it might be assumed, that the miners will modify this rule, and regulate the proper charges to give in each case, the value of such practice, unaided by better *principles*, must be small, where the results are so indistinct. A loud explosion takes place, and the rock is more or less separated, but no proof whatever is afforded that the charge has been precisely, or even nearly, what it should have been; and being regulated by no rule (for in this case of leaving it to the miner's judgment, the only rule is abandoned), the experience, to be valuable, should be of precisely similar cases, whereas in blasting they are constantly varying, in size and depth of hole, and in many other circumstances. If the rock were uniform, and the application of the charge always in similar holes and situations, a tolerable rule of thumb experience might perhaps be obtained; but it is quite otherwise; and among the circumstances that must tend to perplex an ordinary miner workman, would be, that the true principle for charges is, as the *cubes* of the thickness of the resisting medium, but which he would certainly regulate by a much more gradual proportionate increase, such as doubling, trebling, or squaring at most.

In order to quarry with good effect for saving labour and powder, an exposed front, either vertical or horizontal, should, if possible, be established on the rock on which to operate.

principally to obtain a line of least resistance in a different direction from that of the hole bored.

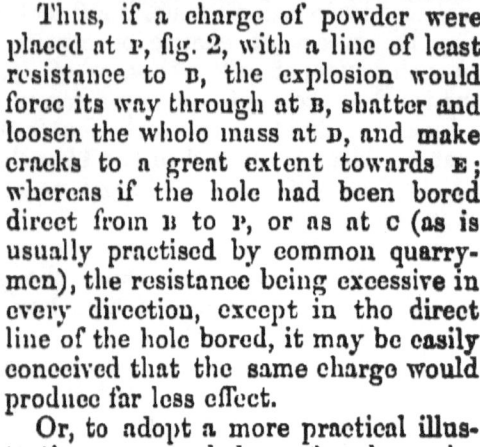

Thus, if a charge of powder were placed at P, fig. 2, with a line of least resistance to D, the explosion would force its way through at B, shatter and loosen the whole mass at D, and make cracks to a great extent towards E; whereas if the hole had been bored direct from B to P, or as at C (as is usually practised by common quarrymen), the resistance being excessive in every direction, except in the direct line of the hole bored, it may be easily conceived that the same charge would produce far less effect.

Or, to adopt a more practical illustration, suppose ledges of rock require to be cleared away to a certain level for a road, navigation, or other object; instead of boring holes + + +, the effect would be far better by inclined holes, A, B, C, fig. 3, applied in succession after the above-mentioned principle.

Where there is a high face of rock, a system of undermining may be advantageously employed: thus a blast at A, fig. 4, would make an opening easy from C to D, and the mass E, if not shaken, which it probably would be, so as to be worked on with crowbars and wedges, would be brought down by very slight subsequent blasts.

When the rock is stratified, and in close parallel beds and seams, the holes should be bored in the direction of the joints, and the powder laid along them as at A, fig. 5, which will

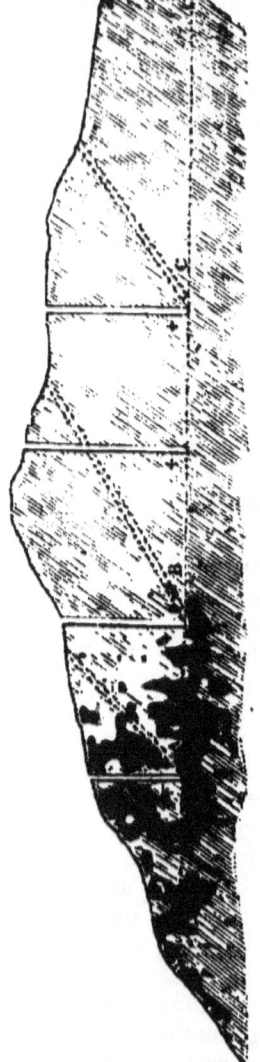

Fig. 3.—(Section.)

have much more effect in lifting large masses than if placed across the grain, and the operation of boring will be easier.

The worst situation for a charge of powder is in a re-entering angle, as at A, fig. 6: the rock exerts such pressure all around it, that very little effect can be expected ; nor is the position much improved at B.

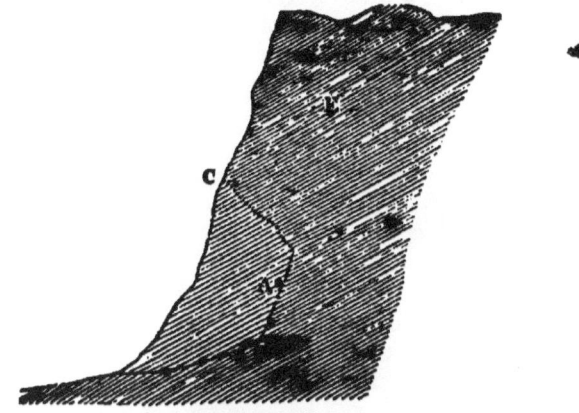

Fig. 4.—(Section.)

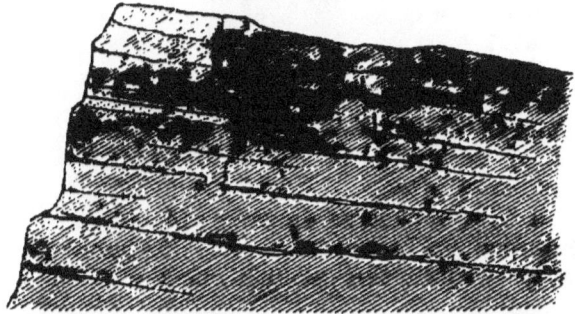

Fig. 5.—(Section.)

Fig. 6.—(Horizontal Section.)

This situation of a re-entering angle occurs very frequently, and should be avoided as much as possible. Thus a charge may be lodged in a hole c, fig. 7, having the same length of line of least resistance as at other holes, A or B; but the effect of the explosion will be greatly reduced by the masses D, E.

Fig. 7.—(Plan.)

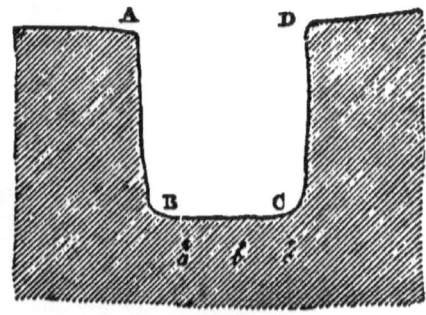

An important illustration of this disadvantageous position for the charge will be experienced in cutting through any narrow confined space A, B, C, D, fig. 8, either horizontally, as in the first drift, or opening, all through a tunnel, or vertically, as in sinking a shaft:

Fig. 8.—(Section.)

blasts at *a*, *b*, or *c*, must be extremely ineffective.

A projection, on the contrary, is the most favourable situation to produce the greatest effect with the smallest

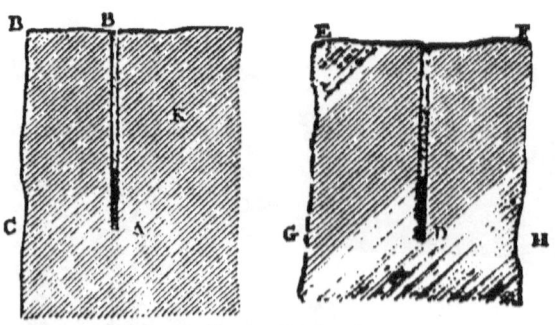

Fig. 9.—(Sections.)

means: a given quantity of powder, for instance, at A, fig. 9, would remove the mass B, B, A, C, and make partial cracks on the side K, but the same quantity at D would remove E, F, G, H, or nearly double the mass*.

Cases, however, frequently occur requiring a deviation from what, under ordinary circumstances, would be the most favourable application of the charge, either owing to the quality of the rock, or where other objects are of more importance than the consumption of powder, or of labour in boring.

The rock may require to be cut to a particular form, as, for instance, when preparing it to receive foundations of masonry; or certain blocks of the stone may be required of particular forms or dimensions: an excess of powder may be applied to increase the shock for bringing down any loose mass in a peculiar state, or *vice versâ*, smaller proportions may from circumstances be sufficient to produce as much effect as is required: these irregularities are very frequent, but it is not the less necessary to understand the correct principles, and not to be carried away with the idea that the whole is a mystery.

It may also be urged that there are cases where the system of working on a line of least resistance, different from that of the hole bored, cannot be followed; such, for instance, as in sinking a shaft, or cutting the first drift-way of a gallery or tunnel.

This is very true, and must cause such operations to be peculiarly costly and slow; and though the rule above recommended for regulating the charges would be inapplicable, still that of taking any proportionate depth of the hole would be quite erroneous.

The system to be adopted in such instances should be to apply the mode of tamping that would give the greatest possible resistance, and to endeavour to obtain by trials the amount of charge by weight that will barely disturb such tamping; in this way the full effect of the powder will act upon the rock, and where that is not very great, a second shot from the same hole will be sure to be very decisive.

Among the cases not admitting of fixed rule, and where a great deal *must* depend upon the intelligence and experience of the directing quarryman, is that of irregularity of joints, or seams.

---

* It will not have quite this effect, as the greater resistance on the side K, in the one case, will increase the effect towards C; but that circumstance does not affect the general consideration of the principle here adverted to.

The following instance will explain this :—

A hole, A, B, fig. 10, of 4 inches diameter and 16 feet deep, was bored to the back of a projecting mass of granite, and 6 feet above a natural slide joint, as shown in the plan and section.

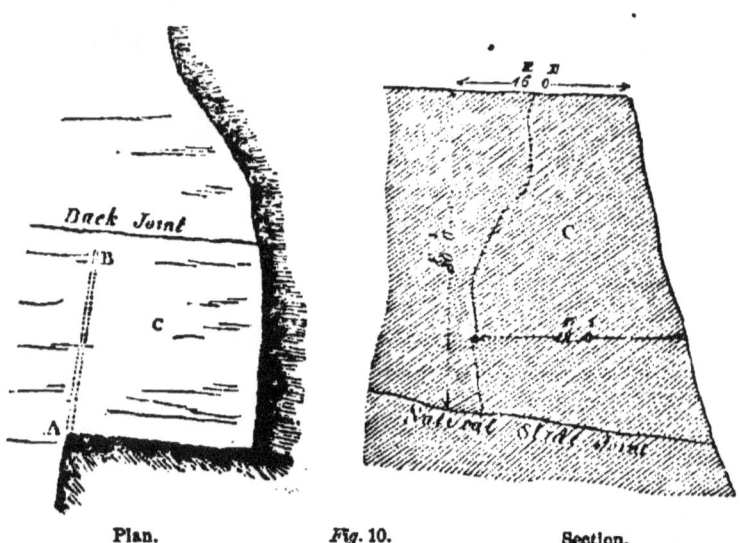

Plan.   Fig. 10.   Section.

Had there been no projection, nor any joint to afford an advantage, it would have required probably 182 lb. of powder to break through a resistance of 18 feet ; but as it was circumstanced, between 35 and 36 lb. (occupying 7 feet of the hole) broke off and overturned an enormous mass c, cutting it down as shown by the dotted lines : the fragments of course were large, one piece containing 80 cubic yards ; and were very appropriate for cutting into ashlar of large dimensions.

Another instance, tried at Dunmore East, near Waterford, may be given of the force of the action of powder, even in an open joint : the same experiment also incidentally serves to illustrate another object of inquiry.

The rock was a very hard conglomerate, in fair parallel beds ; the surface was even ; the side H, H, fig. 11, had been already excavated ; there was a joint or bed, parallel to the surface, and 7 feet below it. A hole a, of 2 inches diameter and 6 feet deep, had been loaded with 1 lb. 14 oz. of powder, (15 inches), and made a straight crack c c, and to k, of 14 feet long, and down to the bed.

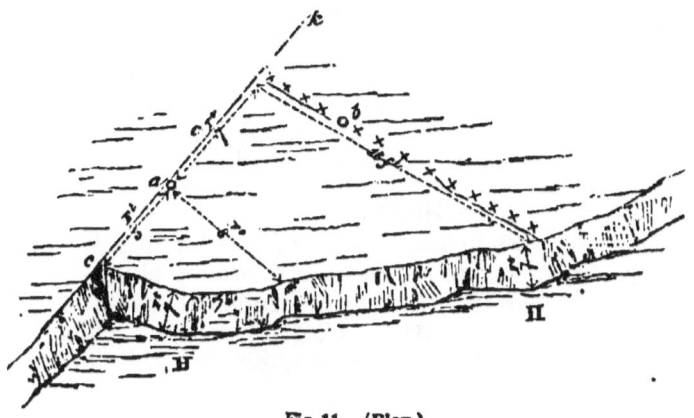

Fig. 11.—(Plan.)

A trial was then made, whether openings might not be directed to particular lines : 13 plug holes were drilled along the line + + + 8 inches deep and 1½ inch diameter ; a 2¼-inch hole was then bored at *b*, to a depth of 5 feet 10 inches, and loaded with 4 lb. (2 feet) of powder : when fired, the line was opened very nearly along the line of the plug-holes ; the separation did not exceed half an inch.

The hole *b* was then cleared out, and loaded with 8 lb. of powder, and the explosion sent the whole mass forward upwards of 2 feet without any new fracture ; the cubic contents of the mass being 663 feet, weighing about 51 tons.

In most extensive quarries of stone, much of the practice must depend upon the intelligence with which advantage is taken of the position and nature of the joints and fissures : still many errors are committed from a want of knowledge of the best application of powder to a perfectly solid mass ; and in cases where the mass to be removed is small, or the openings to be made, confined, but little advantage can be gained by the joints, and the application should be chiefly to given charges for lines of least resistance.

The advantage obtained by joints is one reason for rather reducing the calculated amount of charges, particularly in large explosions ; because, although nothing that is not perceptible can well *augment* the force of resistance, fissures or joints that may not be seen on the surface may have the effect of *reducing* it.

It would be of much advantage, in many cases, if the powder could be placed in a more compact form, than occupying a considerable length of a hole of comparatively small diameter: the position it must assume in these holes is generally unfavourable for producing the best effect, and in some cases renders it impossible to apply so large a charge as would be desirable; but no practical mode of enlarging the space at the bottom of the hole has yet been contrived, except perhaps by successive explosions from the same, as practised at Gibraltar.*

It may be assumed that 1 lb. of powder loosely poured, but not shaken or compressed, will occupy about 30 cubic inches; a cubic foot weighs consequently aboot 57½ lb., although different quantities are given in different tables of specific gravity: if close shaken, powder will go into a smaller compass.

The following Table from Colonel Pasley's (now Major-Gen. Sir Chas. Pasley, K.C.B.) Memoranda on Mining will give the means of calculating the space occupied by any given quantity of powder in round holes of different sizes from 1 to 6 inches:—

Diameter of the hole.	Powder contained in one inch of hole.		Powder contained in one foot of hole.		Depth of hole to contain 1 lb. of powder.
Inches.	lb.	oz.	lb.	oz.	Inches.
1	0	0·419	0	5·028	38·197
1½	0	0·942	0	11·304	16·976
2	0	1·676	1	4·112	9·549
2½	0	2·618	1	15·416	6·112
3	0	3·77	2	13·24	4·244
3½	0	5·131	3	13·572	3·118
4	0	6·702	5	0·424	2·387
4½	0	8·482	6	5·784	1·886
5	0	10·472	7	13·664	1·528
5½	0	12·671	9	8·052	1·263
6	0	15·08	11	4·96	1·061

In practice, the holes are somewhat irregular; this table, however, will be sufficient to ascertain, nearly, the depth required for any charge.

* In the Appendix will be found a memorandum by General Burgoyne on the use, at Marseilles, of nitric acid for the purpose of enlarging the inner end of the hole; and also a brief description of a patent obtained by the Baron Liebhaber for an apparatus for this purpose.—ED.

OF THE POWDER AND THE CHARGE.

Gunpowder used for the blasting of rock is notoriously of inferior strength to that sold for sporting, or manufactured by Government for the army and navy; and there is an impression (I believe nearly universal) that it is right that it should be so, not merely because pound for pound it is cheaper; but because it is thought to be positively better for the object, on account of its less rapid ignition, and assumed quality of giving what the miners call a *heave.*

This opinion appears to be founded on a fallacy.

Inferior powder *cannot* be used in war, or for sporting, without the disadvantage being immediately apparent; while in blasting it can be made to answer the purpose: this, with its comparative cheapness, has led, no doubt, to its being introduced and constantly made use of, without much investigation as to the policy of its employment in preference to a material of superior strength.

The argument used in its favour is, that, by igniting slowly in comparison with the other, the power is more forcibly and efficiently applied for the required object, than by the rapid shock of the superior powder, such as is undeniably requisite for impelling projectiles.

This reasoning would seem to imply that the rock will be opened better by a force of *pressure* than by that of a sudden *shock* or *blow;* which, however, may be disputed, even supposing, what is probably not the case, that the elastic vapour generated by either is the same. Rock being of a brittle nature, it is reasonable to suppose that the sudden violent shock would make more extensive cracks, which is the great object, than a more slow action.

The following are the observations I have been able to collect on this head; and they tend to confirm the impression of the good policy of employing stronger powder for blasting, even at increased prices: more research, however, would be necessary to establish the fact entirely, and to fix the relative value of each gradation in quality.

Having procured from great contractors and respectable dealers eleven samples of Merchants' blasting powder, stated to be that of the principal manufacturers, they were analysed, proved with the éprouvette mortar and éprouvette gun, and compared by the bursting of shells: the results will be seen in the annexed tables.

Qualities and Proofs of eleven samples of Merchants' blasting powder, as compared with Government cannon powder.

Number of samples.		Results of analysis per centage.				Ranges from éprouvette mortar.			No. of degrees and tenths by éprouvette gun.	Remarks.
		Nitre.	Sulphur and Charcoal.	Loss.	Total.	1st.	2nd.	Mean.		
		grs.	grs.	grs.	grs.	ft.	ft.	ft.	degrees.	
1	Said to be of same manufacturers, but procured from different dealers.	72½	25	2½	100	97	93	95	16·6	Highly impregnated with foul salts.
2		66	32½	1½	100	142	137	139½	17·3	Contains foul salts, but not so much as No. 1.—Deficient in nitre.
3	. . . .	66	32	2	100	150	91	120½	18·7	Deficient in nitre, and highly impregnated with foul salts.
4	Two qualities, from the same manufacturers, but procured from different dealers.	66½	31½	2	100	79	99	89	14·6	Same as last.
5		75	24	1	100	125	148	136½	...	Nitre very impure.
6		73½	25½	1	100	83	67	75	...	
7	Two qualities, same manufacturers.	73½	24½	2	100	118	113	115½	17·7	Highly impregnated with foul salts.
8		66	32	2	100	43	55	49	16·9	Do., and deficient in nitre.
9	Three qualities, same manufacturers.	73	25½	1½	100	169	158	163½	12·0	Contain foul salts, but by no means so much as the preceding samples.
10		73	25½	1½	100	128	148	138	to	
11		73	25	2	100	127	107	117	15·2	
	Good Government cannon powder.	75	25	...	100	...	...	265	21·0	Ingredients pure and very intimately mixed.

The best proportion of nitre (the most valuable ingredient) is 75 per cent.

The éprouvette mortar is 8 inches in diameter, and is charged with 2 ounces of the powder, and an iron ball of 68½ lbs. weight; the Government good cannon powder gives an average range of 265 feet. The Government powder somewhat deteriorated, and reserved for blasting, gives a range of 240 feet.

The éprouvette gun is of brass; its bore 1¼ inch in diameter and 27·6 inches long; it weighs 86½ lbs., and is suspended from a frame: being charged with 2 ounces of the powder, without any shot or wadding, it is fired, and the extent of the recoil is measured by an index on a graduated arc.

The éprouvette gun is considered to be rather adapted to try the strength of *fine grained* powder than of the coarse; the fine grained Government Rifle powder will give 25 or 26 degrees; the Government good cannon powder 21 degrees; that tried at the same time with the above, 20·5. It is extremely probable that in many instances of these coarse grained qualities, and of the Merchants' powder, igniting slowly, much of the charges may have been thrown out from the gun in each case unignited, and perhaps in some degree from the mortar.

Some discrepancies will be observed in nearly all proofs of gunpowder, but rarely to the extent that will be noticed in this Table: they show, however, how very unequal may be the qualities of the article as obtained at different times, from different dealers, and subject to a variety in their condition from modes and time of keeping; and they also exhibit a very strong presumption of universal inferiority.

Experiments on the relative strength of Government cannon powder and Merchants' blasting powder, by the bursting of 5½-inch spherical case shells.

Government Cannon Powder.

No. of experiments.	No. of shell.	Charges of powder. (oz.)	Effect.	Observations.
1	1	4	None.	
2	2	6	None.	
3	1	8	Burst.	Loaded and fired warm from previous explosion.
8	5	7	None.	
9	6	8	None.	
10	7	9	None.	
11	8	10	Burst.	
15	12	9	Burst.	Second trial of same shell, but quite cold.
16	3	8	None.	
18	5	9	Burst.	Second trial of same shell, but quite cold.

Merchants' Blasting Powder.

No. of experiments.	No. of shell.	Charges of powder. (oz.)	Effect.	Observations.
4	2	8	None.	Loaded and fired warm from previous explosion.
5	3	10	None.	
6	2	12	Burst.	Third trial of same shell, loaded and fired warm.
7	4	11	None.	
12	9	12	None.	
13	10	14	Burst.	
14	11	13	Burst.	
17	4	12	None.	Second trial of same shell, but quite cold.
19	6	12	Burst.	Second trial of same shell, but quite cold.

The comparative strength by this mode of trial would seem to be about 9 parts of the Government, equal to 13 of the Merchants' powder.

It is very difficult to obtain any very precise results from trials on the rock itself: the effects vary so greatly under circumstances to all appearance precisely similar, that we are driven to reason very much from analogy; and where the blasting is judiciously performed, the tamping but slightly, if at all removed, and the rock merely opened and not violently ejected, it certainly would appear reasonable that the powder showing such superiority of strength in the above-described experiments would be by far the most efficient in its action on the rock.

A few trials that were made at Kingstown to elucidate the point seemed to prove the truth of this reasoning.

Charges calculated on the basis of $\frac{1}{2}$ ounce for 1 foot, and augmented in proportion to the cubes of the lines of least resistance, were exploded in a high face of very solid rock; and the result in every case was very marked in favour of the Government powder, even to the conviction of the miners present, who had previously expressed doubts on the subject.

Although the Government powder was applied to the cases which seemed to present the fewest advantages, the effect was decidedly superior, to the extent of usually dislodging a mass of rock; whereas the Merchants' powder in no instance did more than make cracks and fissures.

If the truth of this suggestion be acknowledged, the following advantages would attend the use of the superior powder.

1. As smaller quantities would go farther, the stock for consumption would be easier to stow away and to carry.

2. Greater effect would be produced with a smaller amount of labour, and, what is of more consequence in many cases, of time in boring holes.

3. By occupying a smaller space in the bottom of a hole, an increased resistance in the tamping would be obtained by its greater proportionate extent.

4. The Government powder, and the superior kind made for sporting, (the former in particular,) are *much less* subject to deterioration from keeping, than the ordinary blasting powder; this would effect a very desirable improvement, but it is not an absolutely necessary consequence of their being stronger, because the best preserving powders are not always the strongest.

According to Dr. Ure's Chemical Analysis, there is not

much difference between the mixtures of the Government Waltham Abbey powder, and those of the *first class of sporting* powder of the private manufacturers; the Government powder, however, resisted rather the best the hygrometric influence, that is, would absorb less atmospheric moisture, and consequently be best for keeping.

In the works carried on by the Royal Engineer department, the powder is usually from the Ordnance stores, sometimes being perfectly good, or even if deteriorated to the degree for its being appropriated to blasting, it is still much stronger than the Merchants' blasting powder.

Fine grained powder made with very superior care, and at superior cost, is manufactured for the Rifle Service by Government, and for shooting by private manufacturers: but it would be too costly in proportion to its increased superiority, and some of its properties not being necessary for blasting, it is considered that the best *cannon* powder would be the most advantageous to employ.

Blasting powder is sold by dealers in the country at from 50*s.* to 75*s.* per 100 lbs.; while nearly as good powder of this nature as can be made, such as the Government cannon powder, might be sold *by the manufacturers* at between 50*s.* and 60*s.*: supposing, therefore, that the cost, including the removal, the *dealers'* expenses and profit, should be one quarter or one third more than at present, the question will be, considering the advantage of using this superior kind, and the proportion which the cost of the powder bears in the general expenditure of blasting, how far, and under what circumstances, it might be desirable to incur that increased expense, making allowance at the same time for the smaller quantity that would be consumed.

Founded on the same reasoning of the advantage of more gradual ignition, and almost leading to the assumption that the blasting powder in its present state is even *too good*, is the assertion that will be found in all books on the subject, namely, that a mixture of fine and dry sawdust of elm or beech with the powder, in the proportion of $\frac{1}{5}$ of sawdust for small charges, and $\frac{1}{8}$ for large, will produce as good results as equal quantities of powder alone.

It is not assumed that the effect is produced by any decomposition of the sawdust, but simply by giving a little more space, and by dividing the particles of the charge, causing them to ignite more gradually, and thus to act with greater force on the rock, than by the more sudden explosion.

No account is given of any defined experiments tending to prove this fact; on the contrary, every trial affording positive results is against it : such a mixture has been tried in guns, and produced no useful effect whatever; and though of very simple application, it does not appear that in any place there has been a continued use of it.

There is indeed a deception in the first instance in the supposed proportions; for a mixture of two equal measures of the two ingredients, the sawdust being, as required, very fine and dry, and the powder of the usual large grain, will not fill above 1¾ of the same measure; consequently, two measures of the mixture will contain nearly ⅛ more powder than calculated upon: thus if two measures, each capable of containing 8 ounces of powder, be filled with the mixture of equal measured proportions, the quantity of powder will be nearer 9 ounces than the 8 calculated upon.

Altogether I feel little doubt of the application of sawdust being of no real value.

Another theoretical refinement, that is to be found in all works on blasting, is, that if a hollow space be left adjoining the charge, a much greater effect will be produced, provided always (and it is essential to bear it in mind) that the tamping be as substantial, and to *as great* extent, in the one case as in the other.

Thus, in two holes of similar dimensions, the charge c, fig. 12, with a hollow space D over it, will produce as good an

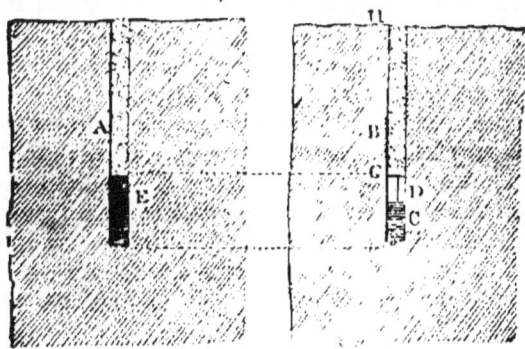

Fig. 12.

effect with ½ or ¾ the quantity, as at the full charge E fully tamped, provided the tamping B, from G to H, be as good and as deep as that at A.

An increased effect will certainly be produced by such

hollow, in the same manner as with guns which are frequently burst by the occurrence of a hollow between the powder and the shot, but there must be great reason to doubt its *practical* utility : no accounts are given of the well-defined result of actual experiment, nor are any rules attempted to be laid down for the extent of the hollow spaces in proportion to the quantity of powder in the charge, &c., to produce useful effect ; and yet these must be matters of consequence ; nor is it any-where stated that it has been ever practically continued to be used, notwithstanding the great saving of powder professed to arise from the adoption of this principle.

In large charges, the space that could be left would be too small to produce any useful effect ; and in small charges, the more simple, quick, and cheap way, would be by using the full charge of powder.

This and the sawdust are among the refinements adverted to in books (on this as on many other subjects), but seldom, if ever, put in practice.

Another mode of improving the power of the charges of powder has been employed, it is said, in America.   It is the mixing of a quantity of quicklime in a proportion of about ¼ with the powder, on the principle that it will absorb any little moisture in the powder, and itself produce some additional vapour in the explosion.   It is stated, however, that it must be used soon after the ingredients are put together, it having been remarked that if left mixed for a whole night the powder was deteriorated, owing, as imagined, to the impurities of the saltpetre of which the powder was composed.*

With reference to the quantities of powder to be employed in blasting, different systems are adopted.

In quarries worked for large stones, and in great quantities, sometimes very large blasts are considered advantageous.

In those near Kingstown, where the granite stones for ashlar work are squared by the contractors to from 40 to 60 cubic feet each, 50, 60, and 70 lb. of powder were frequently exploded in a single blast, sometimes filling two-thirds of a hole of 4 or 3½ inches diameter, and perhaps 20 feet deep.

---

* There are other reasons against this practice.   The absorption of water must be attended with the evolution of heat ; and it is highly probable that, under such circumstances, there would be a reaction between the sulphur and nitre, in the presence of so powerful a base, and the ultimate production of sulphate of lime.   Whilst then, the simplicity of the operation is diminished, the powder is deteriorated ; and, if much moisture be present, not without danger.

They have been applied generally where a projection of considerable height or length, showing joints in large features, offered a prospect of bringing down some enormous mass; and in this way they were usually very successful.

To give an instance of one :—

The hole was 19 feet 7 inches in depth, and 5½ inches diameter : the charge, 75 lb. of powder, filled 8 feet 10 inches of the hole, having consequently 10 feet 9 inches of tamping.

The mass that was brought down, or thoroughly shaken and rent, measured, on a rough calculation, 1200 cubic yards, or 2400 tons. The cost was calculated at £6 15s. 8d., thus :

2 men, 14 days, at 1s. 8d. each	£2	6	8
1 ditto, 14 days, at 1s. 6d.	1	1	0
75 lb. powder	2	0	0
Fuse	0	2	0
Smith's work, iron, steel, &c.	1	6	0
	£6	15	8

Of course there was a great deal of after-work and small blasts required for the separation of the large masses of which this shaken rock consisted, and reducing it to manageable shapes and sizes; but the work was greatly facilitated by this first effect.

At Gibraltar, the military miners under the Royal Engineers work on quite a different system.

The rock there is a peculiarly hard lime-stone marble : to bring down large masses, they bore their holes usually to about the depth of 9 feet with 2½-inch jumpers, and load them with about 4 lb. of powder; the explosion has no apparent effect, but the rock is shaken below: the needle hole is cleared out, and the hole again filled, when it will take perhaps from 8 to 12 lbs., and is fired again; a third charge, with perhaps 20 to 30 lb., is fired in the same manner, and sometimes a fourth, till the rock is very greatly separated and rent to the extent of 10, 20, or 30 feet in different directions. If the needle hole or tamping be deranged before the final explosion, it is bored out and re-tamped.

Under all ordinary circumstances I should much prefer the principle of this system to the other; it is more gradual and systematic, would require less labour in boring, and is less subject to waste of powder, or the violent projecting of stones.

In some rocks it may be liable to one objection, which is, the chance of any of the preliminary explosions tapping a

c

spring or vent for water into the hole; no such springs are found at Gibraltar, but they are at Kingstown.

If the holes should not be vertical, or nearly so (which it seems they always are at Gibraltar), the tamping must be bored out at each explosion, to enable the next charge of powder to be introduced.

The prevailing fault in blasting is the using too much powder.

If the tamping be not blown out by the smaller charges, a very useful effect will have been produced on the rock by every explosion, even although the rock be not *apparently* much affected; the tamping will be easily bored out sufficiently to admit a fresh charge, which, being introduced and re-tamped, will be found to be very efficient.

The object is generally to loosen and bring the rock down in large masses, and not to shatter it into fragments: even for small stone, such as for road metalling, &c., it is better to bring out first large masses, and subsequently to divide them, either by small blasts with powder, or by crowbars and wedges.

OF LOADING.

The ordinary manner in quarries of loading and firing the holes that have been bored is,

I. To dry out the bottom, if necessary, with little wisps of hay.

II. To pour in the powder till it fills a certain number of feet or inches of the bottom of the hole. If the hole be vertical, or very nearly so, the powder will drop in pretty clear to the bottom; but if it be on an inclination, and not very steep, the powder must be scraped down, professedly with a wooden ramrod, but frequently with an iron scraper. If the hole be horizontal, a scoop is used, which is open at top, and by being turned round at the end of the hole leaves the powder there. If the hole incline upwards, a cartridge is employed.

III. A needle is then introduced, the point of which is let well into the charge of powder, and the top with a handle or eye extending to the outside of the hole.

IV. A little wadding, either hay, or straw, or turf, is inserted over the powder.

V. The tamping over the wad is very generally of the small fragments of the quarry stone and its dust (unless there be in it flint or other substance that *notoriously* strikes fire, in which case broken brick is commonly used), rammed down, by one or two inches at a time, by means of an iron rod or tamping-bar; the needle is frequently turned to prevent its becoming fixed.

VI. The last inch or two is filled with damp clay.

VII. The needle is carefully pulled out, and the opening it has left is filled with loose fine-grained powder; or with a long series of connected straws filled with powder, into the upper end of which is inserted a small piece of touch-paper that will burn about half a minute, which is lighted and communicates the fire.

The touch-paper is made by the quarrymen themselves, by soaking coarse paper in a strong solution of saltpetre or gunpowder, and then drying it.

The following is an expressive account of the process, as written by a quarryman of much experience :—

"The method of blasting is in every place nearly the same, as far as I have been able to make observations, and I have had charge of such work in Scotland, England, Wales, America, and, lastly, in Ireland. Different quarrymen may, it is true, not agree in everything; for instance, some prefer a small piece of dry turf for a wad over the powder before they commence ramming; others prefer hay or straw; but in ramming every one uses the same kind of stuff, that is, small pieces of any stone (that has no flint in it) that will go into the drill hole; but, in deep holes, ramming sand will do as well as anything.

"The usual method of blasting is very simple, and is as follows : first, to drill the hole, say 3 feet deep, 1½-inch bore ; in common cases, 6 inches powder will be sufficient in the bottom; then in with your needle, then your wad of turf or hay, &c.; then two or three blows with your rammer, and then in with a handful of small stones; four or five blows more of your rammer; and so on till you fill up the vacuity above the powder within 1 inch of the top; then fill said 1 inch with a bit of moist clay (not too wet), and then extract your needle; lastly, fill up the needle hole with fine powder, or, what is safer, put down straws filled with powder, and apply your match, to which set fire, and run as fast as you can, and you have the whole of it."

Nothing can be more, 1st, uncertain,—2nd, wasteful,—3rd, dangerous.—4th, unscientific, than the whole of this process.

1st. Missing fire occurs frequently,—some obstruction will arise in the needle hole ; any moisture in the hole, or wetness in the atmosphere, will affect so small a quantity of powder as composes the train; loose powder for the train cannot be introduced into any but such as are vertical or very steep, and straws of any length are not easily passed through to the charge. All these and other circumstances must create much uncertainty.

2nd. To say nothing of the guess-work in the proportion of the charge, there must be much waste in the manner of introducing the powder, and in the occasional missing fire.

3rd. With regard to the danger, it manifestly pervades every step from the first handling of the powder.

4th. No rule is adopted for the charge, nor for the size of the holes, nor for the depth of tamping; no knowledge acquired of the best material and mode of tamping, nor any contrivances for accelerating and simplifying the process, or reducing its danger.

To obviate in some degree these defects, the following proceedings have been adopted with success:

To allot every charge by weight, according to a scale adapted to lines of least resistance, or to the circumstances of the case.

The overseer (or, if the work be sufficiently considerable, an express powderman) to have on the spot a strong copper canister containing from 3 or 4, to 10 or 12 lb. of powder, with a large mouth or opening, but thoroughly secured by a well-fitted cover from spilling, accident, or weather, and with a lock and key.

He should have a set of marked copper measures that will contain, when full, just 1 lb., 4 ounces, and 1 ounce of powder, respectively;* a copper cylindrical tube of 3 feet, or 3 feet 6 inches long, by ¼ inch diameter from out to out; a set of three tubes of about an inch in diameter, 3 feet long each, with joints, so as to be screwed at pleasure into one length of 6 or 9 feet, or with more joints if deeper holes are employed, and so constructed that when together the interior should form one smooth surface: a copper funnel, the bowl large enough to contain about 1 lb. of powder, and the neck 2 inches long, by somewhat less than ¼ inch diameter; together with some coils of Bickford's patent fuse.

By means of the measures, the tubes, and the funnel, any

---

* Where the blasting is constant, and the charges vary but little, such as in sinking shafts, driving galleries, &c., it might be found convenient to have charges of the most usual quantities prepared previously in papers, cartridges, or perhaps even in little boxes or chargers.

specific charge of powder may be lodged *clear* to the bottom of any hole; and if horizontal, or nearly so, by pushing it in through the tubes with a wooden stick or ramrod.*

One end of a piece of the patent fuse is inserted well into the powder, the other end cut off about an inch beyond the outside of the hole; a little wadding is then pressed down over the powder with the tamping-bar, and upon that the tamping in the usual manner (but with a proper material) to the top, without any necessity for the moist clay.

Most of the accidents that occur to miners arise from the fir___ows of the tamping-bar over the charge; to obviate th___ e first 2 or 3 inches of the tamping should be merely pressed down gently over the wadding, and then the hard ramming commenced over that: this cannot injure the effect of the explosion, as it is generally acknowledged that a small vacant space about the powder tends, if anything, to increase its power.

If the tamping-bar be tipped with brass, it will add more security, and at *very little* increased expense.

The outer end of the fuse is then lighted; there is neither difficulty, loss of time, nor extra cost or labour, by using these precautions, and obtaining all the consequent advantages; they should therefore never be neglected.

Whenever blasting is to be performed on an extensive scale within a limited space, it will be quite worth while to ascertain by a few experiments the value of the different ingredients that are to be used, or matter to be acted upon in the particular locality, as well as the best modes of applying them; such as the strength of the powder, the tenacity of the rock, the value of the tamping material, &c: it is clear that, by proportioning these justly, so as to obtain the greatest effect with the smallest means, much time and expense may be spared.

OF THE TRAIN AND FIRING.

The inconveniences and loss of time attending the ordinary mode of laying the trains for firing the charge in blasting holes have been mentioned above.

It is the very worst contrived part of the whole operation

---

* It affords one very important medium of security against accidents to deposit the powder quite clear to the bottom of the hole by means of these tubes, instead of allowing grains to hang on the sides, as they must do when it is poured in in the ordinary manner, particularly in holes that are inclined, where it is easy to conceive that a *regular train* may sometimes be left from top to bottom.

of blasting ; but fortunately a most valuable improvement
has been made of late years by the invention of Bickford's
patent safety fuse.*

The use of this article is extremely simple; it is efficient
in damp situations, and even under water, by using the
quality prepared expressly for that object; a miss-fire is
scarcely ever experienced, unless there be great carelessness,
and it is a *very great* protection against accidents.

Whenever accidents have occurred (which are *extremely*
rare), they have been traced to circumstances which could
not be affected by the fuse ; namely, to the first applications
of the tamping-bar over the powder.

So large an opening for the escape of the powder is not
created by the fuse-hole as by the needle ;† and, taking everything into consideration, it is calculated that the use of the
fuse is cheaper than the ordinary priming, even if the very
trifling cost, or at least difference of either, could be deemed
of importance.

SAFETY FUSE.

At Kingstown Harbour it was employed constantly in
working with a diving bell in blasting rock for foundations
in from 20 to 30 feet depth of water, and with complete
success.

The following account of the great value of this invention
is from a Paper by B. Mullins, Esq., an intelligent member
of the firm who have the contract for the Kingstown
Harbour works :—

" Rock-blasting operations have been for many years, and
are now, carried on extensively by my firm. Bickford's
safety fuse has been invariably used in those operations since

---

* This patent was granted on the 6th September, 1831, to W. Bickford,
of Tucking Mill, Cornwall, for " an instrument for igniting gunpowder
when used for blasting rocks, which he denominates the ' Miners' Safety
Fuse.' " This fuse was therein described to be a cylinder of gunpowder
or other explosive compound, inclosed within a hempen cord, which is
first twisted and afterwards overlaid with another cord to strengthen
the casing thus formed, then varnished to preserve the contents from
injury by moisture, and finally covered with whiting, or other suitable
matter, to prevent the varnish from adhering.—[ED.]

† In firing very small charges, the opening made by the needle or fuse-
hole tends very much to reduce the effect. In the tamping experiments
it will be observed that, of clay, and other compact tamping, portions of
the top were frequently carried away; in all these and other partial
removals of tamping it was observed that the principal openings were
always on the side where the fuse had been.

the summer of 1833. It has our entire approval, as being more certain in its effects, less hazardous in its application, and ultimately cheaper, although not apparently so, than priming in the ordinary mode. From the period of its introduction up to the present time, we have not had an accident in any of our works from blasting, although within that period 73,600 lb. of powder have been consumed, and labour equal to that of 288,719 days of one man expended : nor had we more than two or three cases of miss-fire that I can recollect, and those were caused by want of caution in using improper tamping material, having stones in it which cut the fuse and severed the train. We have used of it in the interval 167,322 lineal feet.

"The cost of 167,322 feet of the fuse was 304l. 7s. 9d., while that of the actual quantity of powder required for the same amount of priming, namely, 35 barrels, would be 105l. besides the labour of the application of the latter."

Then follows a comparison between the old system of loading and firing, and the mode with the fuse.

After describing in detail the old practice (that, indeed, still used in most places), the statement continues thus :

"In the application of the fuse the charge may be lodged at any required depth in the rock. We lately drove a hole with a 5-inch gauge 20$\frac{1}{4}$ feet horizontally into the face of the cliff at Dalkey, and charged it with 85 lb. of powder, by which we released 2000 tons of solid rock, a quantity far exceeding what could be displaced by vertical or oblique bores. Straw tubes could hardly be made of so great lengths, and, were it practicable, there is so great a loss of time, and so much uncertainty in using them in horizontal holes of much less depth, that they bear no comparison in facility of use to the fuse, which effectually supersedes the tedious and hazardous employment of the needle, and is a perfect preventive against premature explosion or miss-fire, wherein the old methods are particularly defective.

"It has this further advantage, that any number of shots may be simultaneously fired, whilst with the straw-tubes and match-paper not more than three, with a probable chance of escape to the men employed.

"In wet quarries the fuse is quite as effective as in dry : where wet joints are met with in boring, which frequently happens, the holes fill with water, and must necessarily, by the old methods, before being charged, be rendered perfectly dry ; this is accomplished by wrapping coarse tow or mop

thrums round the end of a stick, and mopping out the water ;
the finest argillaceous clay is then kneaded into a paste, and
worked constantly upwards and downwards by the tamper
struck with the hammer, and continued until the blaster is
satisfied of having staunched the leaky joints in the hole :
this being done, the hole is then cleared out with an iron
scraper, made dry, and charged ; and, after all this labour,
success is doubtful.   A man often spends half a day drying,
tamping, and charging a hole in this way to no purpose, the
powder having got wet.

"In these cases the fuse furnishes an effectual remedy ; a
waterproof bag containing the powder, and having a sufficient
length of fuse closely tied in its mouth, is pushed home to
the bottom of the hole, which is then tamped and fired with
as much certainty and effect as in dry work.

"Blasting in deep water by means of the diving bell is
rendered comparatively easy by the use of the fuse, as compared with the tedious, costly, and ineffective process hereto-
fore practised.

"In the old way, the charge was lodged in a tin canister
in the bored rock ; in this canister a small tube was fixed,
and raised joint after joint, until the bell was elevated above
the water's surface ; then a small piece of iron made red hot
was thrown into the tube to fire the charge in the canister.
What the effect produced may have been, I cannot say of my
own knowledge, not having seen those operations ; but I
have been informed that, except in insulated rocks, it was of
little use.   The canister and the joint of the tube adjoining
were blown to pieces, and most of the joints more remote
were flattened by the collapse of the water, so that new
canisters and tubes were necessary for every shot.

"The fuse employed in blasting under water is somewhat
different, and more expensive than the other, and is called
sump-fuse ; it is used in the following manner :

"A waterproof charger or bag, containing the powder with
a piece of fuse 5 or 6 feet long closely tied in its mouth, is
dipped in boiling pitch * to secure the orifice from wet ; the
charge is then put into the bore-hole, which is tamped with
sand, or the fine chippings of the stone-cutter's waste, and
the fuse, the upper end of which is retained in the diving

---

* A *perfect* waterproof composition for this purpose is made of
8 parts by weight, pitch,
1 do.   do.   bees'-wax, } melted together, but not boiled.
1 do.   do.   tallow,

bell, being set fire to, is thrust out under its edge into the water : the bell is then, by signal, removed 8 or 10 feet out of the way ; the fuse burns through the water, and explosion follows ; the proximity of the bell to the blasted rock, without endangering the workmen, enables them to resume their operations with little or no delay.

"In founding the Commercial Wharf wall (a considerable part on rock) in 22 feet water at low water of spring-tides and in clearing for abutment for setting frame for the eastern pier head in 28 feet at low water (the rise of tide 12 feet) we pursued the method above described with success.

"Having obtained a list of all the men who had been killed, or badly wounded, by the old methods of blasting at the quarries for the Kingstown Harbour works, previous to the use of the fuse, I annex it."

The list referred to of accidents under previous contracts, for the first 15 years, contains the names of 30 individuals, two of whom were twice injured, making 32 casualties, consequently more than 2 per year ; it includes 7 killed, 4 loss of one eye, 1 loss of both eyes, and 20 injuries ; while, during the 8 years of the present contract, there has been but one man injured, and that before the fuse was introduced.

In order to test the extent of applicability of this composition for blasting under water, pieces of the quality prepared for it (called sump-fuse), which is somewhat thicker than the ordinary kind, being about $\frac{3}{10}$ of an inch thick, were kept immersed (except the upper ends) for different periods up to upwards of 16 hours, and were then found to burn throughout with their ordinary force; no trial was made beyond that time.

Pieces 25 feet long (their usual dimension), having one end inserted into a few ounces of powder inclosed in a waterproof bag, were tied to long chains ; the powder-bag was lowered into the water by a weight, and, the other end of the fuse being lighted from a boat, the whole was lowered again until the weight touched the bottom in 39 feet depth, and each time burned through and exploded the powder in 13 or 14 minutes. In order to get a greater length, an extra kind was procured in 51 feet and 52 feet lengths ; it was apparently expressly made, and thicker than the other, being about ⅝ of an inch in diameter.

This succeeded perfectly in every case ; but, being provided for the purpose, it was not considered so satisfactory a trial, and appears to be unnecessary, considering the efficiency of that usually sold.

The common fuse (that not prepared for water) was tried, and on some occasions, when lighted very soon after being immersed, would burn through many feet under water, but frequently only a short distance; it is manifestly not adapted for water (and not assumed to be so), but it is perfectly efficient in damp situations, if fired without much delay.

There is one great merit in this fuse, namely, that the improvement is gained without the least sacrifice of simplicity; on the contrary, it is much easier to apply than any other process.

The only inconvenience attending its use, of which I am aware, is the length of time it takes to burn any but short pieces.

It burns at the rate of from 2 to 3 feet per minute; and as a minute usually affords ample time for the person firing to remove to a sufficient distance, there is a delay and an impatience created in watching the longer terms, particularly when it amounts to 3 or 4 minutes, or more.*

This lengthened time of burning would quite preclude its use for many military mines, where the explosion must take place at a particular instant.

In blasting under water, as it can only be lighted in the bell, or at the surface if the bell be not used in firing and the water deep, the time consumed in burning the fuse would be very inconvenient.

FIRING BY A VOLTAIC BATTERY.

Charges of powder have been fired under ground, as well as under water, and to considerable distances, by the voltaic battery.

It is to be presumed, however, that the distinct machinery for this purpose, the expense, and probably some degree of nicety in its arrangements, even after all the improvements that have been made at Chatham by Colonel Pasley, would render it inapplicable to ordinary purposes; although for firing *very large* quantities of powder, under very peculiar circumstances, it has been considered very useful. The tamping by this mode would be much more complete and substantial, having only two thin wires through it; and by the very instantaneous effect produced, even at varying distances, simultaneous explosions, that are impossible

---

* The fuse burns slower through a tamping of loose sand than through a tough material well rammed, but it is not extinguished by it.

by any other means, might be effected by this mode of ignition.*

MODE OF LIGHTING A TRAIN IN SHAFTS.

Under many circumstances the manner adopted for *lighting* a train is a matter of some consequence.

At the bottom of deep shafts, or of long small galleries where there is no shelter for the man who applies the light, the touch-paper, German tinder, or match of whatever kind, must afford time for him to get completely out of the way. It is attended with some difficulty to secure that object, without wasting time in doing so, by allowing too long an interval; but the latter must be the usual, as the only safe alternative.

The safety fuse has an advantage in this respect, as its period of burning can be more regularly calculated than that of any other match usually resorted to.

A French engineer has proposed and employed a manner of remedying this inconvenience, as far as regards blasting in a shaft, which would appear to be useful where the safety fuse is not employed.

One end of a wire is fixed temporarily into a little powder connected with the train, the other end in a coil being at the surface of the ground.

The wire is carefully straightened up the shaft from any sharp twists or bends; a piece of German tinder is passed round it, forming a very loose ring, and, being lighted, is let go, and drops down on the powder.

The wire may of course be constantly suspended to the side of the shaft, and fixed and applied from time to time as wanted, being lengthened from the coil above as occasion requires.

To facilitate the descent, if necessary, a small weight might be easily added, to the under part of which the lighted match could be fixed.

MEANS FOR PREVENTING SMALL STONES FLYING ABOUT IN BLASTING.

A great loss of time and labour is experienced in quarries and other confined situations, arising from the necessity for

---

* In the Appendix is given a brief account of the successful application of the voltaic firing in removing the Round Down Cliff, at Dover for the works of the South-Eastern Railway.—[ED.]

the workmen to retire to a distance at every blast; not only those engaged in the precise operation, but all others who can be at all supposed to be within reach of its effects.

This is a greater evil than what is perhaps commonly thought.

I have myself been in a great quarry, and in the course of half an hour seen 20 or 30 men, at given signals, retire two or three times from five or six different parts at which they were at work, to which they went leisurely back again after each explosion or ascertained miss-fire.

There is another occasion where the necessary retiring of the miner from the effect of a blast is attended with peculiar inconvenience; that is, from the bottom of a shaft, in which case he has to be drawn up to the top.

When a better mode of applying the charge shall be generally understood, there will be fewer occasions of the projection of stones, but there must always be some; any remedy for this waste of time, therefore, must be very valuable.

QUARRY SHIELDS.

In some quarries in the neighbourhood of Glasgow they are in the habit of frequently applying a piece of old boiler iron, of about 2 feet 6 inches square and $\frac{1}{4}$ inch thick, over the hole when fired, which acts as a shield, and, in small blasts, so far prevents any flying about of loose stones, that the men take much less precaution in moving out of the way on those occasions than when it is not used.

As they have horizontal as well as vertical faces to work on, the shield is suspended over the horizontal holes, and laid flat over those that are vertical; in the latter case a large stone or two, if at hand, is frequently placed upon it.

This application might be very useful under particular circumstances of blasting; for instance, where the blasts are generally small, and in confined situations. In a shaft, where the holes will be all probably vertical, or nearly so, and the blasts not large, a good shield could be placed over every hole, and weighted either with stones, or with one or two half-hundred weights, kept in the shaft for the purpose. On trial at the particular place, this might be found to give such *certain* security, that the miners would not require to be removed more than a very short way above, either by the bucket, or by a ladder, which would lead to a very great saving of time, labour, and expense.

ON TAMPING.

The desideratum in tamping is to obtain the greatest possible resistance over the charge of powder; if it could be made as strong as the rock itself it would be perfection.

If 12 inches of one species of tamping will afford as much resistance as 18 inches of another, the question will be—Does the former, in the application, require as much more time and expense as the operation of boring the additional 6 inches of hole? If not, it will, under most circumstances, be better in the relative proportion of that expenditure.

Where other qualities are equal, that which can be applied in the least space of time will be far preferable, particularly in such operations as sinking shafts, driving long narrow galleries or driftways, and other situations where the progress is necessarily slow.

Different materials are employed for tamping:—

I. The chips and dust of the quarry itself. This is what is most commonly used, unless there be flint or other stone in it that notoriously strikes fire.

II. Sand poured in loose, or stirred up as it is poured in, to make it more compact. This is an approved material in many places, and is recommended to be very fine and dry.

III. Clay, well dried, either by exposure to the sun, or what is more certain and more rapid, by a fire.

Wherever blasting is going on, there must be smiths' forges at work: the clay is formed by the hand into rolls of about 2 inches in diameter, and readily dried by the smiths' fires.

In the course of some experiments, clay was used that was in a state of powder, owing to its having been dried a long time previous, and was not thought so good as when applied in a state just caked enough to remain in lump.

IV. Broken brick is an approved material in some localities, as being less liable to accidents by striking fire than chips of stone.

It is used in small pieces and dust, and is improved by being slightly moistened with water during the ramming.

Vegetable earth, or any small rubbish, is sometimes applied instead of the stone chips, when the latter are considered dangerous. Such are the simple ingredients used in tamping; that is, exclusive of the addition of any mechanical contrivance: of these, the most essential to analyse is the application of sand, since its use has been by many strongly recommended, and, if efficacious, would be most convenient, on account of the rapidity and security with which it can be applied.

In Cachin's Mémoire sur la Digue de Cherbourg, printed in 1820, (a most interesting work as regards the construction of breakwaters,) it is thus stated in a note:—

" In blasting rock at Cherbourg, the use of the needle, and well-rammed tamping, has been long abandoned.

" The priming is in the usual manner, by straws, and the tamping is of very fine dry sand, poured in.

"It has been proved by long experience that the effect of the explosion is as great by this method as by the more laborious tamping in the usual manner."

And in the Journal of the Franklin Institute (United States) for July and August, 1836, after quoting a variety of experiments on the resistance of sand to motion through tubes, made as well in France as in America, and facts regarding the bursting of musket barrels, &c., by charges of sand over the powder, the conclusion come to is, that,

" Experience proves that the resistance offered by sand is quite sufficient for blasting rocks, and it is less troublesome, and more safe, than the usual mode."

It is added, that,

" To ensure success, the space left above the powder should have a length of ten or twelve times as great as the diameter of the hole."

General Pasley, on the contrary, asserts that sand as an ingredient for tamping was found at Chatham to be utterly valueless ; but acknowledges that the opportunities there of blasting were few and on a very small scale. Many other officers of the British Engineers have been long under the same impression.

It does not appear that any of these opinions have been formed upon any more precise experiments than the sensible effect upon stones or rock with the usual charges ; and as these effects are very different under circumstances that are apparently similar, and as they might vary with different proportions of the powder and ingredients used, advantage was taken of the opportunity afforded by the works carrying on at Kingstown Harbour, near Dublin, to try a few experiments that should be somewhat more definite.

The principle which it was thought would be most conclusive was, not to form a judgment by the effect produced on the rock, but to endeavour, if possible, to obtain a charge of powder that should in each case just blow out, or sensibly affect, the *tamping;* and a comparison of the charges to produce that effect would afford a strong proof of the relative value of the different systems; thus—

If it should be shown (as will be found in the following table of experiments) that ¼ of an ounce of powder would blow out the sand tamping which filled a hole of 1 inch diameter and 2 feet deep, while 3 ounces in a similar hole would not disturb a well-rammed clay tamping, it afforded a perfect confirmation of General Pasley's statement, that the sand was good for nothing, as far as the use of it on that scale went.

The experiments detailed in the following Tables were made in granite rock, and, as far as could be judged, where it was firm and without fissures.

The charges were of ordinary merchants' blasting powder, procured from the contractors.

The sand was sharp or gritty, quite dry, and simply poured in over the powder, with a little wad of hay intervening. It was from the sea-shore, and of different qualities.

The finest was a clean running sand, fine enough nearly for an hour-glass, and weighed .   .   .   .   65 lb. per cube foot.

The second quality, a middling gritty sand, and weighed   .   .   93 lb.   „

The third, very coarse, or rather very fine sea shingle, the particles being from the size of a pin's head to that of a pea, and weighed   .   .   98 lb.   „

The clay had been dried at the fire of a smith's forge, and was well rammed down in the usual manner.

Experiments to try the Comparative Value of Sand and Clay for Tamping.

F Sand, fine.   M Sand, middling.   C Sand, coarse.

No. of experiments.	Depth of hole.	Diameter of hole.	Charge of powder.	Description of tamping	Effect and Remarks.
No.	feet	inches.	lb. oz.		
1	2	1	0 2	Clay.	$\frac{1}{2}$ inch of top of tamping removed—rock fractured.
2	2	1	0 2	do.	Tamping remained—rock star-fractured.
3	2	1	0 2	do.	8$\frac{1}{2}$ inches of tamping removed—rock fractured.
4	2	1	0 2	do.	Tamping remained—rock fractured.
5	2	1	0 3	do.	Portions of tamping adhered to sides of the hole—a mass of rock blown off.
6	2	1	0 3	do.	Tamping all remained—rock fractured.
7	2	1	0 3	do.	1$\frac{2}{3}$ inch of tamping removed—rock fractured.
8	2	1	0 3	do.	Tamping remained entire—rock fractured.
9	2	1	0 4	do.	5$\frac{1}{2}$ inches of tamping removed—rock fractured.
10	2	1	0 4	do.	2 inches of tamping removed—rock star-fractured.
11	2	1	0 2	Sand.	Tamping entirely blown out—rock uninjured.
12	2	1	0 1	do.	do. do.
13	2	1	0 1	do.	do. do.
14	2	1	0 0$\frac{3}{4}$	do.	do. do.
15	2	1	0 0$\frac{1}{2}$	do.	do. do.
16	2	1	0 0$\frac{1}{4}$	do.	do. do. This was repeated three times with the same effect. N.B.—By the ordinary miners' rule of allowing $\frac{1}{3}$ depth of hole for the charge, one of 2 feet deep by 1 inch diameter would require 3$\frac{1}{2}$ ounces.
17	4	1$\frac{1}{2}$	0 6	Clay.	1 foot 8-inches of top of tamping removed—rock fractured.
18	4	1$\frac{1}{2}$	0 6	Sand.	Tamping blown clean out—no fracture. N.B.—In hole 4-feet by 1$\frac{1}{2}$ inch, $\frac{1}{3}$ of depth will contain 15 oz. of powder.
19	6	2	0 8	M Sand	Tamping blown out, no fracture.

No. of experiments.	Depth of hole.	Diameter of hole.	Charge of powder.	Description of tamping	Effect and Remarks.
No. 20	feet. 6	inches. 2	lb. oz. 0 8	CSand.	4 ft. 7 inches of tamping blown out, below which was a hard crust of about 4 inches thick, and in the cavity below there remained 8 or 9 inches of the sand, mixed with burnt powder—no fracture in the rock.
21	6	2	0 10	Clay.	Tamping unmoved—rock uninjured.
22	6	2	0 10	Sand.	1 inch of top of sand removed—rock fractured.
23	6	2	0 10	M do.	Tamping blown out—no fracture in rock.
24	6	2	0 12	Clay.	2 inches of tamping removed—rock fractured.
25	6	2	0 12	Sand.	2 ft. 4 inches of sand removed.
26	6	2	0 12	M do.	Tamping all blown out—no fracture.
27	6	2	0 14	Clay.	1 in. removed—rock fractured.
28	6	2	0 14	Sand.	7 inches removed—rock fractured.
29	6	2	1 0	Clay.	Tamping unmoved—rock fractured thoroughly.
30	6	2	1 0	Sand.	Tamping blown out—rock fractured thoroughly.
31	6	2	1 0	C do.	Tamping unmoved—rock lifted—the explosion probably escaped through the joints.
32	6	2	1 4	C do.	Tamping blown out—rock star-fractured.
33	6	2	1 8	C do.	Blown out, rock slightly cracked.
34	6	2	1 8	C do.	Tamping blown out—rock shaken, joints opened.
35	6	2	1 8	C do.	Tamping blown out—no fracture.
36	6	2	1 8	C do.	4 feet 1 inch blown out, then 3 inches of loose sand, and below that a hard crust—no fracture of rock.
37	6	2	1 8	Clay.	Tamping unmoved — rock cracked. N.B.—In hole 6 ft. by 2 inches, ¼ of depth will contain 2 lb. 8 ounces of powder.
38	9	2	0 6	MSand	7 feet 10 inches blown out—no fracture in rock.
39	9	2	0 8	M do.	8 feet 6½ inches do. do.
40	9	2	0 8	C do.	7 feet 4 inches do. do.
41	9	2	0 10	C do.	7 feet 1½ inch. do. do.

No. of experiments.	Depth of hole.	Diameter of hole.	Charge of powder.	Description of tamping	Effect and Remarks.
No. 42	feet. 9	inches. 2	lb. oz. 0 12	M Sand	Tamping blown out, no fracture.
43	9	2	0 12	C do.	7 ft. blown out—no fracture—a hard substance 1 ft. 3 in. above bottom of hole; then a cavity of 2 or 3 inches, and under it sand mixed with burnt powder; the crust required considerable labour to pierce with a 2-inch churn jumper, worked by 2 men.
44	9	2	0 14	C do.	6 feet 10½ inches blown out—no fracture—similar hard crust to preceding No.
45	9	2	3 0	Clay.	Tamping unmoved—rock very slightly cracked. N.B.—⅓ of hole 9 ft. by 2 in. will contain 3¾ lb. of powder.
46	9	2½	1 0	C Sand	3 ft. 11 in. blown out—no fracture—similar hard crust found.
47	9	2¼	1 0	M do.	Blown out, except a small crust of about ⅓ inch thick.
48	9	2¼	1 8	C do.	5 feet 3 inches blown out—rock cracked.
49	9	2½	2 0	C do.	Tamping unmoved.
50	9	2½	3 0	C do.	Tamping unmoved—the explosion found vent by a side joint near the charge—making an extensive fracture.
51	9	2½	3 0	Clay.	Tamping unmoved—rock fractd.
52	9	2½	3 8	C Sand	5 feet 10 inches blown out—no fracture.
53	9	2½	4 0	Clay.	Tamping unmoved—rock fractd.
54	9	2½	4 0	C Sand	3 feet 2 inches blown out—no fracture—the hard crust 5 ft. 7 inches from top of hole was some inches thick.
55	9	2½	4 8	C Sand	Blown all out—rock slightly fractured.
56	9	2½	5 0	C do.	Blown all out—rock fractured.
57	9	2½	5 0	Clay.	Tamping unmoved—rock fractured.
58	9	2½	6 0	do.	Tamping unmoved — rock shaken — explosion escaped through side joints. N.B.—⅓ of depth of hole 9 ft. by 2½ inches would contain 5 lb. 14 oz., or nearly 6 lb. of powder.

In the same paper of the Franklin Institute above referred to, it is stated that the sand was sometimes poured in loose, and sometimes carefully *packed*.

The packing was performed by means of a small sharp stick, which was worked up and down as the sand was slowly poured in.

It is stated, that—

" This method was found to be the best, and is the one always used at Fort Adams, in charging drill holes for sand blasting.

" Sand that was packed presented a much greater resistance than that which was poured in loose."

In order to try the value of thus packing the sand, it was ascertained how much was added to the mass by this mode of condensation; for this purpose we used a tin tube of 24 inches long by $2\frac{1}{8}$ inches diameter at mouth.

$2\frac{1}{16}$ do.   do.   at bottom.

When filled with the different qualities of sand, the weights were respectively—

	Fine	Middling	Coarse.
	oz.	oz.	oz.
Poured in loose . .	65	76	80
Packed by process above described .	74	$83\frac{1}{2}$	84

Many trials in blasting were made with tamping of sand thus packed.

In holes 2 feet deep by 1 inch diameter, each of the three qualities of sand was tried with a $\frac{1}{2}$-ounce and a $\frac{1}{4}$-ounce charge, and in the whole of them the sand was all blown out.

Experiments on Tamping with Packed Sand.

F Sand, fine.   M Sand, middling.   C Sand, coarse.

No. of experiments.	Depth of hole.	Diameter of hole.	Charge of powder.	Description of tamping	Effect and Remarks.
No.	feet.	inches.	lb. oz.		
59	4	1½	0 7	C Sand	Tamping blown out.
60	4	1½	0 7	C do.	Tamping remained—rock fractured.
61	4	1¼	0 6	M do.	2 feet 6¼ inches removed—rock fractured.
62	4	1¼	0 6	M do.	1 foot 5¼ inches removed—rock fractured.
63	4	1½	0 6	C do.	Tamping blown out—but a slight crust adhered to the sides of the hole.
64	4	1¼	0 5	M do.	Tamping blown out.
65	4	1¼	0 5	C do.	Tamping removed—except a hard crust about 12 inches above bottom of hole.
66	4	1¼	0 5	C do.	do. do.
67	4	1½	0 4	M do.	3 in. of tamping only remained.
68	4	1½	0 4	F do.	Tamping blown quite out.
69	6	2	0 7	F do.	In all these, the tamping [blow]n out.
70	—	—	0 6	—	
71	—	—	0 5	—	
72	—	—	0 4	—	
73	—	—	0 3	—	n out but 1½ inch.
74	—	—	0 12	M do.	
75	—	—	0 11	—	
76	—	—	0 10	—	In all these, the tamping blown out.
77	—	—	0 9	—	
78	—	—	0 8	—	
79	—	—	0 7	—	
80	—	—	0 10	M do.	About 1 foot of sand remained rock fractured.
81	—	—	1 0	C do.	Tried twice—in both cases the tamping blown out.
82	—	—	0 15	—	Blown out, except a hard crust 17½ inches from bottom.
83	—	—	0 15	—	2 feet removed—a hard crust, took 2 men 40 minutes to bore through.
84	—	—	0 14	—	16 inches remained — hard crust formed.
85	—	—	0 13	—	Blown out, all but hard crust.
86	—	—	0 13	—	3 feet 6½ inches blown out—hard crust 12 or 14 inches thick, bored through with much labour.
87	—	—	0 12	—	5 feet 4½ inches blown out.

The quality of the sand has not been always noted in these or the former trials ; but all three kinds were employed. The very fine, contrary to the received opinion that it is the best, universally failed : the very coarse, in the larger explosions, was, for a few inches in thickness, generally vitrified or cemented together into a very hard crust.   On trial with an acid, it was found that there were some particles of limestone mixed with this sand, the sudden burning of which might perhaps have assisted in producing this effect.

In all the descriptions of sand, indeed, this cementing process took place at times, more or less, and all of them contained particles of lime.

These last experiments were made at a different period from the former trials of sand, and probably with some variety in the quality of the powder and material, which must account for the apparent inferiority of the packed sand ; whereas the *packed* must be the best, although in too small a degree to remedy the inherent defects in any tamping of sand.

In fact, it is impossible to reduce these kinds of experiments to any very close results *in detail*, although by numerous trials we may come to *general results* that may be well relied on.

The conclusion come to from all these experiments, notwithstanding some discrepancies that will be observed, is, that sand of any description, and however applied, is, when used by itself for small blasts, perfectly worthless, and quite inferior to clay tamping for larger explosions, at least so far as for holes 9 feet deep by 2½ inches in diameter.

The cause of the sand tamping not presenting the same resistance to the explosion of powder in a blasting hole that it does to the mechanical pressure through tubes, is, no doubt, that the explosion penetrates among the particles, and loosens and separates them, instead of wedging them together as when pressed.   The same action will be observed in a subsequent part to produce an extraordinary effect on sand or other loose material when used with iron cones.

No examination was made in any of these or preceding experiments of the quality of the powder, excepting those expressly for that object.   It was in all cases the ordinary merchants' blasting powder ; nor was any account taken of weather, or other such circumstances as might cause discrepancies in trials made at different periods.

The only other materials for tamping, requiring much notice, are—

Broken brick, and
Broken stone, or quarry rubbish.

I. *Broken brick* is a good material for tamping, and gives considerable resistance, though not so much as clay; *vide* Nos. 116, 117, 118, in Table. It will not strike fire with iron, and it is to be procured in most situations.

II. *Broken stone* is of two qualities. Some quarrymen are in the habit of using a rotten kind of stone that is found in most stone countries; not being brittle, it rams into a very firm mass, and is not subject to strike fire; but being *stone* at all, gives an opportunity for careless workmen to apply the harder quality instead, or, at any rate, to mix pieces of the latter with it, by which the operation is subject to the contingencies of the use of the hard material.

The ordinary material used for tamping is the broken stone and rubbish of the quarry itself, unless notoriously subject to strike fire.

This, by experiment with the blue limestone or granite of the neighbourhood of Dublin, was found to be inferior to clay as a resisting medium. *Vide* experiment No. 119.

It is also more liable to cut the safety fuse, or to derange the needle hole, but, above all, it is never, in any rock, entirely free from some danger of giving fire, and causing accidents: this is quite enough to occasion it to be rejected wherever it is possible to procure a substitute.

Experiments with Tamping of Clay, Broken Brick, and Broken Stone.

C Contractor's Powder.　　G Government Powder.

No. of experiments.	Holes.		Charge and description of powder.	Tamping.	Results and Observations.
	Depth.	Diameter			
No.	ft. in.	in.			
88	3　0	2	2 oz. C.	Clay 4 to 16 in.	All blown out.
89	3　0	2	„	Do. 17 in.	A small ⬤ left.
90	3　0	2	„	Do. 18 in.	All blow⬤
91	2　0	2	„	Do. 19 in.	7 inches ⬤ng removed.
92	2　0	2	2 oz. G.	Do. 19 in.	7½ inches removed.
93	3　0	2	2 oz. C.	Do. 20 in.	5½ inches removed.
94	2　0	2	2 oz. G.	Do. 20 in.	8½ inches removed.
95	3　0	2	2 oz. C.	Do. 24 in.	3 inches removed.
96	2　2	2	2 oz. G.	Do. 24 in.	6 inches removed.
97	2　10	2	3 oz. C.	Do. 32¾ in.	Tamping undisturbed — rock well cracked—line of least resistance 19 inches in a favourable position, near a salient angle.
98	3　2	2	3 oz. G.	Do. 37¾ in.	Tamping blown out—rock, to all appearance, not affected—line of least resistance 2 feet, in an unfavourable position, near a re-entering angle.*
99	4　1½	2	2½ oz. C.	Do. 4 ft.	16 inches removed — the clay in this case was very dry, and in powder, and considered to be less efficient than when caked.
100	3　0	2	4 oz. C.	Do. 24 in.	Tamping not disturbed — rock lifted.
101	1　7	2	1 oz. C.	Do. 10 in.	All blown out.
102	1　2½	2	1 oz. C.	Do. 12 in.	About 3 inches of top blown out, and a considerable portion round fuse-hole.
103 to 105	3　0	1	2 oz. C.	Do. 5 & 6 in.	All blown out.
106	3　0	1	2 oz. C.	Do. 7 in.	1½ inch removed.
107	3　0	1	2 oz. G.	Do. 7 in.	All blown out—tried twice.
108	2　9½	1	2 oz. G.	Do. 8 in.	¾ inch removed—rock slightly affected.
109	3　1	1	2 oz. G.	Do. 8 in.	2½ inches removed.
110	4　0	3	2 oz. C.	Do. 14 in.	All blown out.
111	3　9½	3	2 oz. C.	Do. 18 in.	All blown out.
112	2　0	3	2 oz. C.	Do. 20 in.	Very little removed, except on side of fuse-hole.
113	3　10½	3	2 oz. C.	Do. 22 in.	13 inches removed.

* The effect on the tamping in this experiment (No. 98) is so different from all the others, with even superior charges, (*vide* Nos. 100, and 114 to 122,) that there was probably some misapprehension in preparing or recording the experiment.

No. of experiments	Holes.		Charge and description of powder.	Tamping.	Results and Observations.
	Depth.	Diameter			
No.	ft.	in.	in.			
114	4	0½	3	4 oz. C.	Clay 26 in.	17½ inches removed.
115	4	0¼	3	4 oz. C.	Do. 30. in.	22 inches removed.
116	3	2	2	4 oz. C.	Do. 24 in.	Tamping undisturbed — rock slightly cracked.
117	3	2	2	4 oz. C.	Do. 22 in.	3 inches of top of tamping removed—the remainder undisturbed.
118	3	2	2		Do. 21 in.	4 inches of tamping removed—rock burst.
119	3	2	2	4 oz. C.	Do. 20 in.	1 inch removed—rock burst.
120	2	0	2	4 oz. C.	Do. 18 in.	6 inches removed—rock burst.
121	2	0	3	4 oz. C.	Do. 20 in.	Rock burst—enlarged upper part of fuse-hole.
122	2	0	3	4 oz. C.	Do. 18 in.	8 inches removed—rock burst.
123	16	0	4	35 lb. C.	Do. 9 ft.	The charge occupied 7 feet—the rock was separated across the hole, at the outer end of which 4 inches of the tamping was found firmly adhering to the side of the half hole in the solid rock.
124	7	2	2	2 lb. 8 oz. C.	Do. 5 ft. 2 in.	The powder occupied 2 feet—the rock was separated so as to cut the hole longitudinally in two—the tamping was found adhering firmly to 15 inches of the upper end of the half hole.
125	11	0	3	19 lb. 12 oz. C. -	Do. 4 ft.	The powder occupied 7 feet out 11—the face of the rock was blown down along the line of the hole, excepting the upper 2 feet 6 inches, which remained, and in which the tamping continued firmly fixed after the explosion. Fig. 13, p. 49.
126	2	0	2	2 oz. C.	Broken brick, quite dry, 18 in.	All blown out.
127	2	0	2	2 oz. C.	Do. 23 in.	All blown out.
128	2	0	2	2 oz. G.	Broken brick, damped, 23 in.	All blown out, except a slight incrustation on sides near the bottom.
129	2	0	2	2 oz. C.	Broken granite stone, 23 in.	All blown out—the stone was nearly in a state of disintegration.

But few trials were made with broken brick; the object was merely to confirm the opinion that it possessed no decided advantage, in point of resistance, over clay; if anything, it is believed to be somewhat inferior, and requires a little moisture, which is a slight disadvantage; and it is more liable to have particles of stone, or hard material that might strike fire, mixed up with it.

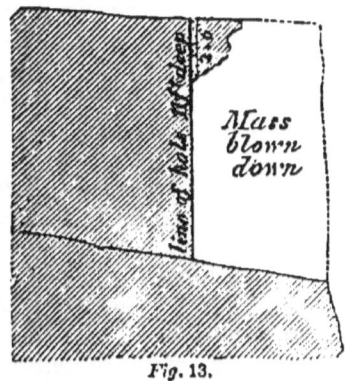

Fig. 13.

The broken stone was tried once or twice besides the instance recorded, and in all showed an inferiority to the clay; the use of it being always attended with more or less of danger, it was not thought advisable even to *experiment* much with it.

It will be perceived that in holes of 2 inches diameter, 2 ounces of powder will blow out about 18 inches of clay, and not more.

In holes of 1 inch diameter, 2 ounces will not blow out above 7 inches.

In holes of 3 inches diameter, 2 ounces will not blow out above 19 or 20 inches.

This comparison, however, is not quite conclusive enough to found a theory on, as the position of so small a quantity as 2 ounces spread on the surface of a 3-inch hole gives it a disadvantage, whereas in a 1-inch hole it lies very compact.

Increase of charges does not produce the increased effect upon good tamping that might be expected. It has been shown (Nos. 90, 91, Table of Experiments,) that in a 2-inch hole 2 ounces of powder will just blow out 18 inches of the tamping; in No. 100, and from 116 to 122, it will be found that 4 ounces, that is, double the charge, had scarcely, if at all, more effect, so far as can be judged under the different circumstances.

When, however, the rock is opened by the explosion, the effect on a tamping of clay or other tough material is greatly reduced; see Nos. 123 and 124, and particularly No. 125, for a remarkable instance of this; also Nos. 97 and 98, for the difference in effect on the tamping caused by the rock yielding, or not, to the explosion. It would appear that the

D

action upon the rock in opening it is much more rapid than on the tamping; even where the rock is separated across the line of the hole itself, the tamping is usually found adhering to one or both sides.

This is a very favourable circumstance in blasting.

It would be interesting to follow up the experiments of the effect of varying charges, with varying depths and diameters, upon one uniform description of clay or other good tamping; it would seem probable that after a certain point, which may be perhaps about 24 inches in a 2-feet hole, the charges to remove increasing depths of such tamping must be increased in a much greater proportion even than as the cubes of those depths: it is very difficult, however, to make such experiments, on account of the bursting of the rock with increasing charges, by which the effect on the tamping is reduced; it could only be done by holes in re-entering angles, *very closely* bound by projecting masses.

After having tried the value of the ordinary modes of tamping with broken stone, sand, brick, and clay, it becomes worthy of consideration whether additional resistance might not be obtained by some mechanical application of a different nature, tending to save time, labour, and chances of accident.

Any such contrivance, to be practically of general service, must be very simple in construction and application, and obtained at an expense not disproportionate to the advantages gained by its use.

The one that naturally suggests itself is some kind of plug or wedge, fixed in the loaded hole in a manner to increase the resistance.

If such a plug could be contrived to give, with sand, or loose small broken stone, or quarry rubbish, equal resistance to the same depth of good clay tamping, a very great advantage would be obtained in rapidity* of the tamping, and in security from accidents.

Many trials were made for this purpose.

The first was with an iron plug two or three inches long, and very slightly coned, the larger end being of somewhat greater diameter than the hole.

It is well known that such plugs, when driven into a hole in rock, and not having perhaps half an inch of contact, will raise from the ground the weight of many tons, showing a

---

* Substantial tamping is usually executed at the rate of from six to twelve inches per minute; nine inches per minute may therefore be calculated upon as a medium for holes of almost any size.

degree of tenacity that it was expected would be very powerful against the explosion from within; but when tried over the sand, although evidently affording much increased opposition, they were still in all cases driven out with sharp explosions, by smaller quantities of powder than would have removed good clay tamping.

Plugs of wood were tried with a similar result.

Iron plugs, of a form *slightly* curved in a barrel shape, and about 3 inches long, were also tried, and with better effect: when tightly driven into the top of the hole they took firm hold, and over loose sand, when properly fitted, appeared to give more resistance than equal depths of clay (*vide* Nos. 130, 131, 132 of Tables); they had a groove along the side for the fuse to pass through (fig. 14), and a strong eye to which

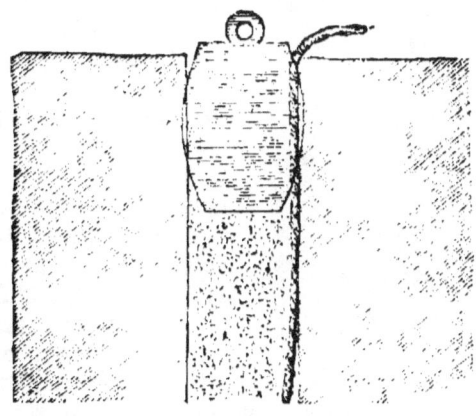

Fig. 14.

a string could be fastened with some object attached, to enable it to be seen and found if the plug was forced into the air.

A few of them were made for 2-inch holes, that is, varying in diameter from a little less to a little more than 2 inches; so that from the set it was easy by trial to find one that would fit with a proper degree of tightness.

The objections to the use of such plugs would be—expense; occasional losses; when blown out, some danger of falling on the by-standers; a degree of difficulty in removing them when not blown out, or the rock cracked precisely across the mouth of the hole; and want of simplicity by requiring an additional implement;—in this case, too, there

D 2

is the chance of the workmen carelessly applying such as would not fit well, by which they would be rendered of little or no service.

Pins formed of cylindrical pieces of iron, 6 inches long, whereof two sides were taken off, each of them of the thickness at top of about a quarter of the diameter of the cylinder, and tapering to nothing at the bottom, so as to form two wedges, were then tried over sand at the upper edge of the hole; and although the pin was driven up against these wedges, and much effect produced, still they were not equal to the clay.

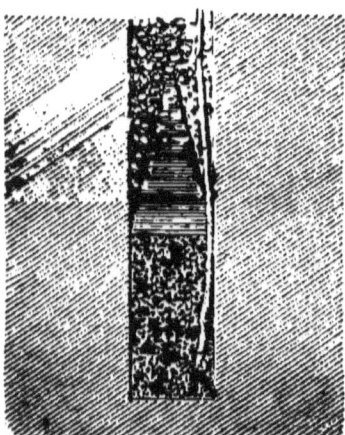

Fig. 15.

A cone placed immediately on the charge of powder, and filled over with stone broken to pieces of about half an inch cube (fig. 15), it was considered would give very powerful effects. Such a cone at the end of a rod of iron, and having only 16 inches of broken stone over it, at Chatham, where the idea originated, was proved to support a weight of 16 tons. A similar trial was made subsequently at Kingstown, and it supported a weight of 10 tons without showing any signs of yielding, and even with fine sand, instead of stone, over it; and although the base of the cone was only $1\frac{3}{4}$ inch in a hole of $2\frac{3}{8}$ inches in diameter, it sustained the same weight perfectly.

Still, notwithstanding this great power, when opposed to the gradual application of a force from above, it was found to give way to the explosion of the powder from below (see Nos. 133 to 145).

It would seem that the explosion penetrates round the sides of the cones, however small the windage (and they cannot be made to fit very tight, on account of the irregular size and shape of the holes), and by the fuse hole, and acts directly on the broken stone or sand above, so as to prevent them from operating as a wedge.

Some of the objections to the barrel-shaped plugs apply to these cones also: it would be attended with great labour to extract them if not disengaged by the explosion; and it would be very difficult to apply them in holes horizontal, or nearly so, unless they were very shallow.

The last contrivance tried, and which, as far as it has gone, has given a greater degree of resistance than any other mode of tamping, has been the application of iron cones, with long iron arrows applied as wedges (fig. 16).

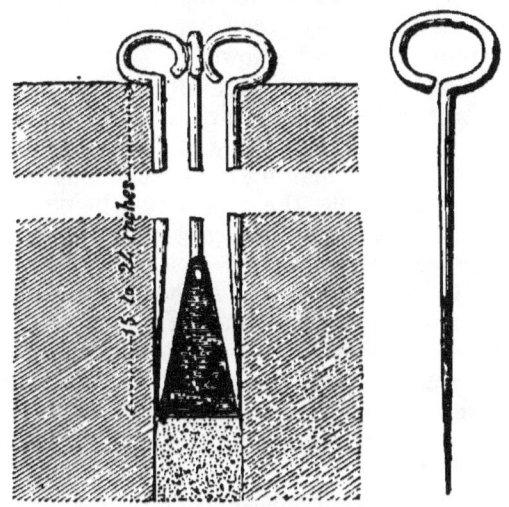

Fig. 16.

The cones may be from 3 to 6 inches long, with a groove for the fuse, and an eye at the top.

The arrows, from 21 inches to 2 feet 6 inches long, made of ½-inch round iron, with a long fine point at one end, and turned to a handle at the other.

The arrows are proposed to be of this shape, as perhaps the cheapest that could be made.

These cones were inserted at from 6 inches to 2 feet below the edge of the hole: for their effects, see Nos. 146 to 163 of the following Tables.

The arrows should not be less than $\frac{3}{8}$ inch thick (see No. 152), nor more than $\frac{5}{8}$; nor fewer in number than 3 for a 2-inch hole, or 5 for a 3-inch (see Nos. 152, and 161, 162).

The cone is let down over the sand, clay, or rubbish, and the arrows are fixed to their position by a slight blow or two with a hammer or stone.

The objections to this implement are in some respects

similar to the others; namely, expense, chance of occasional losses when blown out, or of falling on people's heads; the almost impossibility, frequently, of removing them when not blown out, without breaking open the rock; and want of simplicity in requiring so many additional implements.

The wear and tear of the arrows would be considerable, as they are usually thoroughly flattened near their lower end, and sometimes broken by the explosion.

One remarkable circumstance occurred repeatedly in the trials with these cones and arrows.

With sand laid over the charge of powder, and *under* the cones, the latter were firmly wedged, while the sand (sometimes in considerable quantity) was blown out entirely, or nearly so, by the small opening between the base of the cone and the side of the hole, the cones not being particularly loose, or more so than was necessary to go down freely (see Nos. 146, 149, experiments).

Even clay to the depth of 6 inches was removed in the same manner from *under* the cone (No. 156).

Broken stone could not escape in a similar way, but the explosions through it were observed also to find a vent round the sides of the cones.

From 8 to 12 inches of clay tamping over the sand prevented this effect.

In all cases the powder was poured in by a copper tube to the bottom of the hole, and a very thin covering of one or two folds of paper was the only wadding used.

The rock was not affected, so far as could be perceived, unless where otherwise mentioned.

Clay, and broken brick tamping, were in all cases firmly rammed down.

Sand and gravel in all cases poured in loose.

Broken stone, when employed by itself, was well rammed; and when used with any kind of plugs or cones, it was poured in loose.

Where *portions* of the tamping were removed, it was considered to have been occasioned by the escape of the explosion up the fuse hole, or round the cones, and not by the general concussion.

Experiments on Tamping with different kinds of Iron Plugs or Cones.

No. of experiments.	Holes. Depth. (ft. in.)	Diameter. (in.)	Charge and description of powder.	Description of tamping.	Results and Observations.
130.	2 0	2	2 oz. Contrs.	20 inches of sand, then an iron plug of barrel shape, 3 inches long, driven in very firmly.	Plug not stirred.
131	6 0	2	1 lb. 8 oz. Contractrs.	Fine sand over charge to within 3 in. of top, then barrel-shaped plug.	Plug unmoved—rock cracked—3 feet 4 inches of sand remained in hole.
132	6 0	2	1 lb. 12 oz. Contractrs.	Tamping as in preceding trial.	Plug and tamping unmoved—rock thoroughly rent.
133	2 0	2	1 oz. Contrs.	Iron cone 6 in. long by 1¼ in. diameter at base, over charge, then sand to top.	All blown out.
134	6 0	2	2 oz. Govt.	Iron cone 6 inches, then fine sand to top.	4 feet 5 inches of sand removed, cone and 1 foot of sand remained.
135	3 0	2	2 oz. Contrs.	4 inches fine sand, then iron cone, then sand to top.	All blown out.
136	5 1½	2	2 oz. Govt.	2 inches of sand, then iron cono 2¼ inches long, with sand to top.	Blew all the sand out—the cone remained at the bottom of the hole.
137	2 0	2	2 oz. Govt.	Iron cone 3¾ in. then gravel to top.	All blown out.
138	6 0	2	2 oz. Govt.	Iron cone 6 inches, then gravel to top.	2 feet 9 inches of gravel blown out—the cone and remainder of the gravel remained.
139	2 0	2	2 oz. Govt.	Iron cone 3¾ in. then broken granite stone (about ¼ in. cube) to top.	All blown out.

Experiments on Tamping with different kinds of Iron Plugs or Cones—continued.

No. of experiments.	Holes. Depth. ft. in.	Dia-meter. in.	Charge and description of powder.	Description of tamping.	Results and Observations.
140	2 0	2	2 oz. Gov⁺.	Iron cone 2½ inches, then broken stone (about ½ inch cube) to top.	All blown out.
141	2 0	2	1 oz. Contr⁺.	Iron cone 6 inches, then broken limestone to top.	All blown out.
142	3 0	2	2 oz. Contr⁺.	4 inches broken limestone, then iron cone, with broken stone to top.	All blown out.
143	2 0	2	1 oz. Gov⁺.	5 inches clay, then iron cone 6 inches long, 1¼ inches diameter at base, then sand to top.	All blown out.
144	2 0	2	2 oz. Contr⁺.	8 inches clay, then iron cone 5½ inches, then broken granite to top.	All blown out except about 2 inches of clay at bottom.
145	3 0	2	2 oz. Contr⁺.	14 in. sand, then 4 in. clay, then iron cone 4 inches, with broken stone (about 18 inches) to top.	The cone, broken stone, and some sand blown out, as well as a small portion of the clay.
146	3 0	2	2 oz. Contr⁺.	2 feet fine sand, then iron cone wedged with 3 arrows ⅜ inch thick, then sand to top.	All the sand blown out from *below* as well as above the cone, except about 2 inches, which was partly vitrified; the cone and arrows remained, and more firmly wedged.
147	3 0	2	2 oz. Contr⁺.	Precisely as the preceding, but with broken stone instead of sand.	The stone above the cone blown out, that below remained; the cone more firmly wedged.

Experiments on Tamping with different kinds of Iron Plugs or Cones—continued.

No. of experiments.	Holes.		Charge and description of powder.	Description of tamping.	Results and Observations.
	Depth.	Diameter			
No.	ft. in.	in.			
148	3 0	2	4 oz Govt.	2 feet 2 inches broken limestone, with fine sand intermixed, then cone and 3 arrows, then stone and sand to top.	Stone and sand over the cone blown out; the cone more firmly wedged. It was conceived that the intermixture of fine sand with the broken stone might prevent the explosion escaping round the side of the cone; but it did not.
149	2 0	2	2 oz Govt.	12 inches fine sand, then iron cone 4 inches, with 3 arrows.	The sand all blown out, except about an inch; cone and arrows firmly fixed.
150	2 0	2	2 oz. Contr.	14 inches sand, middling quality, then 4 in. clay, then iron cone, with 3 arrows, and sand to top.	Upper sand blown out—cone wedged very firmly.
151	2 0	2	4 oz Govt.	15 inches sand, then 4 inches clay, then cone, with 3 arrows, and sand to top. N.B.—Only 3 inches for cone and arrows.	Upper sand blown out—cone remained fixed. The clay (4 inches) under the cone was found to be detached from the side of the rock for about half its circumference, the middle of which part was where the fuse had passed.
152	2 0	2	2 oz Govt.	14 in. fine gravel, then cone 4 in. with 4 arrows only ¼ in. thick.	All blown out—the arrows in this experiment were too thin to wedge firmly.
153	2 0	2	2 oz. Govt.	12 inches of small broken stone and its dust, then cone 4 inches, and 3 arrows.	All blown out—this instance of failure could not be accounted for—must have been occasioned by some accidental circumstance—vide next experiment.
154	1 3	2	2 oz Contr.	5 inches broken stone, then cone 5½ inches, and 3 arrows.	Cone raised a little and firmly wedged—the explosion passed round the cone, being observed to escape at the to

Experiments on Tamping with different kinds of Iron Plugs or —— —continued.

No. of experiments.	Holes. Depth. ft. in.	Holes. Diameter. in.	Charge and description of powder.	Description of tamping.	Results and Observations.
155	2 0	2	2 oz. Govt.	6 inches clay, then cone 6 inches, and 3 arrows.	All blown out—one of the arrows found greatly bent.
156	2 0	2	2 oz. Contr.	6 inches clay, then cone 5½ inches, and 3 arrows.	Cone not stirred—nearly all the clay was found to be blown out from *under* the cone.
157	2 0	2	2 oz. Govt.	8 inches clay, then cone 6 inches, with 3 arrows.	Cone and arrows thoroughly wedged—rock uninjured.
158	2 0	2	2 oz. Govt.	10 inches clay, then cone 6 inches, and three arrows.	Cone and arrows thoroughly wedged—rock well cracked.
159	1 2½	2	2 oz. Contr.	4 inches clay, then cone, with 3 arrows.	Cone and arrows thoroughly wedged.
160	3 0	2	1 lb. Contr.	12 inches clay, then cone 4 inches, with 3 arrows.	Rock thoroughly split, and large mass lifted—the clay remained, but opened by splitting of rock—the cone found inside the hole, the arrows thrown out.
161	2 0	3	4 oz. Contr.	6 inches clay, then cone 6 inches, and 4 arrows.	All blown out—broken parts of the arrows found flattened, and side of the hole marked with the arrows—the *number* of arrows evidently insufficient for the 3-inch hole.
162	2 0	3	4 oz. Contr.	8 inches clay, then cone, with 4 arrows.	All blown out—arrows found much bent and flattened.
163	2 0	3	4 oz. Contr.	13 inches clay, then cone, with 5 arrows.	The cone well wedged—about 2 inches of clay removed.

The conclusions which I think may be reasonably drawn from the foregoing experiments and observations on tamping, are,

1. That clay dried to a certain extent is, all things considered, the best material that can be used for tamping.

2. That broken brick, tempered with a little moisture during the operation, is the next best material.

3. That some kinds of rotten stone are as good as either, but that it is not so easy to be sure of always having the proper kind, and the use of it is very likely to lead to an occasional substitution or mixture of stone of other quality, such as is decidedly objectionable.

4. That sand, or any other matter poured in loose, is entirely inefficient.

5. That the stone dust and chippings of the excavation itself (excepting the rotten kind above mentioned) afford less resistance than clay, and being always more or less attended with risk of accidents by untimely explosion, should never be employed.

6. That of the mechanical contrivances by means of plugs or wedges, the most effective of those referred to are, the cone with arrows, and the barrel-shaped plug; both of which, particularly the former, give a great increase of resistance; but that all such contrivances, leading to increased expense, requiring extra arrangements, and some attention to a proper application, such as cannot always be depended upon, are none of them applicable to ordinary purposes, but might be very useful under circumstances where every blast is under great difficulties, or attended with much expense; for instance, under water, or in carrying on shafts, galleries, &c., through very hard rocks; in such cases the additional cost and labour of employing these means would perhaps be well repaid by the improved effect of each explosion.

In the case of blasting in shafts and confined driftways, where the openings made by the explosion *must* necessarily be across the line of the hole, one great difficulty, namely, that of disengaging the cone or plug after the firing, does not occur.

In very confined situations, like the bottom of small shafts, where the greatest possible effect is required from the shallowest holes; the effects from deep holes being counteracted by the infinite resistance of the contiguous masses, these means of increasing the resistance of the tamping might be very useful.

The comparative strength of different kinds of tamping will vary in a small degree in different places; that which is most commonly used, will, in each locality, give, relatively, no doubt, better effects; thus where broken brick or broken stone are commonly employed, they will perhaps on trial be found to give somewhat better results, as compared with clay, than are noted in these Tables, which were drawn up where the clay was in habitual use, and the others were only tried for experiment; but it is apprehended that, although they may vary in degree, in no case would the difference be so great as to alter the relative *order* in which they stand.

TUNNELLING.

By far the most difficult, expensive, and dilatory blasting operations, are those connected with sinking shafts and driving galleries in rock.

The disadvantages under which such work proceeds, arise from—

1. Want of space in which to work to most effect.
2. Want of light.
3. Want of pure air.
4. Penetration of water into the works, sometimes in large quantities.
5. The necessity for securing the parts excavated, on every side, from loose fragments, or other portions that might give way.
6. The inconvenient communication for men and implements, for removing the material, &c., to and from the work during the operation.

These peculiarities are such as to justify and even to require the most perfect arrangements and contrivances to be made use of; some that might be considered for ordinary blasting, as leading to unnecessary refinement and cost.

The easiest tunnels or galleries to open, are those that can be worked from the ends, without requiring any shaft; and more particularly those worked on an ascending inclination, by which any water met with has a natural drainage away.

Sometimes it may be so well circumstanced, as to rise from both ends, and have a summit in the interior.

The disadvantage of blasting in a re-entering angle, surrounded on all sides by great resistance, has been adverted to: this would be the case nearly through the whole progress of a tunnel, if the face were all to be taken out together, and thereforo the following, it is conceived, would bo a better order of proceeding, and has partially been acted upon in some instances.

Commence by a gallery or driftway A (fig. 17), at the apex of the roof,* as small as can conveniently be worked in; viz., about 6 feet high by 3 feet wide. This will be carried on necessarily in tho most disadvantageous way for the effect of tho powder, as previously explained.

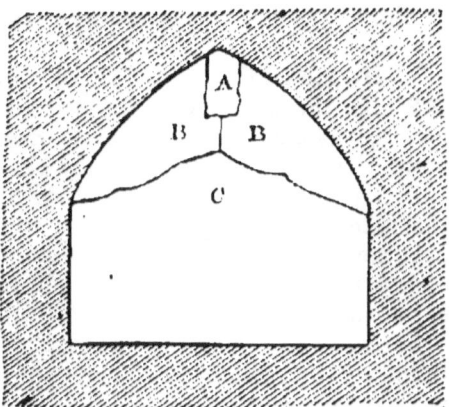

Fig. 17.

The next portion to work out will be B B; and in that some advantage will be obtained from the first opening A, to apply the powder to more effect.

The great mass c will bo then removed almost as favourably as in an open quarry, having a face towards that part of the same portion c, that has been previously removed, to which the lines of least resistance can be directed.

Thus A will throughout be kept well in advance of B, and B in advance of c.

It is probable that each, without checking the progress of the part preceding, may bo made to keep paco with it; and if so, the whole tunnel may be worked out in nearly the same time as would be required for a driftway.

The advantage of beginning at the roof is,—

1. The scaffolding and ladders for working from, become unnecessary.

2. The roof or arch is easily got at, and made sound and secure in the first instance.

3. The drainage is facilitated as the work proceeds, as will be explained.

In tunnels of very great length, the operation would be far too long by working them only from one or even from both

---

* The driftway is more usually carried along the *floor* of the gallery, to give a supposed advantage for drainage; but, as I think, erroneously.

ends: it becomes necessary then to sink shafts to intermediate points, from the bottom of which the tunnel is carried
on in each direction until the whole shall be connected.

This of course will add very greatly to the difficulty and
expense:

1. By the additional labour of excavating the shafts.

2. By the necessity for passing all the workmen, implements, tools, and the materials from the excavation, up or
down the shaft, as the case may be.

3. By the limited space below, particularly as subject to
the interruptions occasioned by the explosions, from which
it is more difficult to obtain refuge.

4. By the probable necessity for increased artificial means
of ventilation.

5. And principally, by the machinery and labour requisite
to keep each distinct shaft, and the galleries connected with
it, free from water.

The expenses will be increased in proportion to the number
of shafts; and the number of shafts will be regulated by the
time to which the execution of the tunnel is limited.

Thus, if the nature of the rock and other circumstances are
such, that the engineer cannot be sure of penetrating faster,
at each head of driving the gallery, than 3 yards per week,
if the tunnel is to be 2 miles long, and the period for its
being opened three years from the commencement; on these
data 468 yards would be the amount that would be opened
during three years in each head of working, requiring consequently between 7 and 8 heads for the whole, or three
shafts, and the two ends. This, however, would be to
suppose that the work commences at once from the *bottom*
of each shaft: the time necessary for sinking the shafts,
however, must be considered, which will consequently
increase the necessary number of them.

A good record of the actual result of working tunnels,
with a minute detail of all particulars, is very much wanted
as a guide for future operations.

Many circumstances will have influence upon the dimensions to be given to tunnels; if for a railway,—the width of
the locomotives and carriages, the height of the former, &c.

Certain dimensions may be deemed fixed: for a railway, for
instance, the height of the vertical side walls suppose 10 feet;
the space between the two tracks, and between each of them
and the walls, suppose 16 feet in all; besides the width of the
track of this space, it might be better to diminish that in the

middle, and to increase those on the sides, suppose 4 feet for the first, and 6 feet for each of the others, because—

1. The side spaces would be more useful for gas or other pipes, or for lamps, or for drains, or for tools or materials during repairs.

2. It is the readiest and most natural position for any person to seek for refuge, should an engine or carriage pass while he may be in the tunnel.

The roof should be as flat as the rock will admit to be secure, provided there be sufficient height for the engine up to *a b*, (fig. 18,) over each trackway.

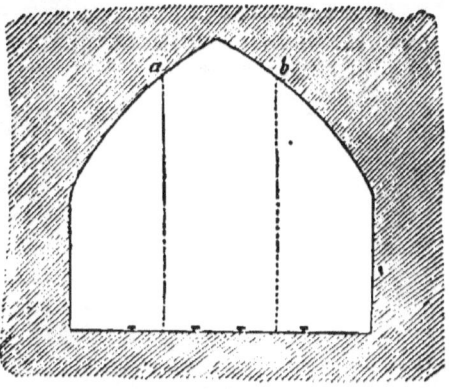

Fig. 18.

Some rocks will bear being cut to an almost straight horizontal roof; this will be particularly the case where the strata are vertical, or nearly so: others require to be high and pointed; when even that form shall be insufficient the very troublesome and costly expedient of lining with brick or masonry must be resorted to

It has been sometimes proposed to construct a double gallery for a tunnel; one for the traffic in one direction, and the other for that in the opposite: the assumed advantages are—

1. That a small roof may be more easily secured than a larger one.

2. That one line can be opened first, and the second worked out by degrees, and at leisure, without interrupting the traffic in the first.

3. That the cross traffic cannot at any time interfere, and that persons who may be accidentally in a gallery while an engine or carriage is about to pass, will find secure refuge in the other, or in the connecting passages.

4. That the subsequent repairs, &c., will be quite safe from any interference with the traffic, which would then be confined to the line not under repair.

In chalk, a material that is easily worked and shaped, and in rocks like it, and in which a large roof may be of doubtful stability, while a small one might be considered secure, this system would be most applicable; but I should think it objectionable in hard rocks requiring to be blasted.

A single tunnel of 28 feet wide will afford as much useful accommodation as two of 18 feet wide each.

Suppose the width of trackway to be 6 feet; then, in either case, there would be a space of 6 feet between each trackway and the wall: but as it is proposed above to allow but 4 feet between the two trackways, it may be considered a more fair comparison to calculate each of the double galleries as only 16 feet wide.

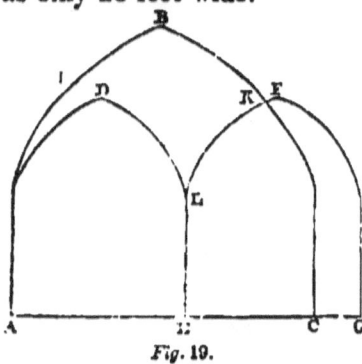

Fig. 19.

The comparison of the relative labour of opening either may be exhibited thus, bringing the two double galleries (which would be several feet asunder in practice) close together for the consideration of the question (fig. 19).

The excavation will in quantity be probably about the same, allowing for the connecting passages between the two smaller ones; but the single will be much easier to work out, because the space to work upon will be larger.

In the trimming work, which, after the first opening or driftway, is the most troublesome, the advantage is greatly in favour of the large gallery; as in the one case there is the amount of trimming the lines F, L, E, and D, L, E, besides the connecting passages, to compare with I, B, K, which they much exceed.

The single gallery will also require but one driftway; the double, two,—a point of great importance as regards labour and expense.

The single also gives additional space and height at the roof, where it is very useful as a receptacle for the vapours of steam and smoke.

It may be mentioned here, that the time and expense consumed in working out a shaft or gallery will be by no means increased in the direct proportion of its size.

One of reduced dimensions would take very nearly the same time in excavating as a larger (unless the difference be excessive), and the expense per cube yard will decrease with the extent of opening,—the first or driftway of a few feet in either case being by far the most costly.*

Where a shaft or gallery is full large, there will be less occasion to be very particular in trimming the sides, by which much time and expense will be saved.

With regard to the floor of a gallery, no particular nicety is required, except to take care to excavate enough: if it should be more, it is of no consequence, as any hollows can be filled up without inconvenience, whereas in sides or roof any excess of rock removed may be troublesome to remedy.

The only assumed advantage of the double gallery worthy of mention, to compensate for the above-stated points of inferiority, is that of the capability of opening them in succession, the second, during the operation, not interfering with the first; but though it has an advantage in that respect, still it is apprehended that the difficulty of doubling the opening of a single gallery, one trackway being previously made good, would not be great.

Should it for any rea-
son be judged inexpe-
dient to open a double
line at once, the mode
will be to open the
driftway 1 (fig. 20), and
then one of the sides 2,
and then 3 on the same
side, leaving the other
portion 4 for subsequent
completion.

The half tunnel 1, 2,
3, will be more easy to
open than one of the
double galleries, on ac-

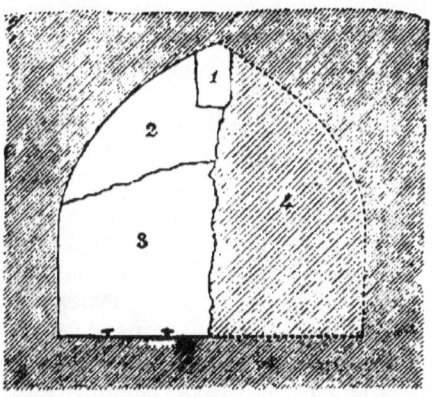

Fig. 20.

count of the *less extent of nice trimming*, &c., and the other half 4 will be far easier than the second small gallery.

The only inconvenience of this proposed mode will be, the danger of incommoding the first line of railway by the materials from the subsequent excavation; but it is apprehended that with moderate precautions this need not be the case.

The work will be gradually performed, the blasts not large;

* An example of the relative expense of this, and of shafts, &c., will be found in the cost of the tunnel of Drenodrohur, page 73.

they may be always fired immediately after the passing of a train, and the line cleared of any little rubbish before the next shall arrive, and a proper system of signals established, by which every train at its entry may be assured that the line is clear.

In the single tunnel, the lower end of the shafts will be in the middle, and form part of it; whereas in the double, however arranged, the shafts cannot be so conveniently placed with reference to both galleries.

SHAFTS.

In sinking shafts, the work is much more disadvantageous than even in the galleries, on account of—

1. The more limited space.
2. The more constrained position of the workmen.
3. The danger of anything, even small articles, falling down upon them.
4. The difficulty of applying any holes for blasting, but such as are vertical, or nearly so.
5. The immediate vicinity of the receptacle for the drainage water, from which it will be almost impossible to keep clear.

It will be found more advantageous probably to sink shafts rather long and narrow (the length crossing the direction of the tunnel at right angles), than circular or square; for instance, 16 feet by 9 feet may be better dimensions to give a shaft than 12 feet each way, provided always that the width is *ample* for working the buckets up and down. By this arrangement it will be easier to apply transverse bearers across the top for machinery; the space for the workmen will be more convenient; the pipes for drawing off the water, for ventilation, &c., will be more out of the way at one end, while the buckets for drawing men and materials, &c., up and down, may be at the other.

The upper surface edge of each shaft must be thoroughly lined, and secured from the possibility of anything falling down; the buckets and windlass of perfect description and arrangement to prevent such accidents, or the striking against each other in meeting, &c.

It is in blasting at the bottom of shafts that the shields described in another part might, it is conceived, be more usefully applied than in any other situation. The holes will be vertical, the blasts small, the shield always close at hand,

and the great labour and loss of time saved of removing tho workmen to the top of the shaft at each blast.

When the shaft is sunk to tho depth of the *driftway* at the *roof* of the galleries, those driftways may be at once commenced to save time; and the remainder of the shaft sunk while the gallery work is going on.

EFFECTS OF STRATA.

In stratified rocks, the direction of the strata in tunnelling will be of much importance.

The most favourable would be vertical, and at right angles with the direction of the line of tunnel, because when the drift A (fig. 21) is carried to sufficient extent, the holes for the subsequent blasts can be bored down the joints, and the explosion made to act in the most favourable manner.

The same principle may be adopted where the strata may be inclined upwards from the miners, as at B (fig. 22), but it will be

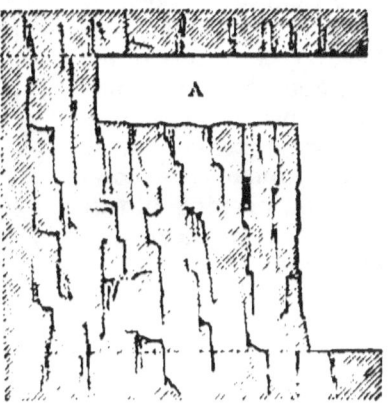

Fig. 21.—(Longitudinal Section.)

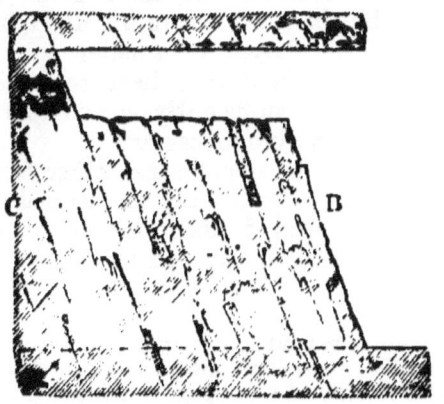

Fig. 22.—(Longitudinal Section.)

more difficult to work with advantage from the other end of the gallery c; as, to follow the same principle, the rock will be always overhanging the workmen.

If the strata be in horizontal beds, it will be worked upon by horizontal boring after the roof is entirely cleared out.

A most unfavourable direction is when the work is proceeding in the same line with vertical strata, which will consequently always present their edges in front.

In that case an opening should be carried down from top to bottom, either at one side at D (fig. 23), or in any other part, and then the holes bored down the strata as at A, or horizontally as at B; the whole roof, however, and opening D, will be worked to much disadvantage.

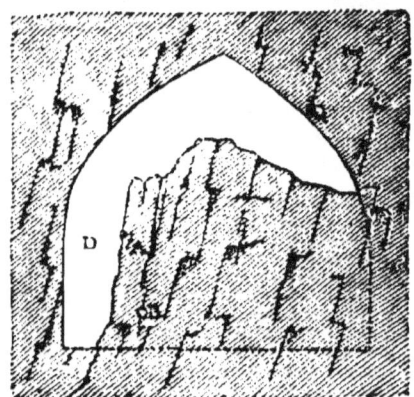

Fig. 23.

DRAINAGE.

An adequate drain will be necessary through the whole length of any tunnel.

A very favourable inclination for a gallery, as respects drainage, would be about 16 feet in a mile (1 in 330).*

The drain will be larger or smaller according to the quantity of water which it may have to discharge, but at 1 in 330 the fall will be sufficiently considerable to render a very large drain probably unnecessary.

In working the *ascending* galleries, either from the end or from a shaft, it will be quite easy to proceed so that there shall be always a natural drainage, at every period, to the receptacles from whence it will run off, or be pumped out, as the case may be.

* Whether for ordinary road or railway, the incline in a tunnel should be easy; as it would be peculiarly inconvenient in that particular part of a line to incur the risk of a stoppage in ascending, or of an accident in descending.

But in each *descending* gallery some little arrangement must be made to assist it.

When the descending meets the ascending gallery, the whole of the drainage will be carried off by the latter; till then, the following arrangement will be better than carrying pipes to the end of the gallery, as must be done if the inclination be steep.

Suppose the descending gallery to be 440 yards in length before it is to meet the other; this, at 16 feet to a mile, will give a perpendicular difference of level of 4 feet: as the gallery will be from 24 to 30 feet high, it is manifest that the far greater portion may have a regular natural drainage out, the same as an ascending gallery; but by sinking a small well-hole at the bottom of the shaft, of 5 or 6 feet deep, from whence the pump may draw the water out, a drain may be cut to it from the very end of such descending gallery, as it progresses, that will carry off the water naturally from its very floor.

That drain will form part of the regular longitudinal drain that must be made at all events, and the only additional labour will be in excavating the well in each shaft, which also might at any rate be desirable.

When the tunnel or gallery is to be horizontal, as it must be for a canal, the drainage will be as described for the *descending* gallery.

In deep sinkings, drainage is sometimes effected, or rather more usually *assisted*, by means of artesian wells or bore-holes sunk from lower levels of the surface ground, down to the lines of strata that shall *descend* from the works. Where the joints shall not be too close, and the distance not too great, the water will be drawn from the works by this self-acting drainage down to the level of the top of the artesian bore-hole; or, *practically*, to nearly that level.

VENTILATION.

The difficulty of working galleries to any extent under ground is occasionally very great, for want of ventilation, or from the presence of foul air.

The remedies are, either to force fresh air to the end of the work, or to draw the foul air off from thence, when the fresh air will rush into the vacuum: the latter is esteemed to be the more easily effected.

In either case there must be an air-tight tube from the

fresh air to the part where the workmen are engaged : and the great difficulty must be to establish such a tube perfectly firm and perfectly air-tight.

In operations on a small scale, such as military miners are engaged in, a small and light tubing is used, and the air forced in by a pair of smith's bellows, or others of about equal power; but to work a gallery of some hundred yards long from the bottom of deep shafts will require tubing more substantial and of larger dimensions, with a continued force applied for exhausting the foul air; or fresh air has frequently been introduced by a fan-wheel.

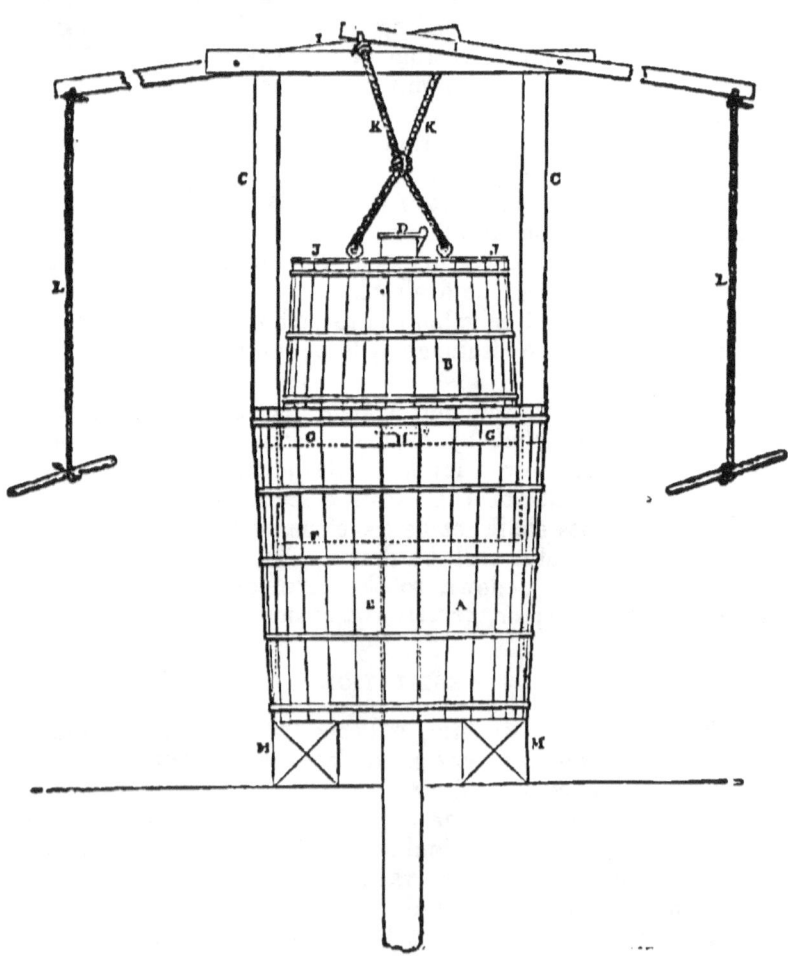

Fig. 24.

In a recent number of the Annales des Ponts et Chausées of France, there is an account of a simple contrivance which enabled the working of a shaft of 5 feet diameter, and 220 feet deep, to be continued after it had been interrupted by the constant collection of carbonic acid gas; all the ordinary measures by bellows, &c., having proved quite ineffectual.

A large tub A (fig. 24) was firmly placed on balks on a level with the top of the shaft, and filled with water to the level G, G.

An air-tight pipe from the bottom of the shaft was brought through the tub A, and had its upper edge a very few inches above the water; it had a valve H on the top.

A smaller tub B, reversed, was suspended within A, by the cords K K, which were made fast to the ends of the levers I I.

B had a very short pipe at top, with a valve D.

The tub B being allowed to descend by its own weight, the air within it was expelled through the opening D; when again raised by pulling the handles attached to the ropes L L, the air was drawn up through the opening H, from the end of the descending tube, and by continuing this reciprocating action, a circulation was created at the very bottom of the shaft.

No dimensions are given; but it is conjectured that the lower tub A would be about 4 feet by 3 feet 6 inches, and the upper one B, about 3 feet by 3 feet.

It was found capable of drawing off 4 cubic yards of air per minute.

No additional men were employed to work it; those at the top of the shaft, who got out the materials from the excavation, were only required to work this pump for about 5 minutes every hour, to keep the air perfectly good at the bottom.

It is in fact an air-exhausting pump of large power and simple construction: if found useful, and required for regular service, it might no doubt be improved, and made more compact, portable, and easy of application.

Instead of using a pump or manual labour for drawing the air from the ends of galleries, the upper ends of the tubes are sometimes made to communicate with a fire kept constantly burning, to which the tubes furnish exclusively the requisite air.

Improved ventilation is said to be obtained by double galleries or driftways, with occasional air-holes connecting them.

The advantage in this respect can hardly be equal to the cost of carrying on the double opening, if not necessary for other objects.

COST.

No kind of work can be more variable in its cost than tunnelling, or driving galleries : so much will depend upon the quality of the rock, the depth at which the gallery is under ground, the facility of communication by more or less of confined galleries, shafts, &c., to and from the actual work,—the amount of necessary ventilation, and the quantity of water to be drawn off,—that the expense may vary from 2*s*. to £2, and much more, per cube yard.

Where the rate is very heavy, it will probably be good economy to adopt the most refined improvements that will forward that portion of the operation which peculiarly leads to the extra expense.

The following is the result of the cost of working out the road tunnel of Drenodrohur, between Kenmare and Glengariff, during 1836 and 1837, in the county of Kerry, under many favourable circumstances.

The piercing of this tunnel, which was 582 feet in length, through the summit ridge of the mountain, saved an ascent, of which the perpendicular height was from 60 to 80 feet, which, reduced from a constant rise of 1000 feet on each side, was of much value.

The rock was stratified, varying in character from a granular to a compact silicious, and to a common clay slate, intersected by veins of quartz. It was all hard, some of it exceedingly so.

The strata in one direction were nearly vertical to the horizon, excepting occasional veins of a few feet in thickness, which were more inclined; and in the other direction, nearly perpendicular to the line of the tunnel.

The rise in the tunnel was from both ends, and at the rate of 1 in 100, forming a summit in the middle, which was consequently nearly 3 feet higher than the entrance.

The passage, as commenced, was meant to be 18 feet wide and 18 feet high ; but subsequently, to save expense, the width of the roof or chord of the arch was reduced to from 15 to 17 feet, and the part below the arch to 12 feet.

The arch stood perfectly without any support, although cut *very* flat, and with a rise or versed sine of only 2 feet.

The cost of the different portions was as follows :—

The roof or arch was first cut out, and contained sectional areas at different parts of about 96 and 90 feet, comprising an excavation of about 2012 cube yards in the aggregate, and cost £6555 16s. 8d., being at the rate of about 6s. 6d. per cube yard.

The body of the gallery under the arch contained sectional areas of about 204 and 144 feet, comprising an excavation of about 3493 cube yards, and cost £599 1s. 11d., being at the rate of about 3s. 5¼d. per cube yard.

A small shaft, 6 feet by 4 feet, was opened to the depth of 33 feet, containing about 29⅓ cube yards, and cost £32 2s. 10d., being at the rate of £1 1s. 10¼d. per cube yard.*

The average cost of tunnel alone per cube yard 4s. 6½d.

  „   „   „   „   and shaft . . . 4s. 8d.

The material from the excavation was deposited in hollows near the entrance at each end.

The total cost of tunnel and shaft £1287 1s. 5d., exclusive of some miners' cottages built, and a few such contingencies.

HEADS OF EXPENSE.

			£	s.	d.
Labour . .	Miners and labourers		620	9	8
„ . .	Smiths (including coals		73	3	3
Iron . . .	13,109 lbs. at 1s. 7d. per lb. . . .		92	16	6
Steel . . .	321 lbs. at 1s. per lb.		16	1	0
Gunpowder .	7946 lbs. at 1s. per lb.		397	6	0
Safety fuse .	1745 coils, of 8 yards each, at 1s.		87	5	0
			£1287	1	5

At the railway tunnel at Liverpool, the excavation of the rock is stated to have cost 4s. per cube yard; the material was a sandstone, and, as it required to be lined nearly throughout with brick-wall and arch, was not probably very hard.

It would form a most useful guide to engineers, if record were kept, and made public, of all the particulars of the actual experience in tunnelling and driving galleries, and sinking shafts: it might be kept without difficulty, and be made to afford very useful checks on the works during the operation.

J. F. B.

* This shaft proved eventually of little or no use, and had better have been omitted.

APPENDIX.

In the following Memorandum, Major-Gen. Sir John Burgoyne describes the mode in use at Marseilles for enlarging the inner end of the hole by means of the action of acid upon the calcareous rocks of that district.

The process for blasting calcareous rocks at Marseilles is extremely simple; it is merely to form a chamber or magazine at the bottom of the drift by means of dilute acid, so as to admit of a larger charge of powder being employed for the blast than is available in the ordinary mode of proceeding, the rock being of a calcareous nature. The apparatus was somewhat rude, but it appeared to answer its purpose very effectually. The rock was pierced in the usual way, by a $2\frac{1}{4}$ inch jumper, to the depth of 5 to 7 feet, generally in a slanting direction, according to the form and mass of the rock to be detached. They then introduced a copper pipe, the size of the bore, in the form sketched on the margin, and pressed the end A, which is open, down to the bottom of the hole, the orifice round the outside of the pipe at B being closed up tight with clay, so that no air could escape; and the bent neck of the pipe c, which is open, hanging downwards, with reference to the slope of the bore. Through the copper pipe at D was introduced a small leaden pipe, e, of about $\frac{1}{4}$ inch diameter, formed with a funnel, f, at the top, and this passed down through the copper pipe to within about an inch of the bottom, the upper orifice of the copper tube round the leaden one at g being filled up with a packing of hemp.

Matters being thus adjusted, dilute nitric acid was poured through the funnel and leaden pipe, and, on arriving at the bottom it produced effervescence, and at the end of a few minutes the frothy substance of the dissolved rock began to run out through the orifice of the bent tube at c. So long as they poured in the dilute acid at f this action continued, and,

whenever they considered from the quantity
of substance delivered through the pipe that
the internal chamber had become of sufficient
magnitude to admit the quantity of gunpowder
required, the pipes were withdrawn; the hole
very soon became dry enough, from the very
action of the acid upon the limestone, to
permit the chamber being charged without
damage to the powder, and the blast was
given in the usual way.

The time occupied would of course vary
according to the size of chamber required.
The foreman of the works informed me that
he had succeeded in forming a chamber capable
of holding 25 kilos. of powder (about 55 lbs.
English) in the space of 4 hours; he showed
an unwillingness to give me the proportions
of acid that he used, or the nature of it, and
I did not therefore press my questions, being
satisfied by the vapour that it was nitric acid,
and the strength of the mixture must in all
cases vary according to the greater or less
proportion of calcareous matter existent in
the rock to be acted upon. This may at all
times be determined in a few minutes by
experiment upon pieces of the stone, with
acids of different degrees of strength.

They were blasting very large masses from
the foot of the hill, on which the Fort of
Notre Dame de la Garde stands, on the south
side of the town, for the purpose, in the first
place, of obtaining sites for building, and at
the same time making use of the *débris* for
forming the new port which is in progress,
and the foreman assured me that this new
process had operated a very large saving to
the MM. Lerm, Frères, who are the parties
that have brought it into action.

In March, 1845, a patent was granted to
William Joseph Conrad Marif, Baron de
Lièbhaber, of Paris, for "Improvements in
blasting rocks and other mineral substances
for mining and other purposes, and in apparatus to be used in such works." The in-
ventor's mode of enlarging the inner end of

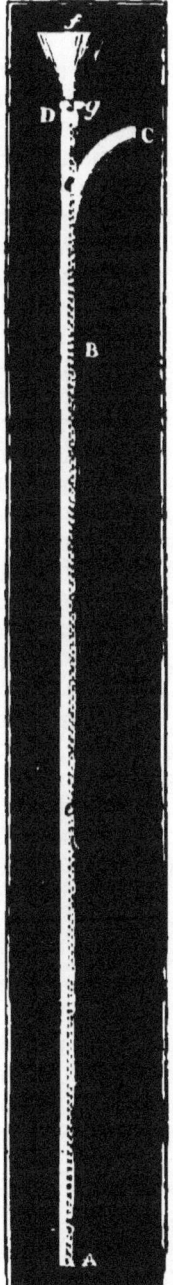

Fig 25.

E 2

the hole was described to consist in dissolving a portion of
the stone by means of muriatic or other acid, diluted with
about three times its weight of water. A tube is inserted in
the hole and externally sealed round at the lower end with
some composition which shall prevent the froth or vapours
from the acid passing between the outside of the tube and the
inside of the hole bored in the rock.   Within this tube there
is a smaller tube, through which the acid passed into the hole.
These tubes are bent over at the top, and terminate in a
vessel containing the acid, and which vessel receives the froth
that passes up between the pipes.   The inner tube is bent
upward at the lower end so as to prevent the froth passing
through the stone.   When the hole is sufficiently enlarged,
the contents of the hole are removed by a siphon or pump
before drying and charging with the powder.

In addition to the important facts given by Gen. Burgoyne,
the following regarding some operations in blasting in the
Jumna and at Delhi, conducted by Lieut. Tremenheere, may
be .quoted as useful and interesting. For the purpose of
blasting in order to improve the navigation of the Jumna, the
jumpers used were 6 feet long, and 2¼ inches in diameter ;
the blasts 5 feet deep, and 4 feet from each other. The rate
of boring varied from 2¼ to 5 feet per day's work for 2 men.
A double-headed jumper was used, to render the hole completely circular for the reception of the canister, about 2½ feet
in length, and 2 inches in diameter, and filled two-thirds with
powder and the rest with sand.   The small tube reaching to
the surface of the water contained quick match with a piece
of slow match at the extremity.   The canister, well greased,
was placed in the hole without any additional tamping.

At Delhi, the blasting was in dry rock, and, economy of
powder being of more importance than economy of time,
tamping was resorted to.   For this a stiff red clay, slightly
moistened, was employed, and the tamping bar was of wood,
the priming wire of copper.   Any dampness which might
exist in the bore was obviated by a tube of coarse paper,
greased on the outside. Fine mealed powder was used as
priming, and a piece of port-fire for ignition. If the firing did
not succeed, a fresh priming hole was bored in the tamping,
or the mine abandoned.   In large irregular masses of rock,
the depth of the bore, or the intervals between the blasts, will
generally represent the line of least resistance ; and the
following results were obtained in the rock at Delhi, which is
hard quartz.   The line of least resistance not exceeding

1 foot, a charge of 2 oz. is sufficient; the line not exceeding 4 feet, and the rock not being highly crystalline, 3 oz. per foot will be sufficient. The charges will vary with the tenacity of the rock, but the following may be a general guide:— the line of least resistance being 1, 2, 3, 4, 5, 6 feet, the charge will be 4, 8, 14, 20, 26, 36 ounces. On comparing the charges used at Delhi, where stiff clay was used as tamping, with those in the Jumna, where sand was used, the following table is the result:—

Line of least resistance.	With clay tamping.	With sand.
2 feet	8	26·8 oz.
2½ „	10	33·5 „
3 „	12	40·2 „
4 „	20	53·6 „

The charges in the last column are to those in the second as 3 to 1, nearly; they are not, however, given as the least required, but are those actually used.*

In the neighbourhood of Plymouth, the limestone, with which that district abounds, is raised in solid masses, of from 3 to 10 tons' weight: it is used most extensively for building, and for lime manure. About 13 cubic feet weigh a ton. It is of a light blue or grey colour, generally free from metallic veins, but with some indications of manganese and ironstone, round pieces of the latter being found in clay beds, intermixed with the rock, and a vein of ironstone 4 inches thick at the surface of the rock, and dipping towards the south, has been opened.

In the blasting of this stone, if a deep hole is required, a 2-inch jumper or bit is used for about 4 feet, and a 1⅞ inch for the next 4 feet by one man; then two men are employed with a 1¾-inch to the depth of 14 feet, a 1⅝-inch to the depth of 21 feet. A constant supply of water is required during the boring. The hole being well dried, about one-third is filled with powder, say 15 lbs.; a needle is introduced as far as possible without driving it; the hole is tamped with dry clay to the top, and then covered with a little wet clay to prevent any of the loose particles falling in when the needle is withdrawn. A reed filled with powder and split at the top, to prevent its falling to the bottom of the hole, is inserted, and a stone laid upon it; the powder being ignited by a piece of touch-paper and a train, the reed flies to the bottom of

* Report of Papers, Inst. Civ. Engineers.

the hole, and ignites the main load. The rock is generally cracked and loosened to a considerable extent, if not thrown; in that case the needle is driven through the tamping, and such a fresh charge is run through the needle-hole as may be requisite. From 6 to 8 tons of rock are generally blasted with 1 cwt. of powder. In July last, however, it was reported that with one charge of 1 cwt. of powder, in a hole 18 feet deep, no less than 1000 tons of the limestone rock, destined for the Plymouth Breakwater, were detached from their bed. We cannot answer for the entire truth of this report; but it is well known that, since the Breakwater quarries were opened in 1811, a great augmentation has been effected in the produce of the blasting there carried on.

In blasting the white limestone of the Antrim coast, in the north of Ireland, it was found that one ounce of powder would rend 14·12 cubic feet of the stone, when in blocks; but the same quantity rent only 11·75 cubic feet of loose whinstone blocks. The specific gravity of the white limestone is nearly 2·76, of the whinstone or basalt about 3·20. The limestone is similar to the chalk of England, in the flints which it contains; but it is exceedingly indurated. The induration may be estimated from the fact that two men will bore one foot in depth in half-an-hour, with jumpers from 1¾ to 2 inches in diameter.

The following account of the method pursued in getting the valuable granites of Scotland is written by a gentleman of extensive practical knowledge of the subject.

The granite quarries of Aberdeen and Peterhead, in the north of Scotland, are comparatively inexhaustible, and the granite which they yield of excellent quality. The manner of extracting the rock in these quarries is by boring, and blasting it with gunpowder. In this process the quarry-men use the ordinary "jumpers," having a piece of steel welded to one end, and made with an edge similar to that of a stone-cutter's chisel, but much more obtuse. They are also made of different lengths—the long ones to follow the short, as the boring proceeds. Three men are employed in this department of the work—one sitting on the rock and turning the "jumper" round, while the other two strike alternately with hammers, each of which is about 12 lbs. weight. These bores are sometimes from 12 to 16, and often 18 feet deep, by about 2½ inches in diameter; and, when charged and fired, they generally loosen a very great quantity of rock, but seldom do much more than merely move it. "Bulling" is then had recourse to, and this consists of filling all the perpendicular cracks or fissures, caused by the former operation, with gunpowder, and firing it; by which means the rock is shifted several inches from its bed, and often thrown some yards forward. The next process is to cut up the rock into the required scantlings, and this is done in the following manner:—A number of holes are cut in a straight line, about 3 inches long, 2 deep, and 3 inches apart, each tapering towards the bottom, into which iron wedges are inserted, and struck with a heavy iron hammer, beginning at one end of the row and striking them from end to end until the block gives way.

Cutting with " Plug and Feather " is also had recourse to, when the block intended to be split is very deep and supposed to be beyond the power of the ordinary wedges. In this case a row of circular holes, about $1\frac{1}{4}$ inch in diameter, 5 or 6 inches deep, and 6 inches apart, are bored with a "jumper;" into each of these are put two "feathers" at opposite sides. (The "feathers," when in position, are merely inverted wedges, having circular backs, so as to fit to the curvature of the holes, the opposite sides being plain, to receive the wedges.) Between these "feathers" long wedges are then introduced, and driven, as in the former case, until the block is split asunder.

In the Seventh Volume of the Professional Papers of the Corps of Royal Engineers,* Capt. Nelson, R.E., has recorded some interesting and useful memoranda on the quarrying of the Plymouth limestone; from which paper some facts may be well quoted. This limestone is described as fine-grained and hard, abounding in organic remains, and varying in colour from light to dark grey. The tools used in these quarries consist of—the "jumper," or "bit," from 8 to 30 feet in length, and from 1 to $2\frac{1}{2}$ inches in width;—the "pitching bar," from 6 to 8 feet long;—the "tamping bar," which is $\frac{7}{8}$ inch diameter for $1\frac{1}{4}$ inch bit;—the "needle," which is from 3 to 13 feet in length;—and the "ripping" or "crow bar," from 6 to 14 feet long, and from $2\frac{1}{2}$ to 3 inches square at the lower end. In addition to these the "feather and tearers" consist of a wedge about 6 inches long, 1 or $1\frac{1}{4}$ inch square at one end and $\frac{1}{4}$ inch square at the other end, and two thin wedges having one flat face and the other segmental; so that the central "feather" with two "tearers," one on each side, serve to fill pretty well a round hole in the

* Weale, 1845.

stone. The quarry-carts arc short and very stoutly built,
lined with strips $2\frac{1}{2} \times \frac{1}{2}$ inch flat iron; they carry from $1\frac{1}{4}$
to $1\frac{3}{4}$ tons—they are 4 feet long, 3 feet 6 inches wide at the
hind end, and 3 feet 4 inches in front; the sides about 1 foot
6 inches high, and the front much higher; they cost about
15l. each, and, with repairs, will last nine years. The navi-
gator-barrows, which are of the common pattern with wooden
wheel, cost 10s. 6d. In the quarry, where they are used all
day, and loaded and worked quietly, they are entirely of
wood; but at the wharf, where the work is shorter and
sharper, a body of plate iron is used on a wooden carriage.
Iron carriages for the barrows would be more economical,
but too heavy for the quarry-men. Iron wheels are considered
too destructive to the planks. The barrows last from three
to five months, according to the work, and without repairs.
The planks, which are of yellow pine, and in the quarry
generally about 25 feet by 14 inches by $2\frac{1}{4}$ inches, hooped
and bolted, cost $4\frac{1}{2}d.$ per superficial foot. At the wharf the
planks used are longer, broader, and thicker; they last about
six months. The "jumpers" cost 5d. per lb. For the removal of heavy stones the "devil cart" is used; this consists
of a pair of large and strong wheels with a stout and well-
braced axle, to which a long central pole is fixed; the front
and lower end of which is carried upon a small wheel or
roller. To this cart the heavy stones are slung by double
chains, one of which is attached to the hinder side of the
axle, and the other to the pole as near to the axle as may be
necessary, according to the dimensions of the stone carried.
The quarry screw-jack is an implement of great power, resembling the ordinary tool of that name, but having a more
extensive series of gearing within; the winch is on a pinion
of four teeth working a wheel of fourteen; on this is another
pinion of four teeth, working a wheel of eighteen, on which is
a three-teethed pinion or triple stud engaged with the vertical
ratchet.

Capt. Nelson's memoranda refer to three quarries in the
neighbourhood of Plymouth, in the two first of which the
limestone is chiefly raised in blocks of from $\frac{1}{4}$ to 1 cwt.,
either to be burned on the spot for lime, or shipped for
different places in the neighbourhood for that purpose.
The stone is likewise wrought for curb-stones and paving
slabs, but cannot be got in masses large enough for wharf
ashlar. In the third quarry the stone is raised in the largest
blocks with heavy charges, and used for breakwaters and

wharf ashlar. The largest block known to have been raised in this quarry weighed about 200 tons; and so variable are the effects of blasting, that, on one occasion, upwards of 1000 tons were detached by a charge of 100 lbs. of powder in a 30 feet hole. It is usually considered that, well stratified as the rock in this quarry is, where the mass to be raised is not jammed at the sides, and where the beds dip to the front of the quarry, a quarter of a pound of powder per ton will dislodge the block sufficiently.

In quarry No. 1, one man raises 5 tons per day, besides loading and unloading the cart, and removing the rubbish produced 50 yards. Wages (in 1839 ?) 15s. per week, on piece work. In jumping, 16 feet, in four 4-feet holes, is considered a good day's work. Powder used, about 4 lbs. for 16 tons; one-fourth of the hole filled with the charge.

In quarry No. 2, one man in one day (10 hours net time) will put down 20 feet with 1½-inch bit, or 15 feet with 2-inch bit; depth of the charge from one-third to one-half that of the hole; half a pound of powder allowed per cubic yard of solid rock. A man will turn out and break up for rubble stone 4 tons, or 56 cubic feet per day; or 6 tons without breaking. When thus broken into pieces of from ½ to ¾ cwt. each, and delivered at the kiln (close to the quarry), he will break it up for burning at one load of 16 tons, or 224 cubic feet per day.

In quarry No. 3, 20 feet of 1½ to 1½-inch bit is reckoned a good day's work, although one man puts down 30 feet, which is very unusual; in deep holes, one man is employed for the first 6 feet, two for the next 10; and, after 16 feet, three men, provided the hole is not more than 10° or 12° out of the perpendicular; if it is, even five or six men are put on after the first 15 feet. In such holes, it is usual to commence with a 2½-inch bit, and end with about 1½ inch. In a 30 feet hole, 2½ inch in diameter, 25 lbs. of powder are used for the first charge. If this does not succeed, it will, at all events, probably disturb the beds beneath sufficiently to allow space for the repetition of the blast, perhaps three or four times over, increasing somewhat every time before the final charge is introduced; as the block, if not well detached on all sides first, will be destroyed by the premature application of the full charge.

SLATE QUARRYING.

In order to understand the peculiar methods adopted in

slate quarrying, it is necessary to refer to the distinguishing geological feature of the slate formation. Slate, besides being divided by fissures which form beds and joints to the masses, as is the case with all stratified materials, is divisible into laminæ or plates of any required thickness, the direction of which laminæ is commonly vertical, or nearly so, but always oblique to, and never coincident with, either the beds or joints. This peculiarity of structure affords the means of splitting the slate and adapting it so suitably to the extensive purposes for which it is employed in great Britain, and, at the same time, determines the most convenient manner of quarrying to be by detaching the masses of slate vertically from the face of a trench or gullet. The cutting of this gullet into the side of the slate mountain is, therefore, the first operation in the working of the quarry. As the trench proceeds, and the height of the surface above becomes greater than convenient (say about 40 feet), a second trench is commenced above the other, and similarly carried onward into the mountain until the height above reaches a similar quantity, when a third trench is commenced, and so on. In the great slate quarries of Bangor,* sixteen of these stages are in progress together; the lower ones being gradually widened, by the getting of the slates, as the upper ones are advanced. In the upper part of the quarry, the slates are removed with crow-bars; but the slates become harder as they are lower from the surface, and require the use of gun-powder to detach the main masses. The miners engaged in drilling the holes for the powder are suspended by ropes from the upper parts of the rock, and are liable to many and severe accidents. After the slates are detached by powder or otherwise, they consume considerable labour in splitting them with wedges and mallets into marketable sizes, and reducing them to the several sizes required for roofing and other purposes. The means of communication between the several stages or levels (each of which in the Bangor quarry

---

* These quarries are about six miles south-east of Bangor, and are worked in the mountain called in Welsh *Y Bron*, a name signifying a *breast* or *pap*, and commonly given to any hill the contour of which has a flowing outline, free from abruptness. This mountain, Y Bron, is on the side of a deep valley, through which the river Ogwen flows towards Lavan Sands, where it falls into the sea nearly opposite Beaumaris. An interesting paper on these quarries, to which we are indebted in preparing this notice, is contained in the Quarterly Papers on Engineering, vol. iii., part 5.—(*Weale*, 1845.)

is about 40 feet high, or nearly 640 feet from bottom to top) are provided by self-acting inclined planes, of great extent, laid from each stage to the contiguous stages. On these planes rails are laid to facilitate the motion of the trucks in which the slate is conveyed. At the head of each plane, a drum and break-wheel are fixed to regulate the velocity of the descent of the loaded trucks towards the level below. From the quarry at Bangor the slates are conveyed upon a railway to the shipping-port, a distance of about seven miles. On the several stages long ranges of sheds are erected for the men employed in cutting and shaping the slates. The slates for roofing are merely split to the required thickness with long iron wedges, and then trimmed with the cutting knife, by being placed on a fixed steel edge.

The dykes of greenstone, with which slate rocks are frequently traversed, are found to injure the slate, and destroy the cleavage of its structure for a considerable breadth. These dykes are usually removed by blasting, and form a very expensive impediment to the operations of the slate-miner.

At the Bangor quarries, about 1000 men are commonly employed, and the profits are understood to amount to about £80,000 per annum.

Some of the slate quarries of France are worked by sub-terranean galleries. In those of Rimogne the main gallery is about 400 feet long, with several lateral galleries, 200 feet in length, on each side of the main gallery. These galleries are about 60 feet high, and contain about 40 feet in height of good slate, the remainder consisting of quartz, or being injured by contact with volcanic substances.

At Angers, in France, are other slate quarries, worked in open cuttings, and which afford blocks, of which most of the houses of that town are built. In the German States there are several slate quarries: at Eisleben, in Saxony; at Ilmenau; Mansfield, in Thuringia; and at Pappenheim, in Franconia. Switzerland is said to possess no slate, except in the valley of Sernst, in the Canton of Glaris. Italy has only one quarry, that at Lavagna, in Genoa, the slate from which is used for lining the cisterns in which olive oil is kept.*

---

* (Papers on Engineering, vol. iii., part 5.) The application of slate here stated in the text is a good proof of the close texture and comparative impermeability of slate. M. Vialet states that he is able to double the natural hardness of this material by baking it in a brick

FIRING MINES BY VOLTAIC ELECTRICITY.

The removal of a large mass of the chalk cliffs near Dover for the works of the South-Eastern Railway Company, by a grand blasting operation effected by three mines, simultaneously fired by electrical communication, was a work of such surpassing magnitude, and so completely successful in its results, that a brief account of the arrangements made and effects produced may be suitably introduced in an Appendix to the valuable treatise of Sir J. F. Burgoyne. We have at the same time the greater pleasure and greater facility in doing this, because the operations have been so well described by the able officer under whose experience they were conducted,* and from whose description the following notice has been abridged.

The Round Down Cliff is situated 2 miles W. of Dover. Its summit is about 380 feet above high-water mark, and 70 feet above that of the Shakspeare Cliff, which is ¾ of a mile nearer to the town. It is composed of a compact chalk, principally without flints, forming the lower bed of the chalk formation. The dip inclines from W. to E. about 40 feet in a mile. The base jutted out to seaward considerably beyond the general line of cliff to the westward, under and along which (from the Abbott's Cliff Tunnel towards Folkestone) a distance of 2 miles of the South-Eastern Railway is passed on an open embankment, defended by a substantial retaining wall of concrete. The Shakspeare Tunnel (which forms the portion of the same line nearest to Dover) had been for some time completed, and its mouth or entrance from Folkestone is about 400 feet eastward of the central part of the base of Round Down. This intervening point, of about 300 feet in length, was therefore to be passed either by a tunnel or an open cutting: the former had been commenced, and the preliminary driftway formed on the upper level, when heavy slips occurring on either side, which partially extended to the cliff in question, materially impaired its stability : the

kiln till it assumes a red colour. Subject to the severe test of Brard's process (boiling in sulphate of soda), slate is found to betray no symptoms of decomposition.

* Account of the Demolition and Removal by Blasting of a portion of the Round Down Cliff, near Dover, in January, 1843. By Lieut. Hutchinson, R.E. Prof. Papers of Royal Engineers, vol. vi. p. 188.—(*Weale.*)

idea of tunnelling was therefore abandoned, and it was determined to remove this point by blasting, and to continue the open railway and sea wall up to the mouth of the Shakspeare Tunnel. For this purpose the principle adopted was to employ large charges, placed a little above the intended level of the railway, which, by blowing out the base of the cliff in their front, would cause the downfall of the superincumbent mass. The result fully justified the adoption of this method.

The experience gained in the many and extensive mining operations on this line of railway led to the adoption of a charge in lbs., bearing the proportion of $\frac{1}{32}$ of the cube of the line of least resistance in feet, corresponding with the rule laid down by Sir J. F. Burgoyne, and which had been found sufficient for the works at Dover for blasts with charges varying from 500 to 1200 lbs. This calculation was therefore adopted in the present instance, and, as the length of face to be removed was great (300 feet) three charges were used, one in the centre at the back of the salient point, the others at the distance of 70 feet on either side. From careful measurements the lines of least resistance were found to be—

Centre . . .	72 feet to face of cliff.	
East and west . .	56 ditto	ditto.

By calculation the quantity of powder required for the centre chamber was found to be 6750 lbs., which was increased to 7500, to provide against contingencies. For each of the two end chambers an allowance of 5500 lbs. was made, and thus the total quantity of powder became 7500 + 5500 + 5500 = 18,500 lbs., or about 8¼ tons. The preliminary driftway already mentioned was used for excavating to the chambers, being about 4 feet wide and 5 feet 6 inches high; but, being cut on the upper level of the intended tunnel, it became necessary to sink shafts a depth of 17 feet to reach the lower level of the chambers 3 feet above that of the railway. These shafts were formed as truncated cones, 5 feet diameter at bottom, and 3 feet at top, thus affording additional security for the retention of the tamping. At the bottom of these shafts, galleries 5 feet 6 inches high were cut at right angles to the driftway, and continued to the points determined for the chambers. These branches also were made of a dove-tailed form, 2 feet wide at the shaft, and 4 feet 6 inches at the other extremity, to assist in securing the tamping. The chambers were excavated at right angles to the galleries, and of the following dimensions, viz.:—

Centre chamber . 13 ft. by 5 ft. 6 in. high, by 4 ft. 6 in.

Two ends of do. . 10 ft. by 5 ft. 6 in. high, by 4 ft.

The voltaic batteries consisted of fifty-four of Daniell's cylinders, being eighteen for each mine. These cylinders were made of sheet copper, 32 oz. to the superficial foot, 1 foot 10 inches long, and 3½ inches diameter, placed in sets of six cach, each set in a deal box 1 foot 4 inches by 1 foot, by 1 foot 9 inches high, with a lid 4 inches deep. The zinc rods were 1 foot 8 inches long, and ¼ inch diameter. These batteries differ from the common plate-battery also in employing two liquids separated by a partition of animal membrane, or plaster of Paris. The liquid into which the zinc rod is plunged is sulphuric acid diluted with eight times its quantity of water. The liquid on the outside of the partition is a saturated solution of sulphate of copper.

Besides the eighteen Daniell's cylinders, two plate-batteries were applied for each mine in order to guard against the injury which it appeared Daniell's apparatus was liable to by the low temperature of the season. In these plate-batteries the solution was weaker, being only 1 of the acid to 12 water. The plate-batteries were contained in boxes 3 feet 2 inches by 12 inches and 8 inches deep, of 1 inch deal, and each divided into 20 cells 1¼ inch wide, by partitions of ⅜ inch deal, the cells being coated with a waterproof composition of spirits of wine and sealing-wax. The 20 pairs of plates forming the series, each composed of a zinc plate ¾ inch thick, in a rectangular case of copper 10 inches long, 1¼ inch wide, and 8 inches deep, without top or bottom, were united by stout copper wire attached to the zinc plate of one pair and the copper plate of the adjoining pair.

For the purpose of firing, it was determined to use three sets of wires and three separate batteries. The total length of wire required was thus 6000 feet, being 2000 for each mine, and ⅛ inch diameter. The wires were coated with a composition of pitch 8 to bees'-wax 1, and tallow 1, and covered with a coarse cotton tape, bound round while the composition was hot. The two wires thus prepared were insulated by being laid one on each side of a 1½ inch rope, and overlaid by a stout packthread turned once round each wire at every coil. The whole was then bound over with 2 yarn-spun yarn, and finally coated with the same composition of pitch, wax, and tallow. One man with a labourer prepared this wire at the rate of 6 feet per hour.

The cartridges or bursting charges were made 9 inches long and 2 inches in diameter, the top and bottom being secured by cork bungs. The priming wires, $\frac{1}{12}$ of an inch in diameter, projected 1 foot 6 inches beyond the top. They were passed through a slip of wood $1\frac{1}{4}$ inch square and $\frac{1}{4}$ inch thick, inserted at the centre of the tube, and their ends clenched on a circular plate $1\frac{3}{4}$ inches diameter, lying over the lower cork bung. The platinum wire was fixed half-way between the two. The powder, which was of the finest sporting quality, was poured in from the top. The upper bung, being in halves, one-half was removed for this purpose, and refixed when the tube was filled: the top and bottom were then coated with a waterproof composition. Two of these cartridges, after being tested by the galvanometer, were attached to each of the conducting wires, the wires being perfectly insulated, and covered with spun yarn. The cartridges were extended to a distance of 3 feet apart, and buried in the centre tier of loose powder in the box. The wires were then carried from the chambers along grooves cut in the sides of the galleries, shafts, and driftway, and covered with wooden troughs.

For the tamping, a dry wall was built in chalk across the end of each chamber, and the galleries and shafts were afterwards filled in with the same material, which was extended in the driftway to 10 feet on each side of the top of the shafts. The tamping occupied about twenty hours with four men to each mine.

For containing the charges of powder, the deal cases were constructed within the chambers of the following dimensions:—

Boxes.—Centre 11 ft. by 4 ft. 3 in. by 3 ft. 6 in.
,,   Ends 10 ft. by 2 ft. 8 in. by 3 ft. 3 in.

The powder was deposited in the boxes, in bags holding 50 lbs. each; the tiers above the centre were placed with their mouths downwards, those below it with their mouths upwards.

The circuit being completed at each battery by pre-arranged words of command, the mines were fired simultaneously on the 26th January, 1843, at 2·20 P.M. The ignition was followed by a deep hollow sound, and the effect was described to resemble the appearance of the fall, or rather flowing, of lava from the side of a mountain, assuming a gently undulating wave-like motion, as the mass slid along the bottom and into the sea. The mass fell 'exactly as had been desired, and the quantity removed was estimated at more than 400,000 cubic yards, being a parallel mass or slice from the inclined face of the cliff, and averaging 380 feet in height by 80 feet in thickness, and 360 feet in length of face. The operation thus successfully conducted and completed, without the slightest accident, saved about 7000*l.* to the South-Eastern Railway Company, and reflects the highest credit upon Lieut. Hutchinson, Messrs. Cubitt, Wright, and Hodges, and all other parties concerned.

PART II.

STONES USED IN BUILDING.

To the architect and the engineer, alike, is a knowledge of the materials which he has to employ, or to deal with, of supreme importance. And, were it worth while to inquire the rank which each class of materials occupies in the scale of professional consideration, we should start upon the fact that those substances which, for their substantial properties and enduring character, are selected as the foundations and the exposed external parts of our buildings and structures, claim our first and most attentive examination. Frequently, indeed, local circumstances will define the limits within which the selection must be made; but there are few, if there are any, cases in which the designer is altogether denied the privilege of selection; while in many instances an acquaintance with the materials at his disposal will open a wide field for the exercise of his judgment in aiming at current economy and permanent preservation.

In the few pages left to us in the present volume, we propose to follow up the account given of the methods of getting or quarrying stones, &c., by describing the several properties of the leading classes of those materials which fit them for the purposes of construction, and which should lead to the adoption of one or other of them, according to the service they may be required for.

Without attempting to observe the classification laid down by geologists, we propose to treat of stones under the four general divisions of *Granites, Slates, Limestones,* and *Sandstones,* including under each of these general heads such constituents or subordinate combinations of each as may appear essential to be noticed in this rudimentary outline of a really extensive and highly important department of practical science.

GRANITE.

This rock, which appears to have originally been a fused mass, and subsequently to have undergone the process of crystallisation, is of a *granular* structure, that is, consisting of separate grains of different substances, united, apparently, without the aid of any intermediate matter or cement. These substances are *quartz, felspar,* and *mica,* each of these being a compound. The infinite variety of proportions in which these several constituent elements are united in the mass, occasions the great diversities of colour and appearance of the several kinds of granite, and also affects in.a much more important manner the enduring characteristics of this valuable material. Thus its colour varies from light grey to a dark tint closely approaching black, and is to be found of all shades of red, and many green. Of the constituents of granite, *quartz* is a substance of a glassy appearance, and of a grey colour, and is composed of a metallic base *silicium* and *oxygen : felspar* is also a crystalline substance, but commonly opaque, of a yellowish or pink colour, composed of silicious and aluminous matter, with a small proportion of lime and potash; *mica,* a glittering substance, principally consists of clay and flint, with a little magnesia and oxide of iron. Instead of the mica, another substance, called *hornblende,* is found in some granites: hornblende is a dark crystalline substance, composed of flint, alumina, and magnesia, besides a large proportion of the black oxide of iron. Granites in which hornblende exists are sometimes called Syenite, having been first found in the island of Syene, in Egypt. A similar rock is found in Scotland, in Aberdeen, and in the Isle of Arran.

Granite is found in mountain-chains, and usually in rugged outlines, in nearly all parts of Europe. In the Pyrenees it is found in masses of piles or columns. In Germany it forms the material of those famed scenes of supernatural tradition, the Brocken and the Hartz Mountains. Granite forms the bold ridges of Switzerland and the Savoy. In England, this valuable rock occurs in Devonshire and

Cornwall, also in North Wales, Anglesea, the Malvern Hills in Worcestershire, Charnwood Forest in Leicestershire, and in Cumberland and Westmorland. Granite rises near the foot of Skiddaw in Cumberland, and there are masses of it on the banks of Ulswater. It is found in the mountains of Armagh and Wicklow in Ireland; and Mr. Bakewell supposes that the same formation of this rock, which occurs on the western side of England, is continued under the Irish Channel, or, if interrupted, it rises again in the Isle of Man, and in the counties of Dublin and Wicklow in Ireland. Granite blocks are found in the beds of some of the rivers in the north-west parts of Yorkshire, and in clay pits in Cheshire and Lancashire, at great distances from any quarries where the stone is obtainable. Most of the granite met with in Charnwood Forest is of the kind called *Sienite*, and already described. A continuation of the same description of rock appears upon the surface, near Bedworth, in Warwickshire.

In the granite of Cornwall the felspar is usually white, but in the Scotch granite it is commonly red. Among the celebrated works of which granite forms the material, may be named the monuments of Ancient Egypt and of Thebes, the celebrated block used as a pedestal for the statue of Peter the Great in St. Petersburgh, the columns in the church of the Casan in the same city ; and in England the columns in the King's library in the Museum, and the bridges of London, &c., &c.

Although all granites are similar in structure, the difference in the proportions of its constituent substances occasions great difference in its enduring and useful properties. Some varieties are exceedingly friable, and liable to decomposition. while others, including that known as Sienite, suffer but imperceptibly from moisture and the atmosphere. Some remarks upon the properties of a Sienite, the " *Herm Granite* " of Guernsey, published in the first volume of the Transactions of the Institution of Civil Engineers, may be here usefully quoted :—

" The Herm granite, as compared with Peterhead, and Moorstone from Devon or Cornwall, is a highly crystallised intermixture of felspar, quartz, and hornblende, with a small quantity of black mica, the first of these ingredients hard and sometimes transparent in a greater degree than that found in other British granites,—the contact of the other substances perfect. It resists the effect of exposure to air, and does not easily disintegrate from the mass when mica does not prevail; but, as this last is usually scarce in Guernsey granites, the mass is not deteriorated by its presence as in the Brittany granites, where it abounds, decomposes, stains, and pervades the felspar, and finally destroys the adhesion of the component parts:—*vide* the interior columns of St. Peter's Port church (Guernsey), which is built of it, for an instance. The quartz is in a smaller quantity, and somewhat darker than the felspar in colour: the grains are not large, but uniformly mixed with the other ingredients, The hornblende, which appears to supply the place of mica, is hard and crystallised in small prisms, rarely accompanied by chlorite: its dark colour gives the grayish tone to this granite, or when abundant forms the *blue* granite of the Vale parish. This substance is essentially superior to mica in the formation and durability of granites for strength and re-sistance; consequently its presence occasions more labour in working or facing the block, and its specific gravity is increased. The mica is inferior in quantity to the hornblende, and usually dispersed in small flakes in the mass;—it may, with chlorite, be considered rare."

"The compact nature of a close-grained granite, such as the Vale and Herm stone, having the felspar highly crystal-lised and free from stained cracks, seems well calculated to resist the effect of air and water. When the exterior *bruised* surface of a block has been blown off, it is better disposed to resist decay;—if the surface blocks of the island are now examined after the lapse of ages, it will be found to have resisted the gradual disintegration of time in a superior degree, when compared with *large grained* or *porphyritic* granite; when exposed to water and air, there is no change beyond the polish resulting from *friction* of the elements. Among the symptoms of decay, disintegration prevails generally among granites, usually commencing with the decomposition of the mica; its exfoliating deranges the cohesion of the grains, and it may be considered then to be the more frequent mode of decay."

"The churches of the Vale and St. Sampson (Guernsey), although much of the materials are French and Alderney, bear many proofs of the above remarks: these erections date A.D. 1100—1150. The ancient buildings of decided Herm and Vale stone must be sought for among the old houses in the northern parishes of Guernsey, where they not only encounter the effect of air and water (rain), but the sea air and burning rays of the sun. Disintegration alone appears going on by slow degrees, but in no case affecting the interior of the stone, and so gradual and general as not to deface the building materially ; indeed, the oldest proofs taken from door-posts, lintels, and arches, have scarcely lost their original sharpness or sculpture. The pier of St. Peter's Port and bridge of St. Sampson's may also be mentioned.

" The shore rocks in like manner do not show any material change of surface by wearing ; where the force of the tide is strongest, a slight smoothness alone may be observed on the exterior, and in many instances each substance possesses this polish *without being levelled down to a face.*"

" Vale stone on the northern point of Guernsey produces a finer grained Sienite than Herm, more hornblende in it, and specific gravity greater. The Herm is somewhat larger grained, but equally good for every erection where durability is the chief point. The *Cat-au-roque* stone in the western part of Guernsey must be considered of a different structure to the above : it is a fair and good stone, and appears to last well; its schistose texture must ally it to the gneiss series. In colour it is much the same as the blue granites, the felspar is brilliant and the hornblende prisms are well defined ; there is more chlorite in it, and it is easier to work."

From the same volume, the following interesting results of experiments upon the relative wear of seven different kinds of granite and one whinstone are extracted, as peculiarly valuable in the choice of materials which will be exposed to similarly destructive forces.

" TABLE *showing the result of Experiments made under the direction of Mr. Walker, on the Wear of different Stones in the Tramway on the Commercial Road, London, from 27th March, 1830, to 24th August, 1831, being a period of seventeen months.*

Name of stone.	Sup. area in feet.	Original weight.			Loss of weight by wear.	Loss per sup. foot.	Relative losses.
		cwt.	qrs.	lbs.	lbs.	lbs.	
Guernsey	4·734	7	1	12·75	4·50	0·951	1·000
Herm	5·250	7	3	24·25	5·50	1·048	1·102
Budle	6·336	9	0	50·75	7·75	1·223	1·286
Peterhead (blue) ...	3·484	4	1	7·50	6·25	1·795	1·887
Heytor	4·313	6	0	15·25	8·25	1·915	2·014
Aberdeen (red)	5·375	7	2	11·50	11·50	2·139	2·249
Dartmoor	4·500	6	2	25·00	12·50	2·778	2·921
Aberdeen (blue)......	4·823	6	2	16·00	14·75	3·058	3·216

"The Commercial Road stoneway, on which these experiments were made, consists of two parallel lines of rectangular tramstones, 18 inches wide by a foot deep, and jointed to each other endwise, for the wheels to travel on, with a common street pavement between for the horses. The tramstones subjected to experiment were laid in the gateway of the Limehouse turnpike, so as of necessity to be exposed to all the heavy traffic *from* the East and West India Docks. A similar set of experiments had previously been made in the same place, but for a shorter period (little more than four months), with, however, not very different results, as the following figures, corresponding with the column of " *relative losses*," in the foregoing table will show.

"Guernsey	.	.	:000	Peterhead (blue) 1·715
Budle	.	.	1·040	Aberdeen (red) . 2·413
Herm	.	.	1·156	Aberdeen (blue) 2·821

All the above stones are granites except the Budle, which is a species of whin from Northumberland, and they were all new pieces in each series of experiments."

The relative hardness, or resistance to crushing, of the several kinds of granite in common use, is exhibited in the following Table of Experiments made with an hydrostatic press on specimens of the sizes stated in the Table.

These experiments were made with a 12-inch press, the pump one inch diameter, and the lever 10 to 1;—the mechanical advantage therefore 144 × 10 = 1440 to 1. The weights on the lever were added by 7 lbs. at a time;—each addition therefore equivalent to 1440 × 7 = 10,080 lbs. or $4\frac{1}{2}$ tons.

In consequence of the smallness of the specimens, the press was filled with blocks to the required height, and with these the surplus effect of the lever was $4\frac{1}{2}$ lbs. at 10 to 1, which strictly should be added to the pressure ; but, as the friction of the apparatus is equal to the effect of the lever, it is dispensed with in the calculation.

The column containing the pressure per square inch required to produce a fracture gives the true value of the stone, as the weight that does so would possibly completely destroy the stone if allowed to remain on for a length of time. It should also be observed that, from the exceedingly short time allowed for the experiments, the results are probably too high.

Table of Experiments on Granite.

Description of Stone.	Weight of each specimen.	Dimensions.	Surface exposed to pressure.	Pressure required to fracture stone.			Pressure required to crush stone.		
				Total to each specimen.	Per sup. inch of surface.	Average per sup. inch.	Total to each specimen.	Per sup. inch of surface.	Average per sup. inch.
	lbs. oz.	Lineal Inches.	Sup. in.	Tons.	Tons.	Tons.	Tons.	Tons.	Tons.
Herm	6 6	4 × 4 × 4	16	80·0	5·00	4·77	116·0	7·25	6·64
	6 6	4 × 4 × 4	16	72·5	4·53		96·4	6·03	
Aberdeen (blue) . .	5 0	4 × 4¼ × 3	17	81·0	4·76	4·13	85·5	5·03	4·64
	5 1½	4 × 4½ × 3	18	63·0	3·50		76·5	4·25	
Heytor	4 7	4 × 4 × 3	16	67·5	4·22	3·94	103·5	6·47	6·19
	4 8	4 × 4 × 3	16	58·5	3·66		94·5	5·91	
Dartmoor	4 10	4 × 4 × 3	16	67·5	4·22	3·52	103·5	6·47	5·48
	4 8	4 × 4 × 3	16	45·0	2·81		72·0	4·50	
Peterhead (red) . .	5 5	4½ × 4 × 3⅛	18	58·5	3·25	2·88	94·5	5·25	4·88
	4 12	4½ × 4 × 3	18	45·0	2·50		81·0	4·50	
Peterhead (blue-grey)	5 3½	4½ × 4⅛ × 3⅛	18·6	58·5	3·14	2·86	85·5	4·60	4·36
	5 4	4½ × 3⅞ × 3⅛	17·5	45·0	2·57		72·0	4·11	
Penryn.	5 7	4⅝ × 4 × 3	18·5	63·0	3·41	2·58	72·0	3·90	3·45
	5 4	4½ × 4 × 3⅛	18	31·5	1·75		54·0	3·00	

The method pursued in quarrying the Peterhead granite has been already described at page 78.

Some experiments upon the granites of Ireland were reported to the Geological Society of Dublin, in January, 1844. These experiments were instituted to show (among other results) the weight of water which the stones would imbibe when immersed in water. The size of the stones immersed was 14 inches long and 3 inches square. They were placed on their ends in 16 inches of water, and were uniformly immersed for 88 hours, having been brought to a dry state before immersion by being kept some time in a room at the ordinary temperature of domestic apartments. They were carefully weighed before and after the immersion. The average weight of several specimens of the stones was 170 lbs. per cubic foot: the maximum being 176, and the minimum 143 lbs. The Newry and Kingston granites absorbed a quarter of a pound of water to the cubic foot ; the Carlow, from 1¼ to 2 lbs. ; and the Glenties, from Donegal (between granite and gneiss), 4 lbs.

Serpentine and *Porphyry* are sometimes classed as varieties of granite ; but more properly as distinct rocks of the same primary character as granite. Serpentine is a valuable material for the ornamental purposes of architecture, being distinguished by its variety and richness of colours ; these are generally light and dark green of various shades, inter-mixed in spots or clouds, resembling the spots on the skins of serpents (whence its name). Some varieties of this rock have also a red colour ; others are found having an inter-mixture of crystalline white marble, and these are known as *verde antique*, highly valued for sculpture of ornamental character. Some kinds of serpentine are crystalline, and are called *schiller spar* or *diallage*. In some of these rocks, magnesia exists in the proportion of 48 per cent.

Serpentine is found in Cornwall with a micaceous rock overlying the granite, and forms part of the promontory called the Lizard Point ; it also occurs in the same county, near Liskeard. It is not met with elsewhere in England ; but in Anglesea beautiful varieties of the red and green-coloured are found in beds of considerable thickness, associated with the common slate rocks of the district. The mixture of serpentine with *talc* or *steatite* becomes soft, and forms the substance called *potstone*, which resists fire, and is used in Switzerland, Lombardy, and Egypt, for culinary and other purposes.

SLATE.

In treating of slate as a material of common utility to the builder, it will be scarcely necessary to do more than enumerate the several varieties which are known under the general term slate, but distinguished one from another, and from the slate of general utility, by a peculiar prefix. Thus, the geologist recognises *mica slate, talcous slate, flinty slate,* and *common,* or *clay slate.* Of these, the last only is a material of extended use in the arts of building and construction. Of the others, the first, or mica slate, is a compound of quartz and mica, with sometimes a little felspar. The several varieties of this rock are dependent on the proportion of mica contained in each, and on the comparative fineness or coarseness of the constituent particles. If the felspar abound, the compound passes into a form of rock known as *gneiss;* and if the mica exist in only small proportion, the material assumes the form of *quartz rock.* The talcous slates are distinguished by their green colour, and contain a large proportion of magnesia. One variety of this kind of slate contains particles of quartz, and is sometimes used for hones, under the name of *whetstone* slate. The third variety on our list, flinty slate, contains a larger proportion of flinty or silicious matter, and assimilates to the scaly structure of flint. Possessing the silicious earth, but *not* the scaly kind of formation, this slate passes into a rock known as *hornstone* by us, and as *petro-silex* by the French. If it contains felspar in crystals, it is distinguished as *hornstone porphyry.* All of these varieties of slate are found alternating with each other in the same rocks in North Wales, and in the Charnwood Forest, Leicestershire. The common or clay slate abounds in the most rocky districts, and is found lying upon granite, gneiss, or mica slate. The several varieties of character—from the extreme crystalline to the extreme earthy—are found occupying positions in regular order, from the primary towards the transition rocks. Clay slate, as its name implies, consists chiefly of clay in an indurated condition, and occasionally containing particles of mica and quartz; and, in some of the coarser kinds, grains of felspar and other fragments of the primary rocks. In the extreme admixture of these foreign substances, clay-slate approaches the nature of the rock known as greywacke. The beds of clay-slate are invariably stratified, the thickness of the strata, however, varying from a fraction of an inch to many feet.

Its laminar texture admits of a ready separation into thin plates, and thus endows it with a supreme value for roofing and other purposes, in which great density and comparative impermeability are required to coexist with a minimum thickness and weight. In our preceding pages, we have quoted a highly interesting description of the method pursued in quarrying this invaluable material. We may here add that, besides the immense quarries which are worked, as there described, at Bangor, in North Wales, slate is also procured from the counties of Westmoreland, York, Leicester, Cornwall, and Devon, and that Scotland is supplied with this useful material from Balahulish and Easdale.

In Ireland slate quarries are worked to a considerable extent at Killaloe, Valentia, and in Wicklow County; the slates from the latter of which are said to resemble those from Bangor in quality and extreme tenacity, and can be raised in blocks 30 feet long, 4 or 5 feet wide, and from 6 to 12 inches in thickness. The weight of slates varies from 174 to 179 lb. per cubic foot; the average weight of several specimens being 177 lb. When immersed in water in the manner already described for granite (page 95), the clay-roofing slate absorbed less than a quarter of a pound of water; while a softer quality of clay slate, from the neighbourhood of Bantry, absorbed nearly 2 lb.

SANDSTONES.

These rocks, belonging, geologically, to various positions in the order of the strata of which the exterior of the earth is composed, and sometimes alternating with the variety of limestones, are widely distributed, or rather frequently met with, superficially, in exploring the surface of our island.

The vast accumulation of beds, known as forming the *Silurian System*, and of which sandstone is the principal member, is found to extend, with some interruptions, from Carmarthenshire and Radnorshire, in the west, to Dudley in Staffordshire, in the central part of England. At the western boundaries of this system the sandstone is known as Llaudillo flagstones; it occurs also at Caer-Caradock in Shropshire, and is there and elsewhere known as Caradock sandstone. Some varieties of this stone are found to contain a large proportion of lime, occasionally in the form of shells, and are hence sometimes called shelly limestones and sandy limestones.

Sandstones are principally silicious, and possess various degrees of induration. The chemical analysis of several

F

specimens of sandstone from four quarries, viz., Craigleith, in Edinburghshire;—Darley Dale, in Derbyshire; Heddon, in Northumberland, and Kenton, in the same county, gives their average constituents thus :—

Silica	95·725
Carbonate of lime	1·065
Iron alumina	2·150
Water and loss	1·060
	100·000

The average weight of these four kinds of stone was found to be 142 lb. 7 oz. per cubic foot. Adopting the same high authority from which these analyses are derived, viz., the scientific Commission appointed to visit quarries and examine the qualities of stones to be used in building the New Houses of Parliament, the composition of these four kinds of sandstone appears to be as follows:—*Craigleith:* Fine quartz grains with a silicious cement, slightly calcareous; occasional plates of mica; colour, whitish gray.—*Darley Dale:* Quartz grains of moderate size and decomposed felspar, with an argillo-silicious cement; ferruginous spots, and plates of mica; colour, light ferruginous brown.—*Heddon:* Coarse quartz grains, and decomposed felspar, with an argillo-silicious cement; ferruginous spots; colour, light brown ochre.—*Kenton:* Fine quartz grains with an argillo-silicious and ferruginous cement; mica in planes of beds; colour, light ferruginous brown.

From the nature of the composition of sandstones, (of which the above four are described as average specimens,) it results that their resistance against, or yielding to, the decomposing effects to which they are subjected, depends to a great extent, if not wholly, upon the nature of the cementing substance by which the grains are united; these latter being comparatively indestructible. From the nature of their formation, sandstones are usually laminated, and more especially so when mica is present, the plates of which are generally arranged in planes parallel to their beds. Stones of this description should be carefully placed in constructions, so that these planes of lamination may be horizontal, for if placed vertically, the action of decomposition will occur in flakes, according to the thickness of the laminæ. Indeed the best way of using all descriptions of stone is in the same position which they had in the quarry, but this becomes a really imperative rule with those of laminated structure.

Uniformity of colour is a tolerably correct criterion of uniformity of structure, and this constitutes, other circumstances being equal, one of the practical excellencies of building stones. The great injury occasioned to these materials by their absorption of moisture, leads properly to a preference for such stones as resist its introduction, for all above-ground purposes. Those which imbibe and retain moisture are especially liable to disruption by frost if exposed. The simplest method of ascertaining the disposition of a stone to imbibe moisture is to immerse it for a lengthened period in water, and to compare the weight of it before and after such immersion.

A method recently introduced of determining the susceptibility of a stone to injury by frost, is to dip the stone in a solution of some salt, and then suspend it for several days over the solution, repeating the process several times, so as to allow the salt to crystallise on the surface of the stone. If the stone can resist frost the solution will remain free from sand or fragments of stone, but if otherwise, the edges of the stone will be found deposited in the vessel beneath.

As examples of the durability of sandstone in buildings, the following may be instanced :—Ecclestone Abbey, built in the thirteenth century, near Barnard Castle, Durham, in which the minute ornaments and mouldings remain still in excellent condition. The circular keep of Barnard Castle (14th century), is also in fine preservation. Tintern Abbey (13th century), built of red and grey sandstones of the vicinity, is for the most part in perfect condition. Whitby Abbey (13th century), is built of stone similar to that in the vicinity, and is generally in good condition, excepting the west front, which is very much decomposed. The stone used is of two colours, brown and white, of which the latter is uniformly in the best preservation. The enrichments on the east front are all in good condition. Of Ripon Cathedral, the west front, the transepts and tower, were built in the 12th and 13th centuries of a coarse sandstone of the vicinity, and remain in very fair condition. Rivaulx Abbey, built in the 12th century, of a sandstone one mile from the ruins, is generally in excellent condition. The west front is slightly decomposed, but the south front is remarkably perfect, even to the preservation of the original tool-marks.

Experiments upon several sandstones to ascertain the force required to crush them, performed with the hydrostatic press, as already described of the specimens of granite (page 93) gave the following results—

F 2

Table of Experiments upon several Sandstones.

Description of Stone.	Weight of each specimen. (lb. oz.)	Dimensions. (Lineal Inches.)	Surface exposed to pressure. (Sup. In.)	Pressure required to fracture stone.			Pressure required to crush stone.		
				Total to each specimen. (Tons.)	Per sup. inch of surface. (Tons.)	Average per sup. inch. (Tons.)	Total to each specimen. (Tons.)	Per sup. inch of surface. (Tons.)	Average per sup. inch. (Tons.)
Yorkshire (Cromwell bottom)	12 8 / 12 6	5¼ × 5 × 5⅛ / 5½ × 5 × 5¼	27·5 / 27·5	81·0 / 76·5	2·95 / 2·78	2·87	121·5 / 95·5	4·42 / 8·47	3·94
Craigleith	11 10 / 11 6	5 × 5 × 5¼ / 5 × 5 × 5⅝	25 / 25	63·0 / 31·5	2·52 / 1·26	1·89	85·5 / 63·0	3·42 / 2·52	2·97
Humbie	17 10 / 17 3	6 × 6 × 6 / 6 × 6 × 6	36 / 36	72·0 / 49·5	2·00 / 1·37	1·69	81·0 / 67·5	2·25 / 1·87	2·06
Whitby	16 10 / 15 12	6 × 6 × 6 / 6 × 6 × 6	36 / 36	36·0 / 36·0	1·00 / 1·00	1·00	40·5 / 36·0	1·12 / 1·00	1·06

LIMESTONES.

The class of limestones, including the magnesian lime-stones and the oolites, is one of extreme importance in the building arts, comprehending some of the most advantageous materials of construction, and combining great comparative durability with peculiar facilities for working, in which they surpass the sandstones ; as those do the rocks of a primary and unstratified character. Of the limestones and the oolites, the principal material is carbonate of lime. The magnesian limestones contain a quantity of carbonate of magnesia, in some cases nearly equal to that of the carbonate of lime. The analyses of four varieties of oolites and three limestones are given below. The oolites were from Ancaster in Lincoln-shire ; from Bath ; from Portland, Dorsetshire ; and from Ketton in Rutlandshire. The three limestones were from Barnack, Northamptonshire ; Chilmark, Wiltshire, and Ham Hill in Somersetshire.

	OOLITES.			
	Ancaster.	Bath.	Portland.	Ketton.
Silica	...	...	1·20	...
Carbonate of lime . .	93·59	94·52	95·16	92·17
Carbonate of magnesia	2·90	2·50	1·20	4·10
Iron alumina . . ·	·80	1·20	·50	·90
Water and loss. . . .	. 2·71	1·78	1·94	2·83

	LIMESTONES.		
	Barnac	Chilmark.	Ham Hill.
Silica	...	10·4	4·7
Carbonate of lime	93·4	79·0	79·3
Carbonate of magnesia . . .	3·8	3·7	5·2
Iron alumina	1·3	2·0	8·3
Water and loss	1·5	4·2	2·5

All of these stones contain a slight trace of bitumen in their composition. The weights of the several kinds are as follow :—Of the oolites, the Ancaster stone, 139 lb. 4 oz. per cubic foot.—Bath, 123 lb.—Portland, top bed, 135 lb.,

best or lower bed, 147 lb., mean, say 141 lb.—Ketton;
128 lb. 5 oz. Of the three limestones, the weights are,
Barnack, 136 pounds, 12 oz.—Chilmark, 153 lb. 7 oz.; and
Ham Hill, 141 lb. 12 oz. The composition of these stones
is described as follows:—First, Oolites.—*Ancaster:* fine
oolitic grains, cemented by compact and often crystalline
carbonate of lime; colour, cream.—*Bath:* chiefly carbonate
of lime in moderately fine oolitic grains, with fragments of
shells. The weather bed of the quarry is generally used for
plinths, strings, cornices, etc.; the corn grit for dressings;
the scallet, which is the finest in grain, is used for ashlar.
Eight quarries are opened on the Box escarpment, many of
them of great antiquity. The colour is that of cream.—
Portland: oolitic carbonate of lime, with fragments of
shells; colour, whitish brown.—*Ketton:* oolitic grains of
moderate size, slightly cemented by carbonate of lime;
colour, dark cream. Secondly, Limestones.—*Barnack:*
carbonate of lime, compact and oolitic, with shells, often in
fragments; coarsely laminated in planes of beds; colour,
light whitish brown. This stone is used for troughs and
cisterns, and is perfectly impervious.—*Chilmark:* carbonate
of lime, with a moderate proportion of silica, and occasional
grains of silicate of iron; colour, light greenish brown.—
Ham Hill: compact carbonate of lime with shells, chiefly
in fragments, coarsely laminated in planes of beds; colour,
deep ferruginous brown.

Of four varieties of magnesian limestone, the following are
the analyses:—

| | MAGNESIAN LIMESTONES. | | | |
	Bolsover.	Huddle-stone.	Roach Abbey.	Park Nook.
Silica	3·6	2·53	·8	...
Carbonate of lime . .	51·1	54·19	57·5	55·7
Carbonate of magnesia	40·2	41·37	39·4	41·6
Iron alumina	1·8	·30	·7	·4
Water and loss . . .	3·3	1·61	1·6	2·3

The weights of these limestones were as follows:—
Bolsover, 151 lb. 11 oz. per cubic foot; Huddlestone,
137 lb. 13 oz.; Roach Abbey, 139 lb. 2 oz.; and Park
Nook, 137 lb. 8 oz. The composition of them is as follows:

—*Bolsover:* chiefly carbonate of lime and carbonate of magnesia, semi-crystalline; colour, light yellowish brown.—*Huddlestone:* similar component parts; colour, whitish cream.—*Roach Abbey:* chiefly carbonate of lime and carbonate of magnesia, with occasional dendritic spots of iron or manganese; semi-crystalline; colour, whitish cream.—*Park Nook:* similar constitution, and of cream colour. Sinks and tanks are made of this stone, but the water wastes in them.

The following structures of magnesian limestones may be distinguished:—Southwell Church, Nottinghamshire, built in the 10th century, and now in perfect condition. Koningsburgh Castle, in Yorkshire (Norman), built of coarse-grained and semi-crystalline magnesian limestone, from the adjacent hill, is in excellent preservation. The mortar has in many parts disappeared, but the edges of the joints remain perfect. The Church at Hemingborough, in Yorkshire (15th century), is in a very perfect state. It is built of a white crystalline magnesian limestone, resembling that from Huddlestone. The entire building is in a perfect state; even the spire, where no traces of decay are apparent.

It is remarked that magnesian limestone appears capable of resisting decomposing action in proportion as its structure is crystalline, and the late Professor Daniell gave it as his opinion, based upon experiments, that "the nearer the magnesian limestones approach to equivalent proportions of carbonate of lime and carbonate of magnesia, the more crystalline and better they are in every respect."

Among the buildings constructed of oolitic and other lime-stones, the following are deserving of notice:—Byland Abbey, Yorkshire, of the 12th century, built partly of a silicious grit (principally in the interior), and partly (chiefly in the exterior) of a compact oolite, from the Wass quarries in the vicinity. The west front, which is of the oolite, is in perfect condition, even in the dog's-tooth and other florid decorations of the doorways, &c. This building is generally covered with lichens.

Bath.—*Abbey Church* (1576), built in an oolite from the vicinity. The tower is in fair condition, the body of the church in the upper part of the south and west sides much decomposed. The lower parts (formerly in contact with buildings) are in a more perfect state: the relief in the west front of Jacob's ladder are in parts nearly effaced.—*Queen's Square,* north side, and the obelisk in the centre, built about 110 years since, of an oolite with shells, in fair condition. *Circus*, built about 1750, of an oolite in the vicinity, generally in fair condition, except those portions which have a west and southern aspect, where the most exposed parts are decomposed.—*Crescent*, built about 60 years since, of an oolite of the vicinity, generally in fair condition, excepting a few places where the stone appears to be of an inferior quality.

Oxford.—*Cathedral* (Norman, 12th century), chiefly of a shelly oolite, similar to that of Taynton. Norman work in good condition; the later work much decomposed.—*Merton College Chapel* (13th century), of a shelly oolite, resembling Taynton stone, in good condition generally.—*New College Cloisters* (14th century), of a shelly oolite (Taynton) in a good condition. The whole of the colleges, churches, and other public buildings of Oxford, erected within the last three centuries, are of an oolitic limestone from Headington, about 1½ mile from the University, and are all, more or less, in a deplorable state of decomposition. The plinths, string-courses, and such portions of the buildings as are much exposed to the action of the atmosphere, are mostly of a shelly oolite from Taynton, 15 miles from the University, and are universally in good condition.

Saint Paul's Cathedral, London. Finished about 1700. Built of Portland oolite, from the grove quarries on the East Cliff. The building generally in good condition, especially the north and east fronts. The carvings of flowers, &c., are throughout nearly as perfect as when executed. On the south and west fronts large portions of the stone exhibit their natural colour, occasioned by slight decomposition of the surface. The stone in the drum of the dome, and in the cupola above it, appears not so well selected as the rest, yet shows scarcely any decay in those parts.

Westminster Abbey. (15th century). Built of several varieties of stone, similar to Gatton or Reigate, much decomposed, and of Caen stone, generally in bad condition. A considerable portion of the exterior, especially on the north side, has been restored at various periods; nevertheless, abundant symptoms of decay are apparent. The cloisters built of several kinds of stone, are in a very mouldering condition, except where they have been recently restored with Bath and Portland stones. The west towers erected in the beginning of the 18th century, with a shelly variety of Portland oolite, exhibit scarcely any appearance of decay;

Henry the Seventh's chapel, restored about thirty years since, with Coombe Down Bath stone, is already in a state of decomposition.*

In *Spofforth Castle* is a striking example of an unequal decomposition of the magnesian limestone and a sandstone; the former used in the decorated parts, and the latter in ashlar and plain facings. Although the magnesian limestone has been equally exposed with the sandstone, it has remained as perfect as when erected, while the sandstone has suffered considerably. In Chepstow Castle, and in Bristol Cathedral, similar contrasted effects are visible upon the magnesian limestones and sandstones employed.

The late Professor Daniell gives the following valuable summary of the results of his experiments upon the stones we have referred to. " If the stones be divided into classes, according to their chemical composition, it will be found that in all stones of the same class there exists, generally, a close relation between their various physical qualities ;— thus it will be observed that the specimen which has the greatest specific gravity possesses the greatest cohesive strength, absorbs the least quantity of water, and disintegrates the least by the process which imitates the effects of weather. A comparison of all the experiments shows this to be the general rule, though it is liable to individual exceptions. But this will not enable us to compare stones of different classes together. The sandstones absorb the least water, but they disintegrate more than the magnesian limestones, which, considering their compactness, absorb a great quantity. The heaviest and most cohesive of the sandstones are the Craigleith and the Park Spring. Among the magnesian limestones that from Bolsolver is the heaviest, strongest, and absorbs the least water. Among the oolites, the Ketton Rag is greatly distinguished from all the rest by its great cohesive strength and high specific gravity."

For durability, for crystalline character, combined with a close approach to the equivalent proportions of carbonate of lime and carbonate of magnesia ; for uniformity of structure ; for facility and economy in conversion ; and for advantage of colour, the commissioners declared their preference for the magnesian limestone of Bolsover and its neighbourhood, and, taking into account the extended range and careful precision of their observations, and the skilful manner in which their

* Report of Commissioners.

experiments were designed and conducted, it will be generally admitted that the opinions thus formed and presented to us are excellent guides for our selection of stone in all architectural constructions, and deserve our most careful consideration, if they do not claim our immediate concurrence.

THE END.

BRIDGES.

45.

In 4 vols. royal 8vo, illustrated by 138 engravings and 92 wood-cuts, bound in 3 vols. half-morocco, price £4. 10s.

THE THEORY, PRACTICE, AND ARCHITECTURE

OF

BRIDGES OF STONE, IRON, TIMBER, AND WIRE:

WITH EXAMPLES ON THE PRINCIPLE OF SUSPENSION.

DIVISIONS OF THE WORK.

THEORY OF BRIDGES. By James Hann, King's College, London.
GENERAL PRINCIPLES OF CONSTRUCTION, &c. Translated from Gauthey.
THEORY OF THE ARCH, &c. By Professor Moseley.
PAPERS ON FOUNDATIONS. By T. Hughes, C.E.
ACCOUNT OF HUTCHESON BRIDGE, GLASGOW, with Specification. By the late Robert Stevenson, C.E.
MATHEMATICAL PRINCIPLES OF DREDGE'S SUSPENSION BRIDGE.
ESSAY AND TREATISES ON THE PRACTICE AND ARCHITECTURE OF BRIDGES. By William Hosking, F.S.A., Arch^t. and C.E.
SPECIFICATION OF CHESTER DEE BRIDGE.
PRACTICAL DESCRIPTION OF THE TIMBER BRIDGES, &c., ON THE UTICA AND SYRACUSE RAILROAD, U. S. By B. F. Isherwood, C. E., New York.
Description of the Plates.—General Index, &c., &c., &c.

LIST OF PLATES.

1. Centering of Ballater bridge across the river Dee, Aberdeenshire.
2. Town's American timber bridge.
3. Do., sections.
4. Do.   do.
5. Ladykirk and Norham timber bridge over the Tweed, by J. Blackmore.
6. Timber bridge over the Clyde at Glasgow, by Robert Stevenson.
7. Elevation of arch of do.
8. Transverse section of do.
9. Section of foot-path on do., &c.
10. Occupation bridge over the Calder and Hebble Navigation, by W. Bull.
11. Newcastle, North Shields, and Tynemouth railway viaduct across Willington Dean, plans and elevations.
12. Do., do.
13. Do., sections.
14. Ditto across Ouse Burn Dean, plan and elevation.
15. Do., do.
16. Isometrical view of the upper wooden bridge at Elysville over the Patapsco, on the Baltimore and Ohio Railroad.
17. Elevation and plan of do.
18. Sections of do.
19. Longitudinal section under the central archway of Old London bridge, showing the sunk weir recommended by Mr. Smeaton to hold the water up for the benefit of the water-works, &c., in 1763; sections of the same.
20. Plan and elevation of timber bridge for Westminster, as designed by Weseley.
21. Half-elevation of ditto for Westminster, as designed by James King.
22. Westminster timber bridge adapted to the stone piers, by C. Labelye.
23. One of the river ribs of the centre on which the middle arch of Westminster bridge was turned, extending 76 feet, designed and executed by James King.
24. Long elevation and plan of Westminster bridge.
25. Elevation of the foot bridge over the Whitadder, at Abbey St. Bathen's.
26. Weymouth bridge, elevation and plan.
27. Very long elevation of Hutcheson bridge, Glasgow, by Robert Stevenson.
28. Longitudinal section of ditto, showing the progress of the works in 1832.
29. Cross section of do., showing the building apparatus and centre frames.
30. Cross section of Hutcheson bridge.
31. Plan of southern abutment of do.
32. Section of abutments of do.
33. Toll-houses of do.
34. Bridge of the Schuylkill at Market Street, Philadelphia.
35. Details of do.

MR. WEALE'S
PUBLICATIONS FOR 1861.

RUDIMENTARY SERIES.

In demy 12mo, cloth, price 1s.

RUDIMENTARY.—1.—CHEMISTRY, by Professor FOWNES, F.R.S., including Agricultural Chemistry, for the Use of Farmers.

In demy 12mo, with Woodcuts, cloth, price 1s.

RUDIMENTARY.—2.—NATURAL PHILOSOPHY, by CHARLES TOMLINSON.

In demy 12mo, with Woodcuts, cloth, price 1s. 6d.

RUDIMENTARY.—3.—GEOLOGY, by Major-Gen. PORTLOCK, F.R.S.. &c.

In demy 12mo, with Woodcuts, cloth, price 2s.

RUDIMENTARY.—4, 5.—MINERALOGY, with Mr. DANA'S Additions. 2 vols. in 1.

In demy 12mo, with Woodcuts, cloth, price 1s.

RUDIMENTARY.—6.—MECHANICS, by CHARLES TOMLINSON.

In demy 12mo, with Woodcuts, cloth, price 1s. 6d.

RUDIMENTARY.—7.—ELECTRICITY, by Sir WILLIAM SNOW HARRIS, F.R.S.

In demy 12mo, with Woodcuts, cloth, price 1s. 6d.

RUDIMENTARY.—7*.—ON GALVANISM; ANIMAL AND VOLTAIC ELECTRICITY; by Sir W. SNOW HARRIS.

In demy 12mo, with Woodcuts, cloth, price 3s. 6d.

RUDIMENTARY.—8, 9, 10—MAGNETISM, Concise Exposition of, by Sir W. SNOW HARRIS, 3 vols. in 1.

In demy 12mo, with Woodcuts, cloth, price 2s.

RUDIMENTARY.—11, 11*.—ELECTRIC TELEGRAPH, History of the, by E. HIGHTON, C.E.

In demy 12mo, with Woodcuts, cloth, price 1s.

RUDIMENTARY.—12.—PNEUMATICS, by CHARLES TOMLINSON.

In demy 12mo, with Woodcuts, cloth, price 4s. 6d.

RUDIMENTARY.—13, 14, 15, 15*.—CIVIL ENGINEERING, by HENRY LAW, C.E., 3 vols.; and Supplement by G. R. BURNELL, C.E.

In demy 12mo, with Woodcuts, cloth, price 1s.

RUDIMENTARY.—16.—ARCHITECTURE, Orders of, by W. H. LEEDS.

In demy 12mo, with Woodcuts, cloth, price 1s. 6d.

RUDIMENTARY.—17.—ARCHITECTURE Styles of, by T. BURY, Architect.

John Weale, 59, High Holborn, London, W.C.

B

2

MR. WEALE'S RUDIMENTARY SERIES.

In demy 12mo, with Woodcuts, cloth, price 2s.

RUDIMENTARY.—18, 19.—ARCHITECTURE, Principles of Design in by E. L. GARBETT, Architect, 2 vols. in 1.

In demy 12mo, with Woodcuts, cloth, price 2s.

RUDIMENTARY.— 20, 21. — PERSPECTIVE, by G. PYNE, Artist, 2 vols. in 1.

In demy 12mo, with Woodcuts, cloth, price 1s.

RUDIMENTARY.—22.—BUILDING, Art of, by E. DOBSON, C.E.

In demy 12mo, with Woodcuts, cloth, price 2s.

RUDIMENTARY.—23, 24.—BRICK-MAKING, TILE-MAKING, &c., Art of, by E. DOBSON, C.E., 2 vols. in 1.

In demy 12mo, with Woodcuts, cloth, price 2s.

RUDIMENTARY.—25, 26.—MASONRY AND STONE-CUTTING, Art of, by E. DOBSON, C.E., 2 vols. in 1.

In demy 12mo, with Woodcuts, cloth, price 2s.

RUDIMENTARY.—27, 28.—PAINTING, Art of, or a GRAMMAR OF COLOURING, by GEORGE FIELD, 2 vols. in 1.

In demy 12mo, with Woodcuts, cloth, price 1s.

RUDIMENTARY.—29.—PRACTICE OF DRAINING DISTRICTS AND LANDS, Art of, by G. D. DEMPSEY, C.E.

In demy 12mo, with Woodcuts, cloth, price 1s. 6d.

RUDIMENTARY.—30.—PRACTICE OF DRAINING AND SEWAGE OF TOWNS AND BUILDINGS, Art of, by G. D. DEMPSEY, C.E.

In demy 12mo, with Woodcuts, cloth, price 1s.

RUDIMENTARY. — 31. — WELL-SINKING AND BORING, Art of, by G. R. BURNELL, C.E.

In demy 12mo, with Woodcuts, cloth, price 1s.

RUDIMENTARY. — 32. — USE OF INSTRUMENTS, Art of the, by J. F. HEATHER, M.A.

In demy 12mo, with Woodcuts, cloth, price 1s.

RUDIMENTARY. — 33. — CONSTRUCTING CRANES, Art of, by J. GLYNN, F.R.S., C.E.

In demy 12mo, with Woodcuts, cloth, price 1s.

RUDIMENTARY. — 34. — STEAM ENGINE, Treatise on the. by Dr. LARDNER.

In demy 12mo, with Woodcuts, cloth, price 1s.

RUDIMENTARY.—35. — BLASTING ROCKS AND QUARRYING, AND ON STONE, by Lieut.-Gen. Sir J BURGOYNE. Bart., G.C.B., R.E.

In demy 12mo, with Woodcuts, cloth, price 4s.

RUDIMENTARY.—36, 37, 38, 39.—DICTIONARY OF TERMS used by Architects, Builders, Civil and Mechanical Engineers, Surveyors, Artists, Ship-builders, &c., vols. in 1.

In demy 12mo, cloth, price 1s.

RUDIMENTARY.—40.—GLASS STAINING Art of, by Dr. M. A. GESSERT. John Weale, 59, High Holborn, London, W.C.

MR. WEALE'S RUDIMENTARY SERIES.

In demy 12mo, cloth, price 1s.

RUDIMENTARY. — 41. — PAINTING ON GLASS, Essay on, by E. O. FROMBERG.

In demy 12mo, with Woodcuts, cloth, price 1s.

RUDIMENTARY. —42.— COTTAGE BUILD-ING, Treatise on.

In demy 12mo, with Woodcuts, cloth, price 1s.

RUDIMENTARY. — 43. — TUBULAR AND GIRDER BRIDGES, and others, Treatise on, more particularly describing the Britannia and Conway Bridges.

In demy 12mo, with Woodcuts, cloth, price 1s.

RUDIMENTARY.—44.—FOUNDATIONS, &c., by E. DOBSON, C.E.

In demy 12mo, with Woodcuts, cloth, price 1s.

RUDIMENTARY. — 45. — LIMES, CEMENTS, MORTARS, CONCRETE, MASTICS, &c., by G. R. BURNELL, C.E.

In demy 12mo, with Woodcuts, cloth, price 1s.

RUDIMENTARY. — 46. — CONSTRUCTING AND REPAIRING COMMON ROADS, by H. LAW, C.E.

In demy 12mo, with Woodcuts, cloth, price 3s.

RUDIMENTARY. — 47, 48, 49. — CONSTRUCTION AND ILLUMINATION OF LIGHTHOUSES, by ALAN STEVENSON, C.E., 3 vols. in 1.

In demy 12mo, with Woodcuts, cloth, price 1s.

RUDIMENTARY.—50.—LAW OF CONTRACTS FOR WORKS AND SERVICES, by DAVID GIBBONS, S.P.

In demy 12mo, with Woodcuts, cloth, price 3s.

RUDIMENTARY.—51, 52, 53.—NAVAL ARCHITECTURE, Principles of the Science, by J. PEAKE, N.A., 3 vols. in 1.

In demy 12mo, with Woodcuts, cloth, price 1s.

RUDIMENTARY AND ELEMENTARY.—53*. —PRACTICAL CONSTRUCTION concisely stated of Ships for Ocean or River Service, by Captain H. A. SOMMERFELDT, N.R.N.

In royal 4to. with Engraved Plates, cloth, price 7s. 6d.

RUDIMENTARY.—53**—ATLAS of 15 Plates to ditto, drawn and engraved to a Scale for Practice.—For the convenience of the Operative Ship Builder the Atlas may be had in three separate Parts. Part I., 2s 6d. Part II., 2s. 6d. Part III., 2s. 6d.

In demy 12mo, with Woodcuts, cloth, price 1s. 6d.

RUDIMENTARY. — 54. — MASTING, MAST-MAKING, AND RIGGING OF SHIPS, by R. KIPPING, A.

In demy 12mo, with Woodcuts, cloth, price 2s. 6d.

RUDIMENTARY.—54*.—IRON SHIP BUILD-ING, by JOHN GRANTHAM, N.A. and C.E.

In demy 12mo, with Woodcuts, cloth, price 2s.

RUDIMENTARY. — 55, 56.— NAVIGATION; THE SAILOR'S SEA-BOOK.—How to Keep the Log and Work it Off—Latitude and Longitude—Great Circle Sailing—Law of Storms and variable Winds; and an Explanation of Terms used, with coloured Illustrations of Flags.

John Weale, 59, High Holborn, London, W.C.

4

MR. WEALE'S RUDIMENTARY SERIES.

In demy 12mo, with Woodcuts, cloth, price 2s.

RUDIMENTARY.—57, 58.—WARMING AND VENTILATION, by CHARLES TOMLINSON, 2 vols. in 1.

In demy 12mo, with Woodcuts, cloth, price 1s.

RUDIMENTARY.—59.—STEAM BOILERS, by R. ARMSTRONG, C.E.

In demy 12mo, with Woodcuts, cloth, price 2s.

RUDIMENTARY. — 60, 61. — LAND AND ENGINEERING SURVEYING, by T. BAKER, C.E., 2 vols. in 1.

In demy 12mo, with Woodcuts, cloth, price 1s.

RUDIMENTARY AND ELEMENTARY.—62. —PRINCIPLES OF RAILWAYS, for the Use of the Beginner in his Studies; with Sketches for Construction. By Sir R. MACDONALD STEPHENSON. Vol. I.

In demy 12mo, with Woodcuts, cloth, price 1s.

RUDIMENTARY.—62*.—RAILWAY WORK-ING IN GREAT BRITAIN, Statistical Details, Table of Capital and Dividends, Revenue Accounts, Signals, &c., Vol. II.

In demy 12mo, with Woodcuts, cloth, price 3s.

RUDIMENTARY.—63, 64, 65.—AGRICULTU-RAL BUILDINGS, the Construction of, on Motive Powers, and the Machinery of the Steading; and on Agricultural Field Engines, Machines, and Implements, by G. H. ANDREWS, 3 vols in 1. —John Weale, 59, High Holborn, London, W.C.

In demy 12mo, cloth, price 1s.

RUDIMENTARY.—66.—CLAY LANDS AND LOAMY SOILS, by Professor JOHN DONALDSON, A.E.

In demy 12mo, with Woodcuts, cloth, price 3s.

RUDIMENTARY. — 67, 68. — CLOCK AND WATCH-MAKING, AND ON CHURCH CLOCKS AND BELLS, by E. B. DENISON, M.A., 2 vols. in 1, considerably extended. Fourth Edition.

In demy 12mo, with Woodcuts, cloth, price 2s.

RUDIMENTARY. —69, 70.— MUSIC, Practical Treatise on, by C. C. SPENCER, Mus. Dr. 2 vols. in 1.

In demy 12mo, cloth, price 1s.

RUDIMENTARY. — 71. — PIANOFORTE, In-struction for Playing the, by C. C. SPENCER, Mus. Dr.

In demy 12mo, with Steel Engravings and Woodcuts, cloth, price 5s. 6d.

RUDIMENTARY.—72, 73, 74, 75, 75*.—RECENT FOSSIL SHELLS (A Manual of the Mollusca), by SAMUEL P. WOODWARD, of the Brit. Mus. 4 vols. in 1, with Supplement.

In demy 12mo., with Woodcuts, cloth, price 2s.

RUDIMENTARY. — 76, 77. — DESCRIPTIVE GEOMETRY, by J. F. HEATHER, M.A. 2 vols. in 1.

In demy 12mo, with Woodcuts, price 1s.

RUDIMENTARY. — 77*. — ECONOMY OF FUEL, by T. S. PRIDEAUX.

In demy 12mo, 2 vols. in 1, with Woodcuts, cloth, price 2s.

RUDIMENTARY.—78, 79.—STEAM AS AP-PLIED TO GENERAL PURPOSES.
John Weale, 59, High Holborn, London, W.C.

M^R. WEALE'S RUDIMENTARY SERIES.

In demy 12mo, with Wood-uts, cloth, price 1s. 6d.

RUDIMENTARY.—78*.—LOCOMOTIVE EN-GINE, by G. D. DEMPSEY, C.E.

In royal 4to, cloth, price 4s. 6d.

RUDIMENTARY. — 79*. — ATLAS OF EN-GRAVED PLATES to DEMPSEY'S LOCOMOTIVE ENGINES.

In demy 12mo, with Woodcuts, cloth, price 1s.

RUDIMENTARY.—79**.—ON PHOTOGRA-PHY, the Composition and Properties of the Chemical Sub-stances used, by Dr. H. HALLEUR.

In demy 12mo., with Woodcuts, cloth, price 2s. 6d.

RUDIMENTARY. — 80, 81. — MARINE EN-GINES AND ON THE SCREW, &c., by R. MURRAY, C.E. 2 vols. in 1.

In demy 12mo, cloth, price 2s.

RUDIMENTARY.—80*, 81*.—EMBANKING LANDS FROM THE SEA, by JOHN WIGGINS, F.G.S. 2 vols. in 1.

In demy 12mo, with Woodcuts, cloth, price 2s.

RUDIMENTARY. — 82, 82*. — POWER OF WATER, AS APPLIED TO DRIVE FLOUR MILLS, by JOSEPH GLYNN, F.R.S., C.E.

In demy 12mo, cloth, price 1s.

RUDIMENTARY.—83.—BOOK-KEEPING, by JAMES HADDON, M.A.

In demy 12mo, with Woodcuts. price 3s.

RUDIMENTARY. — 82**, 83*, 83 (bis) COAL GAS, on the Manufacture and Distribution of, by SAMUEL HUGHES, C.E.

In demy 12mo, with Woodcuts, cloth, price 3s.

RUDIMENTARY.—82***.—WATER WORKS FOR THE SUPPLY OF CITIES AND TOWNS; Works which have been executed for procuring Supplies by means of Drainage Areas and by Pumping from Wells, by SAMUEL HUGHES, C.E.

In demy 12mo, with Woodcuts, cloth, price 1s. 6d.

RUDIMENTARY. — 83**. — CONSTRUCTION OF DOOR LOCKS.

In demy 12mo, with Woodcuts, cloth, price 1s.

RUDIMENTARY. — 83 (bis) — FORMS OF SHIPS AND BOATS, by W. BLAND, of Hartlip.

In demy 12mo, cloth, price 1s. 6d.

RUDIMENTARY.—84.—ARITHMETIC, with numerous Examples, by Prof. J. R. YOUNG.

In demy 12mo, cloth, price 1s. 6d.

RUDIMENTARY. — 84*.— KEY to the above, by Prof. J. R. YOUNG.

In demy 12mo, cloth, price 1s.

RUDIMENTARY. — 85. — EQUATIONAL ARITHMETIC, Questions of Interest, Annuities, &c., by W. HIPSLEY.

John Weale, 59, High Holborn, London, W.C.

MR. WEALE'S RUDIMENTARY SERIES.

In demy 12mo, cloth, price 1s.

RUDIMENTARY.—85*.—SUPPLEMENTARY VOLUME TO HIPSLEY'S EQUATIONAL ARITHMETIC, Tables for the Calculation of Simple Interest, with Logarithms for Compound Interest and Annuities, &c , &c., by W. HIPSLEY.

In demy 12mo, cloth, price 2s.

RUDIMENTARY. — 86, 87. — ALGEBRA, by JAMES HADDON, M.A. 2 vols. in 1.

In demy 12mo, in cloth, price 1s. 6d.

RUDIMENTARY.—86*, 87*.—ELEMENTS OF ALGEBRA, Key to the, by Prof. YOUNG.

In demy 12mo, with Woodcuts, price 2s.

RUDIMENTARY.—88, 89.—ELEMENTS OF GEOMETRY, by HENRY LAW, C.E. 2 vols. in 1.

In demy 12mo, with Woodcuts, cloth, price 1s.

RUDIMENTARY.—90.—GEOMETRY, ANALYTICAL, by Prof. JAMES HANN.

In demy 12mo, with Woodcuts, cloth, price 2s.

RUDIMENTARY. — 91, 92. — PLANE AND SPHERICAL TRIGONOMETRY, by the same. 2 vols. in 1.

In demy 12mo, with Woodcuts, cloth, price 1s.

RUDIMENTARY.—93.—MENSURATION, by T. BAKER, C.E.

In demy 12mo, cloth, price 2s. 6d.

RUDIMENTARY. — 94, 95. — LOGARITHMS, Tables for facilitating Astronomical, Nautical, Trigonometrical, and Logarithmic Calculations, by H. LAW, C.E. New Edition, with Tables of Natural Sines and Tangents, and Natural Cosines. 2 vols. in 1.

In demy 12mo, with Woodcuts, cloth, price 1s.

RUDIMENTARY.—96.—POPULAR ASTRONOMY. By the Rev. ROBERT MAIN, M.R.A.S.

In demy 12mo, with Woodcuts, cloth, price 1s.

RUDIMENTARY.—97.—STATICS AND DYNAMICS, by T. BAKER, C.E.

In demy 12mo, with 220 Woodcuts, cloth, price 2s. 6d.

RUDIMENTARY. — 98, 98*. — MECHANISM AND PRACTICAL CONSTRUCTION OF MACHINES, by T. BAKER, C.E., and ON TOOLS AND MACHINES, by JAMES NASMYTH, C.E.

In demy 12mo, with Woodcuts, cloth, price 2s.

RUDIMENTARY.—99, 100.—NAUTICAL ASTRONOMY AND NAVIGATION, by Prof. YOUNG. 2 vols. in 1.

In demy 12mo, cloth, price 1s. 6d.

RUDIMENTARY. — 100*. — NAVIGATION TABLES, compiled for practical use with the above.

In demy 12mo, cloth, price 1s.

RUDIMENTARY. — 101. — DIFFERENTIAL CALCULUS, by Mr. WOOLHOUSE, F.R.A.S.

John Weale, 59, High Holborn, London, W.C.

MR. WEALE'S RUDIMENTARY SERIES.

In demy 12mo, cloth, price 1s. 6d.
RUDIMENTARY. — 101*. — WEIGHTS AND MEASURES OF ALL NATIONS: Weights, Coins, and the various Divisions of Time, with the principles which determine Rates of Exchange, by Mr. WOOLHOUSE, F.R.A.S.

In demy 12mo, in cloth, price 1s.
RUDIMENTARY. — 102. — INTEGRAL CALCULUS, by H. COX, M.A.

In demy 12mo, in cloth, price 1s.
RUDIMENTARY. — 103. — INTEGRAL CALCULUS. Examples of, by Prof. JAMES HANN.

In demy 12mo, cloth, price 1s.
RUDIMENTARY. — 104. — DIFFERENTIAL CALCULUS. Examples of, by J. HADDON, M.A.

In demy 12mo, with Woodcuts, cloth, price 1s. 6d.
RUDIMENTARY. — 105. — ALGEBRA, GEOMETRY, AND TRIGONOMETRY, Mnemonical Lessons, by the Rev. T. PENYNGTON KIRKMAN, M.A.

In demy 12mo, with Woodcuts, cloth, price 1s. 6d.
RUDIMENTARY. — 106. — SHIPS' ANCHORS FOR ALL SERVICES, by Mr. GEORGE COTSELL, N.A.

In demy 12mo, with Woodcuts, price 2s. 6d.
RUDIMENTARY. — 107. — METROPOLITAN BUILDINGS ACT in present operation, with Notes, and the Act dated August 28th, 1860, for better supplying of Gas to the Metropolis.

In demy 12mo, cloth, price 1s. 6d.
RUDIMENTARY. — 108. — METROPOLITAN LOCAL MANAGEMENT ACTS. All the Acts.

In demy 12mo, cloth, price 1s. 6d.
RUDIMENTARY, — 109. — LIMITED LIABILITY AND PARTNERSHIP ACTS.

In demy 12mo, cloth, price 1s.
RUDIMENTARY. — 110. — SIX RECENT LEGISLATIVE ENACTMENTS, for Contractors, Merchants, and Tradesmen.

In demy 12mo, cloth, price 1s.
RUDIMENTARY. — 111. — NUISANCES REMOVAL AND DISEASE PREVENTION ACT.

In demy 12mo, cloth, price 1s. 6d.
RUDIMENTARY. — 112. — DOMESTIC MEDICINE, PRESERVING HEALTH, by M. RASPAIL.

In demy 12mo, cloth, price 1s. 6d.
RUDIMENTARY. — 113. — USE OF FIELD ARTILLERY ON SERVICE, by Lieut.-Col. HAMILTON MAXWELL, B.A.

In demy 12mo, with Woodcuts, cloth, price 1s. 6d.
RUDIMENTARY. — 114. — ON MACHINERY: Rudimentary and Elementary Principles of the Construction and on the Working of Machinery, by C. D. ABEL, C.E.

In royal 4to, cloth, price 7s. 6d.
RUDIMENTARY. — 115. — ATLAS OF PLATES OF SEVERAL KINDS OF MACHINES, 17 very valuable Illustrative plates.

John Weale, 59, High Holborn, London, W.C.

MR. WEALE'S RUDIMENTARY SERIES.

In demy 12mo, with Woodcuts, cloth, price 1s. 6d.
RUDIMENTARY. — 116. — TREATISE ON ACOUSTICS: The Distribution of Sound, by T. ROGER SMITH, Architect.

In demy 12mo, with Woodcuts, cloth, price 2s. 6d.
RUDIMENTARY.—117.—SUBTERRANEOUS SURVEYING, RANGING THE LINE WITHOUT THE MAGNET. By THOMAS FENWICK, Coal Viewer. With Improvements and Modern Additions by T. BAKER, C.E.

In demy 12mo, with Plates and Woodcuts, cloth, price 3s.
RUDIMENTARY.—118, 119.—ON THE CIVIL ENGINEERING OF NORTH AMERICA, by D. STEVENSON, C.E. 2 vols. in 1.

In demy 12mo, with Woodcuts, cloth, price 3s.
RUDIMENTARY. — 120. — ON HYDRAULIC ENGINEERING, by G. R. BURNELL, C.E. 2 vols. in 1.

In demy 12mo, with 2 Engraved Plates, cloth, price 1s. 6d.
RUDIMENTARY. — 121. — TREATISE ON RIVERS AND TORRENTS, from the Italian of PAUL FRISI.

In demy 12mo, by PAUL FRISI, in cloth, price 1s.
RUDIMENTARY.—122.—ON RIVERS THAT CARRY SAND AND MUD, and an ESSAY ON NAVIGABLE CANALS. 121 and 122 bound together, 2s. 6d.

In demy 12mo, with Woodcuts, cloth, price 1s. 6d.
RUDIMENTARY. — 123. — ON CARPENTRY AND JOINERY, founded on Dr. Robison's Work.

In demy 4to, cloth, price 4s. 6d.
RUDIMENTARY.—123*.—ATLAS of PLATES in detail to the CARPENTRY AND JOINERY. 123 and 123* bound together in cloth in 1 vol.

In demy 12mo, with Woodcuts, cloth, price 1s. 6d.
RUDIMENTARY. — 124. — ON ROOFS FOR PUBLIC AND PRIVATE BUILDINGS, founded on Dr. Robison's Work.

In royal 4to, cloth, price 4s. 6d.
RUDIMENTARY.—124*.—RECENTLY CONSTRUCTED IRON ROOFS, Atlas of plates.

In demy 12mo, with Woodcuts, cloth, price 3s.
RUDIMENTARY.— 125.—ON THE COMBUSTION OF COAL AND THE PREVENTION OF SMOKE, Chemically and Practically Considered, by CHARLES WYE WILLIAMS.

In demy 12mo, cloth. 125 and 126 together, price 3s.
RUDIMENTARY. — 126. — ILLUSTRATIONS to WILLIAMS'S COMBUSTION OF COAL. 125 and 126, 2 vols. bound in 1.

In demy 12mo, with Woodcuts, cloth, price 1s. 6d.
RUDIMENTARY. — 127. — PRACTICAL INSTRUCTIONS IN THE ART OF ARCHITECTURAL MODELLING.

John Weale, 59, High Holborn, London, W.C.

M^R. WEALE'S RUDIMENTARY SERIES.

In demy 12mo, with Engravings and Woodcuts.

RUDIMENTARY.—128.—THE TEN BOOKS OF M. VITRUVIUS ON CIVIL, MILITARY, AND NAVAL ARCHITECTURE, translated by JOSEPH GWILT, Arch. 2 vols. in 1.

In demy 12mo, 128 and 129 together, cloth, price 5s.

RUDIMENTARY. — 129. — ILLUSTRATIVE PLATES TO VITRUVIUS'S TEN BOOKS, by the Author and JOSEPH GANDY, R.A.

In demy 12mo, cloth, price 1s.

RUDIMENTARY.—130.—INQUIRY INTO THE PRINCIPLES OF BEAUTY IN GRECIAN ARCHI-TECTURE, by the Right Hon. the Earl of ABERDEEN, &c. &c.

In demy 12mo, cloth, price 1s.

RUDIMENTARY. — 131. — THE MILLER'S, MERCHANT'S, AND FARMER'S READY RECKONER, for ascertaining at Sight the Value of any quantity of Corn ; toge-ther with the approximate value of Millstones and Millwork.

In demy 12mo, with Woodcuts, cloth, price 2s. 6d.

RUDIMENTARY.—132.—TREATISE ON THE ERECTION OF DWELLING HOUSES, WITH SPECI-FICATIONS, QUANTITIES OF THE VARIOUS MATERIALS, &c., by S. H. BROOKS, Architect. 27 Plates.

RUDIMENTARY SERIES.—ON MINES, SMELTING WORKS, AND THE MANUFACTURE OF METALS, as follows.

In demy 12mo, with Woodcuts, cloth, price 2s.

RUDIMENTARY. — Vol. 1.—TREATISE ON THE METALLURGY OF COPPER, by R. H. LAMBORN.

In demy 12mo, to have Woodcuts, cloth.

RUDIMENTARY. — Vol. 2. — TREATISE ON THE METALLURGY OF SILVER AND LEAD.

In demy 12mo, to have Woodcuts, cloth.

RUDIMENTARY AND ELEMENTARY.— Vol. 3.—TREATISE ON IRON METALLURGY up to the Manufacture of the latest processes.

In demy 12mo, to have Woodcuts, cloth.

RUDIMENTARY AND ELEMENTARY.— Vol. 4.—TREATISE ON GOLD MINING AND ASSAY-ING PLATINUM, IRIDIUM, &c.

In demy 12mo, to have Woodcuts, cloth.

RUDIMENTARY AND ELEMENTARY.— Vol. 5.—TREATISE ON THE MINING OF ZINC, TIN, NICKEL, COBALT, &c.

In demy 12mo, to have Woodcuts, cloth.

RUDIMENTARY AND ELEMENTARY.— Vol. 6.—TREATISE ON COAL MINING (Geology and Means of Discovering, &c.)

In demy 12mo, with Woodcuts, cloth, price 1s. 6d.

RUDIMENTARY. — Vol. 7. — ELECTRO-ME-TALLURGY.— Practically treated by ALEXANDER WATT, F.R.S.A.

John Weale, 59, High Holborn, London, W.C.

NEW SERIES OF EDUCATIONAL WORKS.

In demy 12mo, with Woodcuts, cloth, price 4s.
CONSTITUTIONAL HISTORY OF ENG-
LAND.—1, 2, 3, 4.—By W. D. HAMILTON, of the State P. O.

In demy 12mo, with Woodcuts, cloth, price 2s. 6d.
OUTLINES OF THE HISTORY OF GREECE.
—5, 6.—By W. D. HAMILTON, 2 vols.

In demy 12mo, with Map of Italy and Woodcuts, cloth, price 2s. 6d
OUTLINE OF THE HISTORY OF ROME.—
7, 8.—By W. D. HAMILTON, 2 vols.

In demy 12mo, cloth, price 2s. 6d.
CHRONOLOGY OF CIVIL AND ECCLESI-
ASTICAL HISTORY, LITERATURE, ART, AND CIVI-
LISATION, from the earliest period to the present.—9, 10.—2 vols.

In demy 12mo, cloth, price 1s.
GRAMMAR OF THE ENGLISH LANGUAGE.
—11.—By HYDE CLARKE, D.C.L.

In demy 12mo, cloth, price 1s.
HANDBOOK OF COMPARATIVE PHILO-
LOGY.—11*.—By HYDE CLARKE, D.C.L.

In demy stout 12mo, cloth, price 3s. 6d.
DICTIONARY OF THE ENGLISH LAN-
GUAGE.—12, 13.—A New Dictionary of the English Tongue
as spoken and written, above 100,000 words, or 50,000 more than in
any existing work, by HYDE CLARKE, D.C.L., 3 vols. in 1.

In demy 12mo, cloth, price 1s.
GRAMMAR OF THE GREEK LANGUAGE.
—14.—By H. C. HAMILTON.

In demy 12mo, cloth, price 2s.
DICTIONARY OF THE GREEK AND ENG-
LISH LANGUAGES.—15, 16.—By H. R. HAMILTON, 2
vols. in I.

In demy 12mo, cloth, price 2s.
DICTIONARY OF THE ENGLISH AND
GREEK LANGUAGES.—17, 18.—By H. R. HAMILTON, 2
vols. in 1.

In demy 12mo, cloth, price 1s.
GRAMMAR OF THE LATIN LANGUAGE.
—19.—By the Rev. T. GOODWIN, A.B.

In demy 12mo, cloth, price 2s.
DICTIONARY OF THE LATIN AND ENG-
LISH LANGUAGES.—20, 21.—By the Rev. T. GOODWIN,
B.A. Vol. 1.

In demy 12mo, cloth, price 1s. 6d.
DICTIONARY OF THE ENGLISH AND
LATIN LANGUAGES.—22, 23.—By the Rev. T. GOOD-
WIN, A.B. Vol. II.

In demy 12mo, cloth, price 1s.
GRAMMAR OF THE FRENCH LANGUAGE.
—24.

John Weale, 59, High Holborn, London, W.C.

MR. WEALE'S EDUCATIONAL SERIES.

In demy 12mo, cloth, price 1s.

DICTIONARY OF THE FRENCH AND ENGLISH LANGUAGES.—25.—By A. ELWES. Vol. I.

In demy 12mo, cloth, price 1s. 6d.

DICTIONARY OF THE ENGLISH AND FRENCH LANGUAGES.—26.—By A. ELWES. Vol. II.

In demy 12mo, cloth, price 1s.

GRAMMAR OF THE ITALIAN LANGUAGE —27.—By A. ELWES.

In demy 12mo, cloth, price 2s.

DICTIONARY OF THE ITALIAN, ENGLISH, AND FRENCH LANGUAGES.—28, 29.—By A. ELWES. Vol. I.

In demy 12mo, cloth, price 2s.

DICTIONARY OF THE ENGLISH, ITALIAN, AND FRENCH LANGUAGES.—80, 31.—By A. ELWES. Vol. II.

In demy 12mo, cloth, price 2s.

DICTIONARY OF THE FRENCH, ITALIAN, AND ENGLISH LANGUAGES.—82, 33.—By A. ELWES. Vol. III.

In demy 12mo, cloth, price 1s.

GRAMMAR OF THE SPANISH LANGUAGE. —34.—By A. ELWES.

In demy 12mo, cloth, price 4s.

DICTIONARY OF THE SPANISH AND ENGLISH LANGUAGES.—35, 36, 37, 38.—By A. ELWES. 4 vols. in 1.

In demy 12mo, cloth, price 1s.

GRAMMAR OF THE GERMAN LANGUAGE. —39.

In demy 12mo, cloth, price 1s.

CLASSICAL GERMAN READER.—40.—From the best Authors.

In demy 12mo, cloth, price 3s.

DICTIONARIES OF THE ENGLISH, GERMAN, AND FRENCH LANGUAGES.—41, 42, 43.—By N. E. HAMILTON, 3 vols., separately, 1s. each.

In demy 12mo, cloth, price 7s.

DICTIONARY OF THE HEBREW AND ENGLISH LANGUAGES.—44, 45.—Containing the Biblical and Rabbinical words, 2 vols. (together with the Grammar, which may be had separately for 1s.), by Dr. BRESSLAU, Hebrew Professor.

In demy 12mo, cloth, price 3s.

DICTIONARY OF THE ENGLISH AND HEBREW LANGUAGES.—46.—Vol. III. to complete.

In demy 12mo, cloth, price 1s.

FRENCH AND ENGLISH PHRASE BOOK. —47.

John Weale, 59, High Holborn, London, W.C.

MR. WEALE'S CLASSICAL SERIES.

Now in course of Publication, in demy 12mo, price 1s. per Volume (except in some instances, and those are 1s. 6d. or 2s. each), very neatly printed on good paper. Those priced are published.

GREEK AND LATIN CLASSICS.—A Series of Volumes containing the principal Greek and Latin Authors, accompanied by Explanatory Notes in English, principally selected from the best and most recent German Commentators, and comprising all those Works that are essential for the Scholar and the Pupil, and applicable for the Universities of Oxford, Cambridge, Edinburgh, Glasgow, Aberdeen, and Dublin—the Colleges at Belfast, Cork, Galway, Winchester, and Eton, and the great Schools at Harrow, Rugby, &c.—also for Private Tuition and Instruction, and for the Library, as follows :

LATIN SERIES.

In demy 12mo, boards, price 1s.

A NEW LATIN DELECTUS.—1.—Extracts from Classical Authors, with Vocabularies and Explanatory Notes.

In demy 12mo, boards, price 2s.

CÆSAR'S COMMENTARIES ON THE GAL-LIC WAR.—2.—With Grammatical and Explanatory Notes in English, and a Geographical Index.

In demy 12mo, boards, price 1s.

CORNELIUS NEPOS.—3.—With English Notes, &c.

In demy 12mo, boards, price 1s.

VIRGIL.—4.—The Georgics, Bucolics, with English Notes.

In demy 12mo, boards, price 2s.

VIRGIL'S ÆNEID.—5.—(On the same plan as the preceding).

In demy 12mo, boards, price 1s.

HORACE.—6.—Odes and Epodes ; with English Notes, and Analysis and Explanation of the Metres.

In demy 12mo, boards, price 1s. 6d.

HORACE.—7.—Satires and Epistles, with English Notes, &c.

In demy 12mo, boards, price 1s. 6d.

SALLUST.—8.—Conspiracy of Catiline, Jugur-thine War, with English Notes.

In demy 12mo, boards, price 1s. 6d.

TERENCE.—9.—Andrea and Heautontimorume-nos, with English Notes.

In demy 12mo, boards, price 2s.

TERENCE.—10.—Phormio, Adelphi, and Hecyra, with English Notes.

In demy 12mo.

CICERO.—11.—Orations against Catiline, for Sulla, for Archias, and for the Manilian Law.

In demy 12mo.

CICERO.—12.—First and Second Philippics ; Ora-tions for Milo, for Marcellus, &c.

John Weale, 59, High Holborn London, W.C.

MR. WEALE'S CLASSICAL SERIES.

In demy 12mo.
CICERO.—13.—De Officiis.

In demy 12mo, boards, price 2s.
CICERO.—14.—De Amicitiâ, de Senectute, and Brutus, with English Notes.

In demy 12mo.
JUVENAL AND PERSIUS.—15.—(The indeli- cate parts expunged.)

In demy 12mo, boards, price 3s.
LIVY. — 16. — Books i. to v. in two vols., with English Notes.

In demy 12mo, boards, price 1s.
LIVY.—17.—Books xxi. and xxii., with English Notes.

In demy 12mo.
TACITUS.—18.—Agricola; Germania; and Au- nals, Book I.

In demy 12mo, boards, price 2s.
SELECTIONS FROM TIBULLUS, OVID, and PROPERTIUS.—19.—With English Notes,

In demy 12mo.
SELECTIONS FROM SUETONIUS and the later Latin Writers.—20.

GREEK SERIES, ON A SIMILAR PLAN TO THE LATIN
SERIES.
Those not priced are in the Press.

In demy 12mo, boards, price 1s.
INTRODUCTORY GREEK READER. — 1. — On the same plan as the Latin Reader.

In demy 12mo, boards, price 1s.
XENOPHON. — 2. — Anabasis, i. ii. iii., with English Notes.

In demy 12mo, boards, price 1s.
XENOPHON. —3. — Anabasis, iv. v. vi. vii., with English Notes.

In demy 12mo, boards, price 1s.
LUCIAN. — 4. — Select Dialogues, with English Notes.

In demy 12mo, boards, price 1s. 6d.
HOMER.—5.—Iliad, i. to vi., with English Notes.

In demy 12mo, boards, price 1s. 6d.
HOMER.—6.—Iliad, vii. to xii., with English Notes.

In demy 12mo, boards, price 1s. 6d.
HOMER. —7. — Iliad, xiii. to xviii. with English Notes.

In demy 12mo, boards, price 1s 6d.
HOMER. — 8. — Iliad, xix. to xxiv., with English Notes.

John Weale, 59, High Holborn, London, W.C.

MR. WEALE'S CLASSICAL SERIES.

In demy 12mo, boards, price 1s. 6d.
HOMER.—9.—Odyssey, i. to vi., with English Notes.

In demy 12mo, boards, price 1s. 6d.
HOMER.—10.—Odyssey, vii. to xii., with English Notes.

In demy 12mo, boards, price 1s. 6d.
HOMER.—11.—Odyssey, xiii. to xviii. with English Notes.

In demy 12mo, boards, price 1s. 6d.
HOMER. — 12. — Odyssey, xix. to xxiv. ; and Hymns, with English Notes.

In demy 12mo, boards, price 2s.
PLATO.—13.—Apology, Crito, and Phædo, with English Notes.

In demy 12mo, boards, price 1s. 6d.
HERODOTUS.—14.—i. ii., with English Notes.— Dedicated to His Grace the Duke of Devonshire.

In demy 12mo, boards, price 1s. 6d.
HERODOTUS.—15.—iii. iv., with English Notes. Dedicated to His Grace the Duke of Devonshire.

In demy 12mo.
HERODOTUS.—16.—v. vi. and part of vii. Dedicated to His Grace the Duke of Devonshire.

In demy 12mo.
HERODOTUS.—17.—Remainder of vii., viii., and ix. Dedicated to His Grace the Duke of Devonshire.

In demy 12mo, boards, price 1s.
SOPHOCLES. — 18.— Œdipus Rex, with English Notes.

In demy 12mo.
SOPHOCLES.—19.—Œdipus Colonæus.

In demy 12mo.
SOPHOCLES.—20.—Antigone.

In demy 12mo.
SOPHOCLES.—21.—Ajax.

In demy 12mo.
SOPHOCLES.—22.—Philoctetes.

In demy 12mo, boards, price 1s. 6d.
EURIPIDES.—23.—Hecuba, with English Notes.

In demy 12mo.
EURIPIDES.—24.—Medea.

In demy 12mo.
EURIPIDES.—25.—Hippolytus.

John Weale, 59, High Holborn, London, W.C.

MR. WEALE'S CLASSICAL SERIES.

In demy 12mo, boards, price 1s.

E^{URIPIDES.}—26.—Alcestis, with English Notes.

In demy 12mo.

E^{URIPIDES.}—27.—Orestes.

In demy 12mo.

E^{URIPIDES.}—28.—Extracts from the remaining Plays.

In demy 12mo.

S^{OPHOCLES.}—29.—Extracts from the remaining Plays.

In demy 12mo.

Æ^{SCHYLUS.}—30.—Prometheus Vinctus.

In demy 12mo.

Æ^{SCHYLUS.}—31.—Persæ.

In demy 12mo.

Æ^{SCHYLUS.}—32.—Septem contra Thebas.

In demy 12mo.

Æ^{SCHYLUS.}—33.—Choëphorœ.

In demy 12mo.

Æ^{SCHYLUS.}—34.—Eumenides.

In demy 12mo.

Æ^{SCHYLUS.}—35.—Agamemnon.

In demy 12mo.

Æ^{SCHYLUS.}—36.—Supplices.

In demy 12mo.

P^{LUTARCH.}—37.—Select Lives.

In demy 12mo,

A^{RISTOPHANES.}—38.—Clouds.

In demy 12mo.

A^{RISTOPHANES.}—39.—Frogs.

In demy 12mo.

A^{RISTOPHANES.} — 40. — Selections from the remaining Comedies.

In demy 12mo, boards, price 1s.

T^{HUCYDIDES.} — 41. — I., with English Notes.

In demy 12mo.

T^{HUCYDIDES.}—42.—II.

John Weale, 59, High Holborn, London, W.C.

MR. WEALE'S CLASSICAL SERIES.

In demy 12mo.
THEOCRITUS.—43.—Select Idyls.

In demy 12mo.
PINDAR.—44.

In demy 12mo.
SOCRATES.—45.

In demy 12mo.
HESIOD.—46.

MR. WEALE'S PUBLICATIONS OF WORKS ON ARCHITECTURE, ENGINEERING, AND THE FINE ARTS.

In 1 large Atlas, folio Volume, with fine Plates, price £4 4s.
"BRITISH GOVERNMENT WORK."—THE ARCHITECTURAL ANTIQUITIES AND RESTORATION OF ST. STEPHEN'S CHAPEL, WESTMINSTER (late the House of Commons).

Fine Plates and Vignettes, Atlas folio, price £3 10s.
"NORWEGIAN GOVERNMENT WORK."—THE CATHEDRAL OF THRONDHEIM, IN NORWAY. Text by Professor MUNCH; drawings by H. E. SCHIRMER, Architect.

Large Atlas folio, 4 livraisons, published in Madrid, at 100 reals each, or £1 in England. Illustrated by beautifully executed Engravings, some of which are coloured.
"SPANISH GOVERNMENT WORK."—MONUMENTS ARCHITECTONIQUES DE L'ESPAGNE, PUBLIÉS AUX FRAIS DE LA NATION.—PART I Provincia de Toledo, Granada, Alcalá de Henares.—PART 2. Catedral Toledo, Detailles.—PART 3. Granada, Segovia, Toledo, Salamanca.—PART 4. Santa Maria de Alcalá de Henares, Casa Lonia de Valencia, Toledo, Segovia, &c.—This work surpasses in beauty all other works.

Columbier folio plates, with text also uniform, with gold borders, and sumptuously bound in red morocco, gilt; gilt leaves, £12 12s., Columbier folio plates, with text also uniform, with gold borders, and elegantly half-bound in morocco, gilt, £10 10s.; Plates in Columbier folio, and text in imperial 4to, half-bound in morocco, gilt, £7 7s.; Plates in Columbier folio, and text in imperial 4to, in cloth extra, boards and lettered, £4 14s. 6d.
THE VICTORIA BRIDGE, AT MONTREAL, IN CANADA. — Elaborately illustrated by views, plans, elevations, and details of the Bridge; together with the illustrations of the Machinery and Contrivances used in the construction of this stupendously important and valuable engineering work. The whole produced in the finest style of art, pictorially and geometrically drawn, and the views highly coloured, and a descriptive text. Dedicated to His Royal Highness the Prince of Wales. By JAMES HODGES, Engineer to the Contractors. Engineers: ROBERT STEPHENSON and ALEX. M. ROSS. Contractors: Sir S. MORTON PETO, Bart., M.P., THOMAS BRASSEY, and EDWARD LADD BETTS, Esqrs.
John Weale, 59, High Holborn, London, W.C.

MR. WEALE'S WORKS ON ARCHITECTURE, ENGINEERING, FINE ARTS, &c.

In one imperial folio volume, with exquisite illustrative Plates from costly Drawings made by the most eminent artists, half-bound very neat, price £5 5s. Only 150 copies printed for sale.

PROFESSOR COCKERELL'S WORK.—
THE TEMPLES OF JUPITER PANHELLENIUS AT ÆGINA, AND OF APOLLO EPICURIUS AT BASSÆ, NEAR PHIGALEIA, IN ARCADIA.

It is proposed to publish the Life and Works of the late

ISAMBARD KINGDON BRUNEL, F.R.S.,
Civil Engineer. — The genius, talent, and great enterprise of the late Mr. Brunel has a world-wide fame, his whole life was devoted alone to the science of his profession, not in imitation or copying others, but in invention. In finding out new roads to the onward advancement of his Art, the lifting up from the slow and beating path of Engineering Art, new ideas and realities, and which has or have given to England a name for reference and of renowned intelligence in this Art.

Just published, in 4to, with 100 Engravings, price, bound, 21s.

THE PRACTICAL HOUSE CARPENTER.—
More particularly for country practice, with specifications, quantities, and contracts: also containing—1. Designs for the Centering of Groins, Niches, &c.; 2. Designs for Roofs and Staircases. 3. The Five Orders laid down to a scale; 4. Modern Method of Trussing Girders, Joints of Carpenters' work; 5. Designs for Modern Shop Fronts with their details; 6. Designs for Modern Doors with their details; 7. Designs for Modern Windows, with their details, and for Villa Architecture. The whole amply described, for the use of the Operative Carpenter and Builder. Firstly written and published by WILLIAM PAIN. Secondly, with Modern Designs, and Improvements, by S. H. BROOKS, Architect.

In 1861 will be published a volume in 12mo, entitled

A DIGEST OF PRICES of Works in Civil Engineering and Railway Engineering, Mechanical Engineering, Tools, Wrought and Cast Iron Works, Stone, Timber and Wire Works, and every kind of information that can be obtained and made useful in Estimating, Specifying, and Reporting.

In 4to, 2s. 6d.

AIRY, ASTRONOMER ROYAL, F.R.S., &c.—
Results of Experiments on the Disturbance of the Compass in Iron-built Ships.

In a sheet, 3s., in case, 3s. 6d.

ANCIENT DOORWAYS AND WINDOWS
(Examples of). Arranged to illustrate the different styles of Gothic Architecture, from the Conquest to the Reformation.

In 1 vol. imperial 4to, with 20 fine Plates, neatly half-bound in cloth, £1 5s.

ANCIENT DOMESTIC ARCHITECTURE.—
Principally selected from original drawings in the collection of the late Sir William Burrell, Bart., with observations on the application of ancient architecture to the pictorial composition of modern edifices.

The stained glass fac-simile, 4s. 6d., in an extra case, or in a sheet, 3s. 6d.

ANGLICAN CHURCH ORNAMENT.—
Wherein are figured the Saints of the English calendar, with their appropriate emblems; and the different styles of stained glass; and various sacred symbols and ornaments used in churches.

John Weale, 59, High Holborn, London, W.C.

MR. WEALE'S WORKS ON ARCHITECTURE, ENGINEERING, FINE ARTS, &c.

To 4to, 1s. 6d.

ARAGO, Mons. — Report on the Atmospheric
System, and on the proposed Atmospheric Railway at Paris.

In 4to, with about 500 Engravings, some of which are highly
coloured, 4 vols., original copies, half-bound in morocco, £6 6s.

ARCHITECTURAL PAPERS.

2 Engravings, in folio, useful to learners and for schools, 2s. 6d.

ARCHITECTURAL ORDERS (FIVE) AND
THEIR ENTABLATURES, drawn to a larger scale, with
Figured Dimensions.

4to, 1s.

ARNOLLET, M. — Report on his Atmospheric
Railway.

In 4to, 10 Plates, 7s. 6d.

ATMOSPHERIC RAILWAYS. — THREE RE
PORTS on Improved methods of Constructing and Working
Atmospheric Railways. By R. MALLET, C.E.

In 8vo, 1s. 6d.

BARLOW, P. W. —Observations on the Niagara
Railway Suspension Bridge.

In large 4to, very neat half-morocco, 18s., with Engravings.

BARRY, SIR CHARLES, R.A., &c. —
Studies of Modern English Architecture. By W. H. LEEDS;
The Travellers' Club-House, illustrated by Engravings of Plans,
Sections, Elevations, and details.

In 1 Vol., large 8vo, with coloured Plates, half-morocco, price £1 1s.

BEWICK'S (J. G.) GEOLOGICAL TREATISE
ON THE DISTRICT OF CLEVELAND IN NORTH
YORKSHIRE, its Ferruginous Deposits, Lias and Oolites; with
some Observations on Ironstone Mining.

In 8vo, with Plates. Price 4s.

BINNS, W. S. — Work on Geometrical Drawing,
embracing Practical Geometry, including the use of Drawing
Instruments, the construction and use of Scales, Orthographic Protection, and Elementary Descriptive Geometry.

In 4to, with 105 Illustrative Plates, cloth boards, £1 11s. 6d.

BLASHFIELD, J. M., M. R. Inst., &c. —
SELECTIONS OF VASES, STATUES, BUSTS, &c, from
TERRA COTTAS.

In 8vo, Woodcuts, 1s.

BLASHFIELD, J. M., M. R., Inst., &c. —
ACCOUNT OF THE HISTORY AND MANUFACTURE
OF ANCIENT AND MODERN TERRA COTTA.

In 4to, 2s. 6d.

BODMER, R.; C.E —On the Propulsion of Vessels
by the Screw.

15s.

BRIDGE. — A large magnificent Plate, 3 feet 6
inches by 2 feet, on a scale of 25 feet to an inch, of LONDON
BRIDGE ; containing Plan and Elevation. Engraved and elaborately finished. The Work of the RENNIES.
John Weale, 59, High Holborn, London, W.C.

MR. WEALE'S WORKS ON ARCHITECTURE, ENGINEERING, FINE ARTS, &c.

10s.

BRIDGE. — Plan and Elevation, on a scale of 10 feet to an Inch, of STAINES BRIDGE; a fine Engraving. The work of the RENNIES.

In royal 8vo, with very elaborate Plates (folded), £1 1s.

BRIDGES, SUSPENSION. — An Account, with Illustrations, of the Suspension Bridge across the River Danube, by Wm. T. CLARK, F.R.S.

In 4 vols., royal 8vo, bound in 3 vols., half-morocco, price £4 10s.

BRIDGES. — THE THEORY, PRACTICE, AND ARCHITECTURE OF BRIDGES OF STONE, IRON, TIMBER, AND WIRE; with Examples on the Principle of Suspension; Illustrated by 138 Engravings and 92 Woodcuts.

In one large 8vo volume, with explanatory Text, and 68 Plates comprising details and measured dimensions. Bound in half-morocco, uniform with the preceding work, price £2 10s.

BRIDGES. — SUPPLEMENT TO "THE THEORY, PRACTICE, AND ARCHITECTURE OF BRIDGES OF STONE, IRON, TIMBER, WIRE, AND SUSPENSION."

---

1 large folio Engraving, price 7s. 6d.

BRIDGE across the Thames.—SOUTHWARK IRON BRIDGE.

---

1 large folio Engraving, price 5s.

BRIDGE across the Thames. — WATERLOO STONE BRIDGE.

---

1 very large Engraving, price 5s.

BRIDGE across the Thames. — VAUXHALL IRON BRIDGE.

---

1 very large Engraving, price 4s. 6d.

BRIDGE across the Thames.—HAMMERSMITH SUSPENSION BRIDGE.

---

1 large Engraving, price 4s. 6d.

BRIDGE (the UPPER SCHUYLKILL) at PHILADELPHIA, the greatest known span of one arch, covered.

---

1 large Engraving, price 3s. 6d.

BRIDGE (the SCHUYLKILL) at PHILADELPHIA, covered.

---

1 large Engraving, price 3s. 6d.

BRIDGE. — ON THE PRINCIPLE OF SUSPENSION, by Sir I. BRUNEL, in the ISLAND OF BOURBON.

---

1 large Engraving, price 4s.

BRIDGE. — PLAN and ELEVATION of the PATENT IRON BAR BRIDGE over the River Tweed, near Berwick.

---

84 Plates, folio, £1 1s., boards.

BRIGDEN, R. — Interior Decorations, Details, and Views of Sefton Church, Lancashire, erected in the reign of Henry VIII.

John Weale, 59, High Holborn, London, W.C.

MR. WEALE'S WORKS ON ARCHITEC-
TURE, ENGINEERING, FINE ARTS, &c.

1 large Engraving, price 3s. 6d.
BRITTON'S (John) VIEWS of the WEST
FRONTS of 14 ENGLISH CATHEDRALS.

1 large Engraving in outline, price 2s. 6d.
BRITTON'S (John) PERSPECTIVE VIEWS of
the INTERIOR of 14 CATHEDRALS.

In 4to, 2s. 6d.
BRODIE, R., C.E. — Rules for Ranging Rail-
way Curves, with the Theodolite, and without Tables.

1 large Engraving, price 4s. 6d.
BROWN'S (Capt. S.) CHAIN PIER at Brighton,
with Details.

The Text in one large volume 8vo, and the Plates, upwards of 70
in number, in an atlas folio volume, very neatly half-bound,
£2 10s.
BUCHANAN, R. — PRACTICAL ESSAYS
ON MILL WORK AND OTHER MACHINERY; with
Examples of Tools of modern invention; first published by
ROBERT BUCHANAN, M.E.; afterwards improved and edited
by THOMAS TREDGOLD, C.E.; and re-edited, with the im-
provements of the present age, by GEORGE RENNIE, F.R.S.,
C.E., &c., &c. The whole forming 70 Plates, and 103 Woodcuts.
John Weale, 59, High Holborn, London, W.C.

Text in royal 8vo, and Plates in imperial folio, 18s.
BUCHANAN, R. — SUPPLEMENT. —
PRACTICAL EXAMPLES ON MODERN TOOLS AND
MACHINES; a Supplementary Volume to Mr. RENNIE'S
edition of BUCHANAN "On Mill-Work and Other Machinery,"
by TREDGOLD. The work consists of 18 Plates.

In 8vo, with Plates, 2nd Edition, 1s. 6d.
BURN, C., C.E.—On Tram and Horse Railways.

In one volume, 4to, 21 Plates, half-bound in morocco, £1 1s.
BURY, T., Architect. — Examples of Ancient
Ecclesiastical Woodwork.

7s. 6d.
CALCULATOR (THE): Or, TIMBER MER-
CHANT'S AND BUILDER'S GUIDE. By WILLIAM
RICHARDSON and CHARLES GANE, of Wisbeach.

In 8vo, Plates, cloth boards, 7s. 6d.
CALVER, E. K., R.N.—THE CONSERVATION
AND IMPROVEMENT OF TIDAL RIVERS.

In 8vo, Woodcuts, 1s 6d.
CALVER, E.K., R.N.—ON THE CONSTRUC-
TION AND PRINCIPLE OF A WAVE SCREEN,
designed for the Formation of Harbours of Refuge.

In 4to, half-bound, price £1 5s.
CARTER, OWEN B., Architect.—A SERIES
OF THE ANCIENT PAINTED GLASS OF WINCHES-
TER CATHEDRAL, Examples of. 28 Coloured Illustrations

In 4to, 17 Plates, half-bound, 7s. 6d.
CARTER, OWEN B., Architect. —ACCOUNT
OF THE CHURCH OF ST. JOHN THE BAPTIST,
at Bishopstone, with Illustrations of its Architecture.
John Weale, 59, High Holborn, London, W.C.

MR. WEALE'S WORKS ON ARCHITECTURE, ENGINEERING, FINE ARTS, &c.

In 4to. with 19 Engravings, £1 1s.

CHATEAUNEUF, A. de, Architect. — Architectura Domestica; a Series of very neat examples of Interiors and Exteriors of residences in the Italian style.

Large 4to, in half-red morocco, price £1 8s.

CHIPPENDALE, INIGO JONES, JOHNSON, LOCK, and PETHER.—Old English and French Ornaments: comprising 244 designs on 105 Plates of elaborate examples of Hall Glasses, Picture Frames, Chimney-pieces, Ceilings, Stands for China, Clock and Watch Cases, Girandoles, Brackets, Grates, Lanterns, Ornamental Furniture, Ornaments for brass workers and silver workers, real ornamental iron work Patterns, and for carvers, modellers, &c., &c., &c.

4to, third Edition with additions, price £1 11s. 6d.

CLEGG, SAM., C.E.—A PRACTICAL TREATISE ON THE MANUFACTURE AND DISTRIBUTION OF COAL GAS, Illustrated by Engravings from Working Drawings, with General Estimates.

In 4to, Plates, and 76 Woodcuts, boards, price 6s.

CLEGG, SAM., C.E.—ARCHITECTURE OF MACHINERY. An Essay on Propriety of Form and Proportion. For the use of Students and Schoolmasters.

In 8vo, 1s.

COLBURNS, Z.—On Steam Boiler Explosions.

One very large Engraving, price 4s. 6d.

CONEY'S (J.) Interior View of the Cathedral Church of St. Paul.

In 4to, on card board, 1s.

COWPER, C.—Diagram of the Expansion of Steam.

In one vol. 4to, with 20 Folding Plates, price £1 1s.

CROTON AQUEDUCT. — Description of the New York Croton Aqueduct, in 20 large detailed and engineering explanatory Plates, with text in the English, German, and French languages, by T. SCHRAMKE, C.E.

In demy 12mo, cloth, extra bound and lettered, price 4s.

DENISON.—A Rudimentary Treatise on Clocks and Watches, and Bells; with a full account of the Westminster Clock and Bells, by EDMUND BECKET DENISON, M.A., Q.C. Fourth Edition re-written and enlarged, with Engravings.

In royal 4to, cloth boards, price £1 11s. 6d.

DOWNES, CHARLES, Architect.—Great Exhibition Building. The Building erected in Hydo Park for the Great Exhibition, 1851; 28 large folding Plates, embracing Plans, Elevations, Sections, and Details, laid down to a large scale, and the Working and Measured Drawings.

DRAWING BOOKS.—Showing to Students the superior method of Drawing and Shadowing.

DRAWING BOOK. — COURS ELEMENTAIRES DE LAVIS APPLIQUÉ À L'ARCHITECTURE; folio volume, containing 40 elaborately engraved Plates, in shadows and tints, very finely executed, by the best artists in France. £2. Paris.

John Weale, 59, High Holborn, London, W.C.

MR. WEALE'S WORKS ON ARCHITECTURE, ENGINEERING, FINE ARTS, &c.

DRAWING BOOK. — COURS ÉLÉMENTAIRES DE LAVIS APPLIQUÉ À MÉCHANIQUE.) folio volume, containing 50 elaborately engraved Plates, in shadows and tints, very finely executed, by the best artists in France. £2 10s. Paris.

DRAWING BOOK. — COURS ÉLÉMENTAIRES DE LAVIS APPLIQUÉ À ORNEMENTATION; folio volume, containing 20 elaborately engraved Plates, in shadows and tints, very finely executed, by the best artists in France. £1. Paris.

DRAWING BOOK. — ÉTUDES PROGRESSIVES ET COMPLÈTES D'ARCHITECTURE DE LAVIS, par J. B. TRITON; large folio, 24 fine Plates, comprising the Orders of Architecture, mouldings, with profiles, ornaments, and forms of their proportion, art of shadowing doors, balusters, parterres, &c., &c., &c. £1 4s. Paris.

In 12mo, cloth boards, lettered, price 5s.

ECKSTEIN, G. F. — A Practical Treatise on Chimneys; with remarks on Stoves, the consumption of Smoke and Coal, Ventilation, &c.

Plates, Imperial 8vo, price 7s.

ELLET, CHARLES, C. E., of the U. S. — Report on the Improvement of Kanawha, and incidentally of the Ohio River, by means of Artificial Lakes.

In 8vo, with Plates, price 12s.

EXAMPLES of Cheap Railway Making, American and Belgian.

In one vol. 4to, 49 Plates, with dimensions, extra cloth boards, price 21s.

EXAMPLES for Builders, Carpenters, and Joiners; being well-selected Illustrations of recent Modern Art and Construction.

With Engravings and Woodcuts, price 12s.

FROME, Lieutenant-Colonel, R.E. — Outline of the Method of conducting a Trigonometrical Survey, for the Formation of Topographical Plans; and Instructions for filling in the Interior Detail, both by Measurement and Sketching; Military Reconnaissances, Levelling, &c., &c., together with Colonial Surveying.

In 4to, with Plates, price 7s. 6d.

FAIRBAIRN, W., C.E., F.R.S. — ON WATER-WHEELS, WITH VENTILATED BUCKETS.

In royal 8vo, with Plates and Woodcuts, Second Edition, much improved, price, in extra cloth boards, 16s.

FAIRBAIRN, W., C.E., F.R.S. — ON THE APPLICATION OF CAST AND WROUGHT IRON TO BUILDING PURPOSES.

In imperial 8vo, with fine Plates, a re-issue, price 16s., or 21s. in half-morocco, gilt edges,

FERGUSSON'S (J.) Essay on the Ancient Topography of Jerusalem, with restored Plans of the Temple, &c.

In 8vo, sewed in wrapper, price 2s.

GILL, J. — ESSAY ON THE THERMO DYNAMICS OF ELASTIC FLUIDS, by JOSEPH GILL, with Diagrams.

John Weale, 59, High Holborn, London, W.C.

MR. WEALE'S WORKS ON ARCHITECTURE, ENGINEERING, FINE ARTS, &c.

Plates, 8vo, boards, 5s.

GWILT, JOSEPH, Architect.—TREATISE ON THE EQUILIBRIUM OF ARCHES.

In 8vo, cloth boards, with 8 Plates, 4s. 6d.

HAKEWELL, S. J.—Elizabethan Architecture ; illustrated by parallels of Dorton House, Hatfield, Longleat, and Wollaton, in England, and the Palazzo Della Cancellaria at Rome.

8vo, with a Map, 1s.

HAMILTON, P. S., Barrister-at-Law, Halifax Nova Scotia—Nova Scotia considered as a Field for Emigration.

In imperial 8vo, Third Edition, with additions, 11 Plates, cloth boards, 8s.

HART, J., On Oblique Bridges. — A Practical Treatise on the Construction of Oblique Arches.

In 4to, with Woodcuts, 3s. 6d.

HEALD, GEORGE, C.E.—System of Setting Out Railway Curves.

Royal 8vo, Plates and Woodcuts, price 12s. 6d.

HEDLEY, JOHN. — Practical Treatise on the Working and Ventilation of Coal Mines, with Suggestions for Improvements in Mining.

Two Vols., demy 12mo, in cloth extra boards and lettered, price 12s. 6d.

HOMER. — The Iliad and Odyssey, with the Hymns of Homer, Edition with an accession of English notes by the Rev. T. H. L. LEARY, M.A.

In 8vo, with Engravings, cloth boards, Third Edition, 10s. 6d.

HOPKINSON, JOSEPH, C.E.—The Working of the Steam Engine Explained by the use of the Indicator.

In 8vo, in boards, 18s.

HUNTINGTON, J. B., C.E. — TABLES and RULES for Facilitating the Calculation of Earthwork, Land, Curves, Distances, and Gradients, required in the Formation of Railways, Roads, and Canals.

Separate from the above, price 3s.

HUNTINGTON, J. B., C.E. — THE TABLES OF GRADIENTS.

10 Plates, 8vo, bound, 5s.

INIGO JONES.—Designs for Chimney Glasses and Chimney Pieces of the Time of Charles the 1st.

In a sheet, 2s.

IRISH.—Plantation and British Statute Measure (comparative Table of), so that English Measure can be transferred into Irish, and vice versâ.

In 4to, with 8 Engravings, in a wrapper, 6s.

IRON. — ACCOUNT OF THE CONSTRUCTION OF THE IRON ROOF OF THE NEW HOUSES OF PARLIAMENT, with elaborate Engravings of details.

In Imperial 4to, with 50 Engravings, and 2 fine Woodcuts, half-bound in morocco, £1 4s.

IRON. — DESIGNS OF ORNAMENTAL GATES, LODGES, PALISADING, AND IRON-WORK OF THE ROYAL PARKS, with some other Designs.

John Weale, 59, High Holborn, London, W.C.

MR. WEALE'S WORKS ON ARCHITEC-
TURE, ENGINEERING, FINE ARTS, &c.

In 4to, with 10 Plates, 12s.

J EBB'S, Colonel, Modern Prisons.—Their Construction and Ventilation.

In 3 vols. 8vo, with 26 elaborate Plates, cloth boards, £2 2s.

J ONES, Major-Gen. Sir John, Bart. — Journal
of the Sieges carried on by the Army under the Duke of Wel-
lington in Spain, between the years 1811 and 1814, with an Account
of the Lines of Torres Vedras. By Major-Gen. Sir JOHN T.
JONES, Bart, K.C.B. Third Edition, enlarged and edited by
Lieut.-General Sir HARRY D. JONES, Bart.

16mo, cloth boards, 2s. 6d.

K ENNEDY AND HACKWOOD'S Tables for
Setting out Curves.

In 4to, 37 Plates, half-cloth boards, 9s.

K ING, THOMAS.—The Upholsterer's Guide;
Rules for Cutting and Forming Draperies, Valances, &c.

Illustrated by large Draughts and Engravings. In 1 volume 4to,
text, and a large atlas folio volume of Plates, half-bound, £6 6s.

K NOWLES, JOHN, F.R.S.—The Elements and
Practice of Naval Architecture; or, A Treatise on Ship
Building, theoretical and practical, on the best principles established
in Great Britain; with copious Tables of Dimensions, Scantlings,
&c. The Third Edition, with an Appendix, containing the princi-
pl's of constructing the Royal and Mercantile Navies, by Sir
ROBERT SEPPINGS.

---

41 Plates of a fine and an elaborate description in large atlas folio
half-bound, £2 12s. 6d.; with the text half-bound in 4to.

L OCOMOTIVE ENGINES. — The Principles
and Practice and Explanation of the Machinery of Locomotive
Engines in operation.

In 12mo, sewed, 1s.

M AIN, Rev. ROBERT. — An Account of the
Observatories in and about London.

4to, in boards, 15s.

M ANUFACTURES AND MACHINERY. —
Progress of, in Great Britain, as exhibited chiefly in Chrono-
logical notices of some Letters Patent granted for Inventions and
Improvements, from the earliest times to the reign of Queen Anne.

16mo, 2s. 6d.

M AY, R. C., C.E.—Method of setting out Railway
Curves.

Imperial 4to, with fine Illustrations, extra cloth boards, £1 5s., or
half-bound in morocco, £1 11s. 6d.

M ETHVEN, CAPTAIN ROBERT.—THE LOG
OF A MERCHANT OFFICER, Viewed with Reference
to the Education of Young Officers and the Youth of the Merchant Service. By ROBERT METHVEN, Commander in the
Peninsular and Oriental Company's Service.

In royal 8vo, 1s. 6d.

M ETHVEN, CAPTAIN ROBERT.—NARRA-
TIVES WRITTEN BY SEA COMMANDERS, ILLUS-
TRATIVE OF THE LAW OF STORMS. The "Blenheim"
Hurricane of 1851. with Diagrams.

Part 1, large 8vo, 5s. Part 2, in preparation.

M URRAY, JOHN, C.E. — A Treatise on the
Stability of Retaining Walls, elucidated by Engravings and
Diagrams.

John Weale, 59, High Holborn, London, W.C.

MR. WEALE'S WORKS ON ARCHITEC-TURE, ENGINEERING, FINE ARTS, &c.

On a large folio sheet, price 2s. 6d.

NEVILLE, JOHN, C.E., M.R.I.A. — OFFICE HYDRAULIC TABLES: for the use of Engineers engaged in Water Works, giving the Discharge and Dimensions of River Channels and Pipes.

In 8vo, Second and much Improved Edition, with an Appendix, cloth boards, price 16s.

NEVILLE, JOHN, C.E., M.R.I.A.—HY-DRAULIC TABLES, COEFFICIENTS, AND FORMULÆ; for Finding the Discharge of Water from Orifices, Notches, Weirs, Pipes, and Rivers, with Extensive Additions, New Formulæ, Tables, and General Information on Rain-Fall Catchment-Basins, Drainage, Sewerage, Water Supply for Towns and Mill Power.

On 33 folio Plates, 12s.

ORNAMENTS. — Ornaments displayed on a full size for Working, proper for all Carvers, Painters, &c., containing a variety of accurate examples of foliage and friezes.

Plates, 8vo, 2s. 6d.

O'BRIEN'S, W., C.E. — Prize Essay on Canals and Canal Conveyance.

In demy 8vo, cloth, boards, 12s.

PAMBOUR, COUNT DE. — STEAM ENGINE; the Theory of the Proportions of Steam Engines, and a series of practical formulæ.

In 8vo, cloth, boards, with Plates, a second edition, 18s.

A PRACTICAL TREATISE ON LOCOMO-TIVE ENGINES UPON RAILWAYS. — With practical Tables and an Appendix, showing the expense of conveying Goods by means of Locomotives on Railroads. By COUNT F. M. G. DE PAMBOUR.

4to, 72 finely executed Plates, in cloth, £1 16s.

PARKER, CHARLES, Architect, F.I.B.A. — The Rural and Villa Architecture of Italy, portraying the several very interesting examples in that country, with Estimates and Specifications for the application of the same designs in England; selected from buildings and scenes in the vicinity of Rome and Florence, and arranged for Rural and Domestic Buildings generally.

Price, complete, £2 2s. In 4to.

POLE, WILLIAM, M. Inst., C. E. — COR-NISH PUMPING ENGINE; designed and constructed at the Hayle Copper House in Cornwall, under the superintendence of CAPTAIN JENKINS; erected and now on duty at the Coal Mines of Languin, Department of the Loire Inférieur, Nantes. Nine elaborate Drawings, historically and scientifically described.

With Plate. 10s. 6d.

AN ANALYTICAL INVESTIGATION OF THE ACTION OF THE CORNISH PUMPING ENGINE. — This Third Part sold separately from above.

28s. bound in 4to size.

PORTFOLIO OF ENGINEERING ENGRAV-INGS. — Useful to Students as a Text Book, or a Drawing Book of Engineering and Mechanics; being a series of Practical Examples in Civil, Hydraulic, and Mechanical Engineering. Fifty Engravings to a scale for drawing.

John Weale, 59, High Holborn, London, W.C.

MR. WEALE'S WORKS ON ARCHITECTURE, ENGINEERING, FINE ARTS, &c.

50 Plates, 28s., boards.

PORTFOLIO OF GREEK ARCHITECTURE.
—Or, Dilettanti Drawing Book; Architectural Engravings, with descriptive Text. Being adapted as studies of the best Classic Models in the Grecian style of Architecture.

50 Plates, £1 8s., bound.

PORTFOLIO OR DRAWING BOOK OF GOTHIC CHURCH ARCHITECTURE.
—Of the periods of the 14th, 15th, and 16th centuries. Useful to Architects, Builders, and Students.

25 Plates, folio. 25s.

PORTFOLIO OF ARCHÆOLOGICAL COLLECTIONS.
—Of curious, interesting, and ornamental subjects and patterns for stained glass windows, from York.

18 Plates, 10s. 6d. Small folio.

PORTFOLIO OF ANCIENT CAPITAL LETTERS, MONOGRAMS, QUAINT DESIGNS, &c.
—Beautifully Coloured and Ornamented.

153 Plates, folio, half-bound in morocco, very neat, £4 4s.

PUBLIC WORKS OF GREAT BRITAIN.
—Consisting of Railways, Rails, Chairs, Blocks, Cuttings, Embankments, Tunnels, Oblique Arches, Viaducts, Bridges, Stations, Locomotive Engines, &c.; Cast-Iron Bridges, Iron and Gas Works, Canals, Lock-gates, Centering, Masonry and Brickwork for Canal Tunnels; Canal Boats: the London and Liverpool Docks, Plans and Dimensions, Dock gates, Walls, Quays, and their Masonry; Mooring-Chains; Plan of the Harbour and Port of London, and other important Engineering Works, with Descriptions and Specifications.

In two Parts. Imperial folio.

PUBLIC WORKS OF THE UNITED STATES OF AMERICA.
And the text in an 8vo Volume, price together £2 6s.

REPORTS, SPECIFICATIONS, AND ESTIMATES OF PUBLIC WORKS OF THE UNITED STATES OF AMERICA;
explanatory of the Atlas Folio of Detailed Engravings, elucidating practically these important Engineering Works. The Plates are Engraved in the best style.

Imperial 8vo, 50 Engravings, £1 5s.

PAPERS AND PRACTICAL ILLUSTRATIONS OF PUBLIC WORKS OF RECENT CONSTRUCTION—BOTH BRITISH AND AMERICAN.
Supplementary to previous Publications, and containing all the details of the Niagara Suspension Bridge.

Half-bound in morocco, finely coloured Plates, price £3 3s.

RAWLINSON'S, ROBERT, C.E.—Designs for
Factory, Furnace, and other Tall Chimney Shafts. Tall chimneys are necessary for purposes of Trade and Manufactures. They are required for Factories, for Foundries, for Gas Works, for Chemical Works, for Baths and Wash-houses, and for many other purposes.

Third Edition, in royal 8vo, boards, with 13 Charts, &c., 12s.

REID, Major-General Sir W., F.R.S., &c.—AN ATTEMPT TO DEVELOP THE LAW OF STORMS
by means of facts arranged according to place and time; and hence to point out a cause for the variable winds, with a view to practical use in navigation.

John Weale, 59, High Holborn, London, W.C.

MR. WEALE'S WORKS ON ARCHITECTURE, ENGINEERING, FINE ARTS, &c.

In royal 8vo, uniform with the preceding, 9s., with Charts and Woodcuts. The work together in 2 vols., £1 1s.

REID, Major-General Sir W., F.R.S., &c. — THE PROGRESS OF THE DEVELOPMENT OF THE LAW OF STORMS AND OF THE VARIABLE WINDS, with the practicable application of the subject to navigation.

Illustrated with 17 Plates, Third Edition, 8vo, cloth, 7s. 6d.

RICHARDSON, C. J., Architect. — A Popular Treatise on the Warming and Ventilation of Buildings; showing the advantage of the improved system of Heated Water Circulation. And a method to effect the combination of large and small pipes to the same apparatus, and ventilating buildings.

Bound in 2 vols., very neat, half-morocco, gilt tops, price £18.

RENNIE'S, Sir JOHN, F.R.S., Work on the Theory, Formation, and Construction of British and Foreign Harbours, Docks, and Naval Arsenals. This great work may now be had complete, 20 parts and supplement, price £16.

In 8vo, 2s.

RÉVY, J. L., C.E. — THE PROGRESSIVE SCREW AS A PROPELLER IN NAVIGATION.

12mo, cloth boards, 3s. 6d.

SIMMS, F. W. — Treatise on the principal Mathematical and Drawing Instruments employed by the Engineer, Architect, and Surveyor; with a description of the Theodolite, together with Instructions in Field Works.

4to, with fine Plates, a New Edition, extended, sewed, 5s.

SMITH, C. H., Sculptor.—Report and Investigation into the Qualifications and Fitness of Stone for Building Purposes.

In 1 vol. 8vo, in boards, 7s. 6d.

SMITH'S, Colonel of the Madras Engineers, Observations on the Duties and Responsibilities Involved in the Management of Mines.

8vo, cloth boards, with Index Map, 5s.

SOPWITH, THOMAS, F.R.S. — THE AWARD OF THE DEAN FOREST COMMISSIONERS AS TO THE COAL AND IRON MINES.

16 large folio Plates, £1 4s. Separately, 2s. each.

SOPWITH, THOMAS, F.R.S.—SERIES OF ENGRAVED PLANS OF THE COAL AND IRON MINES.

12 Plates, 4to, 6s. in a wrapper.

STAIRCASES, HANDRAILS, BALUSTRADES, AND NEWELS OF THE ELIZABETHAN AGE, &c.— Consisting of — 1. Staircase at Audley-end Old Manor House, Wilts; 2. Charlton House, Kent; 3. Great Ellingham Hall, Norfolk; 4. Dorfold, Cheshire; 5. Charterhouse; 6. Oak Staircase at Clare Hall, Cambridge; 7. Cromwell Hall, Highgate; 8. Ditto; 9. Catherine Hall, Cambridge; 10. Staircase by Inigo Jones at a house in Chandos Street; 11. Ditto at East Sutton; 12. Ditto, ditto. Useful to those constructing edifices in the early English domestic style.

Large atlas folio Plates, price £2 2s.

STALKARTT, M., N.A. — Naval Architecture; or, The Rudiments and Rules of Ship Building: exemplified in a Series of Draughts and Plans. No text.

John Weale, 59, High Holborn, London, W.C.

MR. WEALE'S WORKS ON ARCHITEC-
TURE, ENGINEERING, FINE ARTS, &c.

With Illustrative Diagrams. In 8vo, 7s. 6d.
STEVENSON'S, THOMAS, C.E., of Edinburgh,
Description of the Different kinds of Lighthouse Apparatus.

8vo, 2s. 6d.
STEVENSON, DAVID, C.E., of Edinburgh. —
Supplement to his Work on Tidal Rivers.

Text in 4to, and large folio Atlas of 75 Plates, half-cloth boards,
£2 12s. 6d.
STEAM NAVIGATION. — Vessels of Iron and
Wood; the Steam Engine; and on Screw Propulsion. By
WM. FAIRBAIRN, F.R.S., of Manchester; Messrs. FORRESTER,
M.I.C.E., of Liverpool; JOHN LAIRD, M.I.C.E., of Birkenhead;
OLIVER LANG, (late) of Woolwich; Messrs. SEAWARD, Lime-
house, &c. &c. &c. Together with Results of Experiments on the
Disturbance of the Compass in Iron-built Ships. By G. B. AIRY,
M.A., Astronomer Royal.

10s.
ST. PAUL'S CATHEDRAL, LONDON, SEC-
TION OF. — The Original Splendid Engraving by J.
GWYN, J. WALE, decorated agreeably to the original intention
of Sir Christopher Wren; a very fine large print, showing distinctly
the construction of that magnificent edifice.

Size of Plate 4½ feet in height, 10s.
ST. PAUL'S CATHEDRAL, LONDON, GREAT
PLAN. — J. WALE and J. GWYN'S GREAT PLAN,
accurately measured from the Building, with all the Dimensions
figured and in detail, description of Compartments by engraved
Writing.

Second Edition, greatly enlarged, royal 8vo, with Plates, cloth
boards, price 16s.
STRENGTH OF MATERIALS.—FAIRBAIRN,
WILLIAM, C.E., F.R.S., and of the Legion of Honour of
France. On the application of Cast and Wrought Iron to Building
Purposes.

With Plates and Diagrams. New Edition. The work complete
in 2 vols., bound in 1 vol., price, in cloth boards, 16s. The
second portion of the work, containing Mr. Hodgkinson's Experi-
mental Researches, may be had separately, price 9s.
STRENGTH OF MATERIALS.—HODGKIN-
SON, EATON, F.R.S., AND THOMAS TREDGOLD,
C.E. A PRACTICAL ESSAY ON THE STRENGTH OF CAST
IRON AND OTHER METALS; intended for the assistance of
engineers, ironmasters, millwrights, architects, founders, smiths
and others engaged in the construction of machines, buildings, &c'
By EATON HODGKINSON, F.R.S.

To be published in 1861, in crown 8vo, bound for use.
STRENGTH OF MATERIALS.—POLE, WIL-
LIAM, C.E., F.R.S.—Tables and popular explanations of
the Strength of Materials, of Wrought and Cast Iron with other
metals, for structural purposes; developing in a systematic form,
the strengths, bearings, weights, and forms of these materials, whether used as girders or arches, for the construction of bridges and
viaducts, public buildings, domestic mansions, private buildings,
columns or pillars, bressummiers for warehouses, shops, working
and manufacturing factories, &c. &c. &c. The whole rendered of
easy reference for architects, builders, civil and mechanical engineers, millwrights, ironfounders, &c. &c. &c., and forming Ready
Reckoner or Calculator.

John Weale, 59, High Holborn, London, W.C.

MR. WEALE'S WORKS ON ARCHITEC-
TURE, ENGINEERING, FINE ARTS, &c.

90 very elaborately drawn Engravings. In large 4to, neatly half-bound and lettered, £1 1s. A few copies on large imperial size, extra half-binding, £1 11s. 6d.

TEMPLE CHURCH.—The Architectural History
and Architectural Ornaments, Embellishments, and Painted Glass, of the Temple Church, London.

Part I., with 26 Engravings on Wood and Copper, in cloth boards, 4to, 15s.

THAMES TUNNEL.—A Memoir of the several
Operations and the Construction of the Thames Tunnel, from Papers by the late Sir ISAMBARD BRUNEL, F.R.S., Civil Engineer.

Fourth Edition, with a Supplementary Addition, large 8vo, 12s. 6d.

THOMAS (LYNALL), F.R.S.L.—Rifled Ordnance.
—A Practical Treatise on the Application of the Principle of the Rifle to Guns and Mortars of every calibre; to which is added a New Theory of the Initial Action and Force of Fixed Gunpowder plates.

In 4to, complete, cloth, Vol. I., with Engravings, £1 10s.; Vol. II., ditto, £1 8s.; Vol. III., ditto, £2 12s. 6d.

TRANSACTIONS OF THE INSTITUTION
OF CIVIL ENGINEERS.

---

8 vols., numerous Engravings of Sections of Coal Mines, &c., large folding Plates, several of which are coloured, in large 8vo, half-bound in calf, price £1 1s. per volume.

TRANSACTIONS OF THE NORTH OF
ENGLAND INSTITUTE OF MINING ENGINEERS.—
Commencing in 1852, and continued to 1860.

A New Edition revised by the translator, and with additional Plates, in demy 12mo, India proof Plates and Vignettes, half-bound in morocco, gilt tops, price 12s. Only 25 printed on India paper.

VITRUVIUS. — The Architecture of Marcus
Vitruvius Pollio in 10 Books. Translated from the Latin by JOSEPH GWILT, F.S.A., F.R.A.S.

In 4to, with Plates, 7s. 6d.

WALKER'S, THOMAS, Architect. — Account
of the Church at Stoke Golding.

£1 10s.

WEALE'S QUARTERLY PAPERS ON EN-
GINEERING. — Vol. VI. (Parts 11 and 12 completing the work.) Comprising, "On the Principles of Water Power." Plates. Experiments on Locomotive Engines. Coloured Plates. On Naval Arsenals. On the Mode of Forming Foundations under water and on bad ground. Plates. On the Improvement of the River Medway and of the Fort and Arsenal of Chatham. On the Improvement of Portsmouth Harbour. An Analysis of the Cornish Pumping. Plates. On Water Wheels. Plates.

Text in 8vo, cloth boards, and Plates in atlas folio, in cloth, 16s.

WHITE'S, THOMAS, N.A., Theory and Prac-
tice of Ship Building.

In 8vo, with a large Sectional Plate, 1s. 6d.

WHICHCORD, JOHN, Architect. —
OBSERVATIONS ON KENTISH RAG STONE AS A BUILDING MATERIAL.

John Weale, 59, High Holborn, London, W.C.

MR. WEALE'S WORKS ON ARCHITEC-
TURE, ENGINEERING FINE ARTS, &c.

4to, coloured Plates, in half-morocco, 7s 6d.

WHICHCORD, JOHN, Architect.—HIS-
TORY AND ANTIQUITIES OF THE COLLEGIATE
CHURCH OF ALL SAINTS, MAIDSTONE.

In 4to, 6s.

WICKSTEED, THOMAS, C.E. — AN EXPE-
RIMENTAL INQUIRY CONCERNING THE RELA-
TIVE POWER OF, AND USEFUL EFFECT PRODUCED
BY, THE CORNISH AND BOULTON & WATT PUMPING
ENGINES, and Cylindrical and Waggon-Head Boilers.

In 8vo, 1s.

WICKSTEED, THOMAS, C.E. — FURTHER
ELUCIDATION OF THE USEFUL EFFECTS OF
CORNISH PUMPING ENGINES; showing the average work-
ing for long periods, &c., &c., &c.

£2 2s.

WICKSTEED, THOMAS, C.E. — THE
ELABORATELY ENGRAVED ILLUSTRATIONS OF
THE CORNISH AND BOULTON & WATT ENGINES erected
at the East London Water Works, Old Ford. Eight large atlas
folio very fine line engravings by GLADWIN, from elaborate
drawings made expressly by Mr. WICKSTEED; folio, together
with a 4to explanation of the plates, containing an engraving, by
LOWRY, of Harvey and West's patent pump-valve, with specification.

With numerous Woodcuts.

WILLIAMS, C. WYE, Esq., M. Inst. C. E.—
THE COMBUSTION OF COAL AND THE PREVEN-
TION OF SMOKE, chemically and practically considered.

Imperial 8vo, with a Portrait, 2s. 6d.

WILLIAMS, C. WYE, Esq., M. Inst. C. E. —
PRIZE ESSAY ON THE PREVENTION OF THE
SMOKE NUISANCE, with a fine portrait of the Author.

With 3 Plates, containing 51 figures, 4to, 5s.

WILLIS, REV. PROFESSOR, M.A.—A
system of Apparatus for the use of Lecturers and Experi-
menters in Mechanical Philosophy.

In 4to, bound, with 26 large plates and 17 woodcuts, 12s.

WILME'S MANUALS. — A MANUAL OF
WRITING AND PRINTING CHARACTERS, both
ancient and modern.

Maps and Plans, in 4to, plates coloured, half-bound morocco, £2.

WILME'S MANUALS. — A HANDBOOK
FOR MAPPING, ENGINEERING, AND ARCHITEC-
TURAL DRAWING.

Three Vols., large 8vo, £3.

WOOLWICH. — COURSE OF MATHEMA-
TICS. This course is essential to all Students destined
for the Royal Military Academy at Woolwich.

8vo, 1s.

YULE, MAJOR-GENERAL.—ON BREAK-
WATERS AND BUOYS of VERTICAL FLOATS.
John Weale, 59, High Holborn, London, W.C.

FOREIGN WORKS, KEPT IN STOCK AS FOLLOWS:—

Large folio, 32 plates, some coloured, and 12 woodcuts, 50 francs. £2 10s.

ARCHITECTURE SUISSE.—Ou Choix de Mai- sons Rustiques des Alpes du Canton de Berne, par GRAF-FINRIED et STÜRLER, Architectes. Berne, 1844.

Small folio, 52 most interesting and explanatory plates of Public Works, Bridges, Iron Works, &c., &c., &c., very neatly half-bound in morocco, £1 10s.

BAUERNFEIND, CARL MAX.—VORLEGE- BLAETTER ZUR BRUCKENBAU KUNDE. München.

Large folio, 36 plates of Byzantine capitals, 12s.

BYZANTINISCHE CAPITAELER.—München.

Second edition, 126 plates, large folio, best Paris edition, 100 f., printed on fine paper, half-cloth boards, £4 4s.

CALLIAT, VICTOR, ARCT.—Parallèle des Mai- sons de Paris, construites depuis 1830 jusqu'à nos jours.—1857.

Large folio, 60 francs, 60 plates, and several vignettes, £2 8s.

CANÉTO, F.—Sainte-Marié d'Auch. Atlas Mono- graphique de Cette Cathédrale. The Plates consist principally of outline drawings of the Painted Glass Windows in this Cathedral.

120 plates, elegant in half-morocco extra, interleaved, £5 15s. 6d.

CASTERMAN, A.—PARALÈLLE des MAI- SONS de BRUXELLES et des PRINCIPALES VILLES de la BELGIQUE, construites depuis 1830 jusqu'à nos jonrs, représentés en plans, élévations, coupes et détails intérieurs et extérieurs. —Paris.

Small folio, 48 plates of edifices. £1 1s.

DEGEN, L. — LES CONSTRUCTIONS EN BRIQUES, composées et publiées. 8 livralsons.—1858.

Small folio, 48 plates of houses, parts of houses, details of all kinds of singularly beautiful woodwork, coloured plates in imitation of the objects given, £1 1s.

DEGEN, L.—LES CONSTRUCTIONS ORNA- MENTALES EN BOIS, 8 livraisons.

In 3 very large folio parts, 35 fine plates, £1 11s. 6d.

GAERTNER, F. V.—The splendid works of M. GAERTNER of Munich, drawn to a very large size, consisting of the library in plans, elevations, interiors, details, and sections, and coloured ornaments. The church, with details, ornaments, &c.—München.

Small folio, 86 fine plates of the Architecture, ornament, and detail of the houses and churches of Germany during the middle age, very neatly half-bound in morocco, £2 12s. 6d.

KALLENBACH, C. C.—Chronologie der Deutsch- Mittelalterlichen Baukunst.—München. Fine Work.

The works of the great master KLENZIE of Munich, in 5 parts very large folio, 50 plates of elevations, plans, sections, details and ornaments of his public and private buildings executed in Munich and St. Petersburg, £2 2s.

KLENZE, LEO VON. — Sammlung Arthitec- tonisher Entwürfe, für die Ausführung bestimmt oder wirklich ausgeführt. Published in Munich.

John Weale, 59, High Holborn, London, W.C.

FOREIGN WORKS KEPT IN STOCK AS
FOLLOWS :—

Upwards of 100 plates, large 4to, £2 12s. 6d.

PETIT, VICTOR.—CHATEAUX DE FRANCE.
Architecture Pittoresque, ou Monuments des quinzième et seizième siècles. Paris.

Livraisons 1 à 18, very finely executed plates, large imperial folio, £5 8s.

CHATEAUX DE LA VALLÉE DE LA
LOIRE DES XV, XVI, ET COMMENCEMENT DU XVII SIECLE.—Paris, 1857—60.

4to, 96 plates, 72f. ; £2 10s.

RECUEIL DE SCULPTURES GOTHIQUE.—
Dessinées et graveés à l'eau forte d'après les plus beaux monuments construits en France depuis le onzième jusqu'au quinzième siècle, par ADAMS, Inspecteur des travaux de la Sainte Chapelle. Paris, 1856.

4 parts are published, price 11s.

RAMÉE.—HISTOIRE GÉNÉRALE DE L'AR-
CHITECTURE. L'Histoire générale de l'Architecture, par DANIEL RAMÉE, forme 2 vol. grande in 8vo, publiés en 8 fascicules.

5 vols., large 8vo, numerous fine woodcuts, half morocco.

VIOLET-LE-DUC. — DICTIONNAIRE RAI-
SONNE, de l'Architecture Francaise du quinzième au seizième siècle. Paris, 1854-8.

2 vols., extra imperial folio, price £6 16s. 6d.

BADIA D'ALTACOMBA.—Storia e Descrizione
della Antico Sepolchro dei Reali di Savoia, fondita da Amedio III. rinnovata da Carlo Felice e Maria Christina.

79 livraisons in large 4to, 200 engravings, £8 18s. 6d.

BELLE ARTI.—Il Palazzo Ducale di Venezia,
illustrato da Francesco Zanotto. Venezia, 1846—1858.

2 vols. large 4to, 62 very neatly engraved outline Plates, £1 5s.

CANOVA.—Le Tombe ed i Monumenti Illustri
d'Italia. Milano.

2 vols. 4to, 67 elaborate Plates, £1 16s.

CAVALIERI SAN-BERTOLO (NICOLA).—
ISTITUZIONI DI ARCHITETTURA STATICA E IDRAULICA. Mantova.

2 vols. imperial folio, in parts of eight divisions, &c., New and much Improved Edition, comprising 259 Plates of the Public Buildings of Venice, plans, elevations, sections, and details, £8 18s. 6d.

CICOGNARA (COUNT).—Le Fabbriche e i Monu-
menti Cospieni di Venezia, illustrati da L. Cicognara, da A. Diedo, e da G. A. Selva, edizione cou copiose note ed aggiunte di Francesco Zanotto, arricchita di nuove tavole e della Versione Francese. Venezia nello stab. naz. di G. Antonelli a spese degli edit. G. Antonelli e Luciano Basadonna, 1858. The elaborately descriptive text is in French aud Italian, beautifully printed.
Copies elegantly half-bound in morocco, extra gilt, library copy and Interleaved, £12 12s. Venezia, 1858.

Folio, Portrait, and 147 Plates, consisting of subjects of public buildings, executed at Verona, plans, elevations, sections, details, and ornaments, with some executed works at Venice. &c., £4 4s.

FABBRICHE.—CIVILI ECCLESIASTICHE
E MILITARI DI MICHELE SAN MICHELE diseguate ed Incise da RONZANI FRANCESCO e L. GIROLAMO.

John Weale, 59, High Holborn, London, W.C.

FOREIGN WORKS KEPT IN STOCK AS
FOLLOWS.

Large folio, containing a profusion of Plates of the palaces, theatres, hôtel de villes, and other public buildings in several parts of Italy. Elegantly half-bound in red morocco, extra gilt and interleaved, £6 6s.

FABBRICHE.—E DISEGNI D'ANTONIO
DIEDO, NOBILE VENETO. Venezia.

36 livraisons, price £12 12s.

GALLERIA DI TORINO (LA REALE). —
Illustrata da R. D'AZEGLIO, Memb. dell' Accad., &c. &c.
Copies, Indian proofs, £18 18s.
. Bound copies in elegant half-morocco binding, India proof, £23 2s.

2 vols. folio, complete, 177 Plates of outline elevations, plans, interiors, details, &c., first impression, 150 francs, half-bound. £6 6s.

GAUTHIER, M.P., Architecte. — Les PLUS
BEAUX ÉDIFICES de la VILLE de GENES et des ses ENVIRONS. Paris, 1830-2.

Folio, 109 Plates of plans, elevations, sections, and details, £2 8s.

GRANDJEAN de MONTIGNY et A. FAMIN.
— ARCHITECTURE TOSCANE, ou palais, maisons, et autres édifices, de la Toscane. Paris, 1815.

Oblong folio, containing a profusion of picturesque views of palaces and public buildings and scenes of Venice, executed in tinted lithography, with full descriptions attached to each. Elegant in half extra morocco, interleaved, £4 14s. 6d.

KIER, G.—VENEZIA MONUMENTALE PIT-
TORESCA. Venezia.

Large folio, 61 livraisons or 3 vols., with 3 vols. of text in 4to, £18 18s.

LETAROUILLY, P. — Édifices de Rome Mo-
derne. Paris, 1825-55.

Fine Plates of the New Palace of Justice, Senate House, &c., plans, elevations, sections, doors, &c., details of the several parts, &c., £1 1s.

MICHELA, IGNAZIO.—DESCRIZIONE e
DISEGNI del PALAZZO del MAGISTRATI SUPREMI di TORINO. Torino.

Large folio, 94 Plates, bound in extra half-morocco, gilt and interleaved, price £6 10s.

REYNAUD, L.—Trattato di Architettura, con-
tenente nozioni generali sui Principii della Construzione e sulla storia dell' Arti, con annot. per cura di Lorenzo Urbani. Venezia, 1857.

4 imperial bulky 8vo volumes, printed and published under authority, and treats of the early foundation of Venice and establishment as a kingdom, its wealth and commerce, and its once great political position, with Plates, £3 3s.

VENEZIA.—E le sue Lagune. Venezia, 1847.

VENEZIA.—Copies elegantly bound and gilt,
£4 14s. 6d. Venezia, 1847.

In 2 large folio volumes, numerously and elaborately drawn Plates, very well executed in outline, altogether a very fine work. Very elegantly half-bound in morocco, extra gilt and interleaved, £12 12s.

ACCADEMIA DI BELLI ARTI. — Opere dei
Grandi Concorsi Premiate dall' I. R. Accademia delle Belle: Arti, in Milano, e publicate, per cura dell' Architetto, G. ALUISETTI— per la Classi di Ornano—per le Classi di Architettura, figura ed Ornato. Milano, 1825-29.

John Weale, 59, High Holborn, London, W.C.

FOREIGN WORKS, KEPT IN STOCK AS FOLLOWS:—

Atlas folio, very fine impressions, complete in 3 parts, Columbier folio, £3 13s. 6d Elegantly half-bound in extra morocco and interleaved. £5 15s. 6d.

ALBERTOLLI, G.—Alcune Decorazioni di Nobili Sale ed Altri Ornamenti. Milano, 1787, 1824, 1838.

To be had separately, £1 8s.

ALBERTOLLI, G.—Part III., very frequently required to make up sets.

2 vols., folio, 80 Plates of the most exquisite kind in colours, far superior to any existing work of the present day, £7 10s.

HOFFMAN, ET KELLERHOVEN. — Recueil de Dessins relatifs à l'Art de la Décoration chez tous les peuples et aux plus belles époques de leur civilisation, &c., destinés à servir de motifs et de matériaux aux peintres, décorateurs, peintres sur verre, et aux dessinateurs de fabriques.

Price £1 1s.

HOPE, ALEXANDER J. BERESFORD, Esq.— Abbildungen der Glasgemälde in der Salvator-Kirche zu Kilndown in der Graffschaft Kent. Copies of paintings on glass in Christ Church, Kilndown, in the county of Kent, executed in the Royal Establishment for Painting on Glass, Munich, by order of ALEXANDER J. BERESFORD HOPE, Esq., published by F. Eggert, Painter on Glass, München. The work contains one sheet with the dedication to A. J. B. HOPE, Esq., and fourteen windows; in the whole fifteen, beautifully engraved and carefully coloured.

In large folio, 80 Plates, containing a profusion of rich Italian and other ornaments. Elegant in half-morocco, gilt, and interleaved, £6 6s.

JULIENNE, E.—Industria Artistica o Raccolto di Composizioni e Decorazioni Ornamentali, come suppellettili, tappezzerie, armature, cristalli, soffitti, cornici, lampade, bronzi, ec. Venezia, 1851—1858.

Prix 50f., in folio, £3.

LE PAUTRE.—Collection des plus belles Com- positions, gravées par DE CLOUX, Archte. L'Ouvrage contient cent planches. Paris.

This unique collection is in 2 Vols. 4to, had its commencement in 1812, and contains upwards of 500 rich Designs. Price £5 5s.

METIVIER, MONS., Architecte.—The original Sketches, Drawings, and Tracings, in pencil and pen and ink, of executed Works and Proposals, displaying the genius of Mons. Metivier, as an architect of high attainments, whose recent death was much regretted in Bavaria. He was a native of France, and was induced to settle in Munich by the late Duke of Leuchtenberg, under whose patronage he was much employed in the construction of private edifices for the Bavarian nobility and gentry; and for decoration and fittings of them; his interiors are still much in admiration. He built a mansion for Prince Charles, in a most simple and elegant style (in Brienner Street), which is still now considered one of the purest buildings of Munich. The above Sketches are his professional life and practice.

Twelve Parts, in small oblong 4to, 60 coloured Plates of 90 elaborately coloured and gilt ornaments. £1 1s.

ORNAMENTENBUCH.—Farbige Verzierungen für Fabrikanten, Zimmermaler und andere Baugewerke. München.

John Weale, 59, High Holborn, London, W.C.

FOREIGN WORKS, KEPT IN STOCK AS FOLLOWS:—

410 Plates, in two thick large 4to. Vols., designed and engraved by MM. Relster Argel, d'Hautel, de Wailly, Wagner, L. Feuchére et Regnier, &c. £5 5s.
ORNEMENTS.—Tirés ou imités des Quatre Écoles. Paris.

Six Parts, large folio, Plates beautifully coloured, in fac-similes of the Interiors, Ornaments, Compartments, Ceilings, &c. £2 12s. 6d. Also, elegantly half-bound in morocco gilt, £4 4s.
ROTTMANN, L.—Ornamente aus den vorzüglichsten Bauwerken München. München.

Very elegant. in half red morocco, gilt, and interleaved, £7 17s. 6d.
ZANETTI, G.—STUDII ARCHITETTONICO ORNAMENTALI, dedicati all' J. R. Accademia Veneta delle Belle Arti, seconda edizione con aggiunte del Prof. L. URBANI, 56 livraisons, in Imperial folio, about 200 of most elaborately designed subjects of Architecture and Interior Fittings, Designs for Chimney Pieces, Iron Work for Interiors and Exteriors, Gates and Wooden Gates, Garden Decorations, &c., &c., including the Appendices. Venezia.

A Catalogue, of 40 pages, to be had gratis; printed in demy 8vo.

Export Orders executed either for Principals abroad, or Merchants at home.

In Atlas of Plates and Text, 12mo, price 25s. together,

IRON SHIP BUILDING.

WITH

PRACTICAL ILLUSTRATIONS.

BY

JOHN GRANTHAM, N.A.

DESCRIPTION OF PLATES.

1. Hollow and Bar Keels, Stem and Stern Posts.

2. Side Frames, Floorings, and Bilge Pieces.

3. Floorings continued — Keelsons, Deck Beams, Gunwales, and Stringers.

4. Gunwales continued — Lower Decks, and Orlop Beams.

5. Angle-Iron, T Iron, Z Iron, Bulb Iron, as rolled for Iron Ship-Building.

6. Rivets, shown in section, natural size, Flush and Lapped Joints, with Single and Double Riveting.

7. Plating, three plans, Bulkheads, and modes of securing them.

8. Iron Masts, with Longitudinal and Transverse Sections.

9. Sliding Keel, Water Ballast, Moulding the Frames in Iron Ship-building, Levelling Plates.

10. Longitudinal Section, and Half-breadth Deck Plans of large Vessels, on a reduced scale.

11. Midship Sections of Three Vessels of different sizes.

12. *Large Vessel*, showing details.— *Fore End* in Section, and End View, with Stern Post, Crutches, Deck Beams, &c.

13. *Large Vessel*, showing details. — *After End* in section, with End View, Stern Frame for Screw, and Rudder.

14. *Large Vessel*, showing details. — *Midship Section*, Half breadth.

15. *Machines* for Punching and Shearing Plates and Angle-Iron, and for Bending Plates; Rivet Hearth.

16. *Machines*. — Garforth's Riveting Machine, Drilling and Counter Sinking Machine.

17. *Air Furnace* for Heating Plates and Angle-Iron; various Tools used in Riveting and Plating.

18. *Gunwale*, Keel, and Flooring; Plan for Sheathing Iron Ships with Copper.

19. Illustrations of the Magnetic Condition of various Iron Ships.

20. Gray's Floating Compass and Binnacle, with Adjusting Magnets.

21. Corroded Iron Bolt in Frame of Wooden Ship; Caulking Joints of Plates.

22. *Great Eastern*—Longitudinal Sections and Half-breadth Plans.

23. *Great Eastern*—Midship Section, with details.

24. *Great Eastern*—Section in Engine Room, and Paddle Boxes.

This Work may be had of Messrs. LOCKWOOD & Co., No. 7, Stationers' Hall Court, and also of Mr. WEALE; either the Atlas separately for 1l. 2s. 6d., or together with the Text price as above stated.

Bradbury and Evans, Printers Whitefriars.

www.ingramcontent.com/pod-product-compliance
Lightning Source LLC
Chambersburg PA
CBHW021128020726
47500CB00003B/975